ASHES FLY BACK

ASHES FLY BACK
A NOVEL

MARTHA JANE PETERSEN

Faraway Publishing
Black Mountain, N.C.

Cover design by Martha Jane Petersen

Published by
FARAWAY PUBLISHING
125 Spring View Drive
Black Mountain, N.C. 28711

Printed in the United States of America
10 9 8 7 6 5 4 3 2 1
ISBN-13: 979-8-9881761-2-1(paper)
ISBN-10: 8-9881761-2-1(paper)

Library of Congress Control Number: 2023950861

DEDICATION

This book is dedicated to my three adult children: Harry IV, Martha Lynne, and John Morgan, all born overseas. International news, friendships, and discussions have swirled around them since birth. It is also dedicated to the memory of my late husband, "Pete," who affirmed whatever project I found myself involved in and who befriended the world.

I am most grateful to Rev. Drs. Beverly and George Thompson and Roberta Binder, who urged the publication of this book, and to Randolph Shaffner, who enabled it to happen.

Ashes always fly back in the face of the one who throws them.

—Yoruba Proverb

CONTENTS

FOREWORD

In today's shrunken world, few geographic areas can be considered remote. Prejudices and practices sown in one community can reap ruinous results globally. My novel pictures repercussions in Africa from racism in Georgia through the experiences of a missionary sent by a southern USA church to Ilaria, an imaginary country in West Africa.

I was emboldened to pursue a "missionary story" after I recently encountered *Protestants Abroad: How Missionaries Tried to Change the World but Changed America* (Princeton University Press, 2017), by David Hollinger, which cited Joel Alvis's *Religion and Race: Southern Presbyterians, 1946-1983,* 1994. Here, I learned that 202 southern Presbyterian missionaries in the 1960s actively protested how segregation in their supporting USA churches undermined their efforts abroad.

Autobiographical pieces abound in this story, as my husband initially served as a Chaplain in an African University, as does the novel's protagonist. Although it was fifty years ago that I wrote this novel while in Ghana, today I have inserted the terms Black and White, referring to race, which may not have been used then but is preferred language now.

I have been encouraged to bring this story to light, saying it may be more relevant today than when it was written. So here it is.

Chapter 1

My decision to go to Ilaria, West Africa, occurred a month after Martin Luther King, Jr., was assassinated. For this reason, friends say that what I did was a copout, that anybody with sense should have known where the action was as well as the need: namely, the southland of America, right where I was living and had lived all my life. Furthermore, according to them, the White man's usefulness in Africa was finished.

In spite of the times and the opinions of friends, however, I forged ahead with my determination to serve abroad. For one thing, my decision was based on no sudden whim. I had leaned toward overseas service since age fifteen. For another, that spring found me unexpectedly relieved of my job as assistant pastor in a large church. And still another, Ilaria had deeply interested me through my associations with Moses Awulu, a national of that country.

With these motivations propelling me, we landed in Ilaria in September, 1970. By we, I mean my wife Kay and I; David, aged three; and Lisa, a year and a half. I felt as conspicuous as a small white spot on a large black cat. For having come from a White dominated society, I found the shoe uncomfortable and strange on the other foot. The process of becoming odd-man-out began with our flight from Kennedy with a third of the passengers Black. A filtering out of White people began with our first stop at Dakar in the steamy light of early dawn. More Black people boarded the plane, as well as an African replacement crew. Further sifting occurred in Monrovia so that by the time we reached Kwa, Ilaria's capitol, only we and a handful of White people remained. Clutching briefcase, purse, bookbag, and teddy, the four of us disembarked and moved efficiently through customs, manned by Black policemen and women in black uniforms.

"Hank and Kay Lattimer. Welcome, welcome!" a voice drawled, as we entered the waiting room. A tall man, tanned, with striking white hair and beard, stepped forward. He introduced himself as Rod Allen, Coordinator of the Presbyterian Mission in Ilaria. His pert wife, Edith, wore a dress of the same African print as her husband. Beside them stood Rev. Timothy Aketu and Rev. Daniel Quaina, Ilarian pastors, both wearing clerical collars and heavy suits. Rev. Aketu, a foot shorter than his colleague, welcomed us with a moist handshake and an eager grin.

"Welcome, Rev. and Mrs. Lattimer. Welcome to Ilaria." When he talked, his bushy eyebrows rose and fell with each inflection of a simulated British accent. "On behalf of the United Christian Church of Ilaria, we extend to you a most cordial and heartfelt welcome," he continued, holding my hand limply, as if posing for a photographer. Rev. Quaina, angular and intense, echoed similar sentiments but with less ceremony. I appreciated their presence, for they were my bosses. Rev. Aketu acted as chairman of the Church's Personnel Committee, which had invited me to Ilaria. And Rev. Quaina was chairman of the Western Region churches. I would be working near him as Protestant Chaplain at Western University, located at Charlestown.

In Rod's car, we followed the Ilarian pastors to a hotel for lunch. My eyes hungrily sought to pick up every sight in our new environment. But my tired mind refused to soak it in. I barely remember white-helmeted, white-gloved policemen directing traffic from pedestals, plus barefoot women with loads on their heads, babies on their backs.

"A driver from the University will shuttle you on over to Charlestown after lunch. It's about two hours from here. Are you game?" Rod asked on the way.

"Sure," I said. "The suspense of finally getting there is killing us all!"

Rod and Edith laughed. "I'm sure it must be," said Edith.

"What's the town like?" Kay asked. "Is it very big?"

"Oh, about 50,000 but with few amenities," said Rod. "I go there mainly to show visitors the castle."

"I've read about the castle," I said. "Used to hold slaves, didn't it?"

"Right," answered Rod. "For a couple of centuries. Then it became the seat of the British government until the whole kit and kaboodle was transferred to Kwa. Charlestown now proudly rests on its historical laurels. Aside from the castle, its main claim to fame is the University."

"Have you ever been to the University?" I asked.

"Nope. Only seen it from the highway." After a pause at a roundabout, Rod said, "We're awfully glad you're going there, Hank. It's a strategic piece of work among the future leaders of the country. We've long sought such an opportunity. You'll be the only one of the Mission in university work."

"Are there any other missionaries stationed nearby?" asked Kay.

"Only Luella Watson, who teaches at the Training College in Buasi. That's about thirty miles from you. But, unfortunately, she's on furlough right now. Won't be back 'til April. The rest of the Mission—a couple of dozen of us—live mostly in Kwa and up in the interior. Still, we can offer you plenty of moral support."

"We'll need that, I'm sure," laughed Kay.

"Any problems about life and work will go directly to the University or the Church," went on Rod. "About the only thing the Mission decides these days is where to assign you according to the needs of the church!"

"If you ever need us, though," Edith turned to look at us, "just holler. We're only too glad to help in any way."

By then we had arrived at the hotel. It seemed staffed and patronized exclusively by Ilarians, though the menu displayed a three-course European dinner. Rev. Aketu trundled sprightly ahead of us into a breezy dining room alongside a small garden. After we were seated, he ordered for the group and had the head waiter bring several pitchers of cold water to the table.

While we waited for our meal, Rev. Aketu carried the conversation. He asked about our trip over and our activities in America prior to it. "I believe you did a course in African Studies last academic year, is that correct?" he said, smiling broadly,

"Yes. At Northwestern University," I answered.

"I don't think I'm familiar with that one," he chuckled and fingered his napkin.

"It's one of the best in that field," declared Rev. Quaina. I turned to look at him and met his penetrating gaze offset by a warm smile. "And you're one of the few of your Mission who has done such a course." He seemed to approve.

I shrugged. "I don't know about that!"

"The only one, I believe," put in Rod.

"You know," Rev. Aketu flashed a smile, "I have been to your country, and I know many of the leaders of your church!"

"It was before the days of church union in Ilaria. When Rev. Aketu was a Presbyterian," explained Rod. "Our Mission Board sponsored him in a three-month exchange program."

"Yes," Rev. Aketu said, nodding vigorously. "I had a marvelous time, really. Why, I visited almost all the Southern states, where your denomination is located. From Texas to Maryland and down to Florida."

During most of our meal, Rev. Aketu mentioned the names of many Board heads and leading ministers he had met on his visit in 1962. He listed cities he had visited, as well as their congregations. I asked where he had been in Georgia, my home state.

"Only Atlanta, I'm afraid," he sighed. "I was advised not to venture into the more rural areas of the State." He giggled and rubbed his pudgy hands together. "It was during a time of upheaval in the South, and your church didn't want . . . uh, how shall I say . . . uh, any unpleasantries," he said with a smile.

"It's still in upheaval," commented Rod, "from that point of view."

"Yes," said Rev. Quaina. "Only two years ago an Ilarian had an unfortunate episode happen to him . . . in a Georgia church."

I figured whom he meant, and my mouth went dry. He didn't say it scornfully or even critically. "Do you mean . . . Moses Awulu?"

He looked sharply at me. "Yes. Did you know him by chance?"

I paused. "Yes, I did. He was once a friend of mine." I tried to sound casual, as I waited for some incriminating outburst from him.

But he responded only with, "I see."

What does that mean? I thought, in a turmoil. *What does he know about Moses and my connection with him?*

But the subject veered away. Rev. Aketu talked about others in the Ilarian church who had studied in America, as he stirred his after-dinner tea. I wanted to ask him more about the University and Charlestown, but I was too tired to pump him with questions.

....

After dinner, we headed west with a University car and driver, arranged by Rev. Aketu. The car had no springs in the seats, nor shock absorbers. That, with the uneven, hole-pocked road, tried every stiff joint and weary muscle. Again, I wanted to view the scenery, but eventually my eyes closed, and my head sagged. From time to time, I was awakened abruptly by a slam of the brakes to avoid a stray sheep or a vehicle hidden around a curve. I vaguely remember giant termite mounds and clumps of hump-backed cattle. Villages, all brown with mud. Half-naked people. Sacks of charcoal and piles of tomatoes sold at the roadside. Then, as the road edged the coastline, the masses of coconut palms framing the bright glint of ocean beyond. And the silvery fish drying in the sun and smelling like vomit.

At one point, the rickety car ground to a halt at what appeared to be a bus stop. Bedka, our Ilarian driver, got out. "Charlestown is near to halfway. I'm coming," he said to me and turned away.

"Looks to me like he's *going*, not *coming*," I remarked to Kay, as I watched him disappear. Around us, busses and open-sided lorries or "mammy wagons" received and discharged passengers. Fascinating slogans emblazoned their sides: "Save me, O God," "Fear Woman," "World Without End." From atop their heads, swarms of Black women were selling things to eat: baked bread loaves, kebab covered with red pepper, peeled oranges, hard-boiled eggs, doughnut-like balls. A few of the women sat at crude tables calling to potential buyers. Children, sheep, and chickens scampered about. Motors revved. People yelled and pushed through the crowds.

"Only halfway!" moaned Kay from the back seat. Lisa and David pressed against her in a sweaty sleep.

"You look swamped. Can't I take one of them up here with me?"

"Heavens, no!" she exclaimed. "You'd bounce right through the windshield. Besides, you look cramped yourself."

"You're so right," I said. "I think this car was made for midgets." I moved my legs across the driver's seat to unkink them.

"Why don't you get out and stretch?" Kay suggested.

"Are you kidding? They'd make hamburger out of me!" I said, referring to the dozen or so black faces staring in at us. Mostly children with an occasional adult lurking in the background. They laughed, pointed, and commented about us. We sat and breathed like ordinary people, wore clothes, and had arms and legs as they. Only our skin was so glaringly white. We were the foreigners, the minority, their stares indicated. Not they. When some of the girls started pushing their hands through the windows to feel Lisa's hair, we quickly rolled them up. "*Fama, fama,*" they chanted. I wondered what it meant.

Kay squirmed. "Where did our driver go? I wish he'd hurry up. What was he wearing? I don't think I could recognize his face again."

"Well, now, let me see," I said. "I think he had black hair, brown skin, brown eyes, a round face and . . . ."

"Oh, go on!" she punched my back.

I shrugged. "You asked. I tried." Admittedly I couldn't remember his face either.

Eventually the crowd thinned out, and Bedka climbed back into the car. We struggled on toward our destination. Bedka aroused us as we approached Charlestown. It consisted of gawky two-storied houses towering over narrow streets, which rambled off in odd directions. We pushed through swarms of Black people, buying and selling, cooking and eating, visiting with neighbors, getting water at a community pump. I glanced at my family. David, wide awake, sat by the window, his eyes glued to what he saw in the street. Kay looked at me with an I-don't-know-what-I've-gotten-myself-in-for-but-I'll-do-my-best expression. I dropped my hand from the back of the seat to squeeze hers.

We angled out of town and zoomed under a tunnel of coconut palms for about three miles. A vine-covered archway met us with "Western University" written at the sides. Ahead of us on a hill sloping from the sea marched cluster after cluster of academic buildings, white stuccoed with red tile roofs. Most of them were set in quadrangles complete with lily pools and flowering shrubs.

I tried to absorb as much as possible, as we whizzed past the faculties of chemistry, engineering, architecture. At the top of the hill loomed a great building with a tall tower. We took an abrupt turn down beside it and headed out into an open field, where the faculty houses stood. Their white walls glared in the late afternoon sun. We pulled into the drive of one and got out.

A cook, on loan to us by the University for three days, helped us unload. Then with our belongings inside and Bedka on his way, we surveyed our new quarters. It was one story, set around a large courtyard. Kay poked among the three bedrooms, closets, kitchen, and flower beds. At suppertime, practically hidden behind a mammoth stew the cook had prepared, the children blinked at their new surroundings. In a small voice, David asked, "Are we home, Daddy?"

I reached over and grabbed his hand. "Yes, David. This is our new home."

After supper, the darkness fell with scarcely a pause between it and daylight. Accompanying it came the sound of crickets, frogs, and the ping-ping-ping of a fruit bat. In the distance we could hear the ocean surging on the shore. A University night watchman came, wearing a flowing robe, skull cap, and a grim expression, which would deter any nighttime invader. Moments later, we heard him chanting his Muslim prayers.

We tumbled into bed, overcome with fatigue. But sleep came reluctantly. Dozens of assorted pictures and impressions of the last few months flickered across my mind. I was still caught up in the momentum of getting to Ilaria. Exhausted in the achievement, I couldn't relax just yet, knowing that bigger hurdles of adjustment lay ahead. But we were home! I found it hard to believe. After the last year and a half of suitcase living, we once more could put down roots. I found it equally hard to believe that out of all the Ilarians who lived in this strange land, I would so soon hear the name of Moses Awulu.

For the next few days, we concentrated on regaining our strength. David startled us the second morning upon his discovery of "little snakes." Upon rushing outside, we realized he meant large, varicolored lizards which attacked each other sideways. Each afternoon Joseph, our cook, served us a very English tea—definitely his idea, not ours. After that, we walked down the road. We took in the names of other faculty members on signboards at the driveways: Larson, Pela, Vandenburg, Woods. We wondered which of them were expatriates, since a third of the faculty came from abroad.

But we saw no one. The doorways covering the open ends of the courtyards and the garages remained formidably closed. No child played in neighboring yards or open fields. Only a rare car came down the dusty road and disappeared beyond our vision. Twice a day a squad of women with buckets on their heads sallied into the campus area from a distant village to get water. Still, aside from neighbors, I halfway expected a student or faculty member or administrator to come and officially greet us. Someone among them knew of our arrival, else we would never have been picked up in Kwa. When Joseph left the evening of the third day, our isolation was complete.

The next morning, I decided to go out exploring. Kay badly wanted to go. But we both saw the difficulties of marching two preschoolers across two miles of treeless fields to the academic site. I solemnly promised her I'd bring any food I found, and I'd tell her everything I did and saw. She and the kids waved me out of sight as I left.

Upon my return, I fulfilled my promise to Kay. I spilled out a bag full of canned beans, fruit, and luncheon meat, along with a blow-by-blow account of my outing. With no radio, TV, newspaper, telephone, friends, books, odd house jobs to distract, we revived the delicate art of conversation. I told of the long hike under the blazing sun. Few cars had passed, and I had not thought to flag anyone down for a lift.

"The kids would never have made it, huh?" Kay commented.

"No chance," I said. I then described the campus on the other side of the hill that separated the academic from the housing site. The cool sea breezes. The ocean several thousand yards away, fringed by leaning coconut palms. The fishing canoes on it. Fort San Paulo jutting out to the east.

Kay looked puzzled. "Fort San Paulo?"

"Sure. The Portuguese fort. Some 400 years old. Don't you remember reading about it along with Charlestown Castle?"

"Vaguely. Then what?"

"I wandered over the campus." I paused. "It's pretty."

She sighed. "Specifics, dear. Specifics."

"Oh, flowers and trees and bushes everywhere. Fancy walkways and trellises. Like a botanical garden."

"What about the buildings?"

"Wide open. Lots of windows and lattice work. I suppose to encourage coolness. Terrazzo floors. Chairs and lecterns in not too good shape."

"Did you meet anybody?"

"I'm coming, I'm coming. Don't rush me," I said with a smile. I described various dorms, departments, libraries, and shops. "After a while, I found the auditorium, which also serves as chapel, a few levels from the hilltop. Looks like back-home stuff: stationary seats, big curtains on stage, a piano. When I went in, a fellow was playing the piano. He came over to me and asked if I happened to be the new chaplain. He welcomed me and said he was Kwafu somebody—a second-year student. He asked where we lived and when we had arrived. A real friendly chap."

"Great! Your first real-live student," exclaimed Kay.

"He asked if I had transport, and I said no. Then he said he thought there was a bus, which could take us back and forth from here to there. That I should find out its schedule." I pronounced the last word like Kwafu did: "shedule."

"It's what?" Kay broke up with laughter.

"You heard me. That's what he said. I could hardly keep a straight face."

"Must be English English," she said.

"He took me up to the Administration Building, the one at the top of the hill with the tower," I explained. "We went from one crowded little office to another. Nobody knew anything about a bus. We finally found the Transport Yard and were told the bus was strictly for students when the term began. I asked the head guy there what a carless family could do. He and the others shrugged and looked at each other and had no suggestions."

"Yuk," muttered Kay. "So, we warm up our hiking muscles 'til our car gets here. When . . . by Christmas?"

"Just wait, there's more. I asked Kwafu other things. Like when services began on campus. Where to get the mail, to cash checks. Where David will go to school."

"What about fresh fruits and vegetables?"

I blinked. "I didn't think about that."

"Weren't there any in the campus shop?"

"I didn't see any."

Kay sighed, "So, we eat out of cans from now on?" There must be something somewhere. The local people certainly don't eat out of cans!"

"Sure. But how do we find it before we starve?"

"Well, Kwafu has volunteered to take us to town, for a start. On Tuesday. He's living there with his brother and will borrow his brother's car to take us. How does that sound?"

"Brimming with possibilities," she glowed.

"After I had thoroughly grilled Kwafu with all these questions, I started out for home. I got a lift, though, in a Land Rover. Was an Irish fellow, Sean Finnegan, teaches in Engineering. Kay, what a character!"

"How so?"

"Bushy red hair. African shirt. Beard. Been in Ilaria for four years. Swears like a sailor, all with an intriguing accent. He doesn't talk to you: he booms. He told me that the Transport Yard could furnish us with a car and/or driver."

"I thought you said they had nothing."

"I did. And I told Sean that. Well, he just roared. 'I knew it, the bloody blokes,' he boomed. He said it's no point just asking for things in general. You have to nail 'em down with specifics. So I guess I'll go back to see if we can get something."

"Why isn't all this written down somewhere for newcomers?" Kay frowned.

"I asked Sean that. He about wrecked us with laughing. 'They don't give a damn,' he said. 'Ye have to stumble into things for yoorself.'" I tried imitating his speech.

That was on Friday. The weekend crept by in uneventful slow motion. We had nothing to occupy our minds with except the rudiments of daily living. Eating, sleeping, cleaning up, child tending. On Monday morning, I hiked back to the Transport Office to see about cars and drivers. But they had nothing to offer, not until the term began, four long weeks away. Cars were "spoiled," and drivers, "on leave." I left and checked the mail. A letter from Kay's mother arrived: our first from back home.

I hitched a ride with an Ilarian fellow who expressed surprise to learn that a fulltime chaplain had been appointed. "Many of us feel that ministers from the Region coming to the campus part-time have been entirely adequate!" he exclaimed.

The conversation solidly reduced my morale. At home, I shared the letter with Kay. But instead of cheering her up, it dissolved her into sudden tears.

On Tuesday, we anticipated Kwafu's visit with mounting excitement. At least it would be something to do. An hour after he said he would arrive, Kwafu lurched into our driveway in a battered car. We climbed in, and the car coughed and sputtered out onto the road. The window handles were broken off and we had to tie the doors shut with a cord. Passing fields of cassava plants and stretches of brilliant green grass as tall as I, we slowly made our way into town. In the back seat, Kay grimly clutched the children on either side of her.

We entered town on a hill arched over with flamboyant trees and coasted down the other side into the melee of Charlestown's central market. Kwafu indicated that we'd return here after our visit to the historic castle. Along the sides of the market, makeshift shops spilled out their wares into the road. Cans of nails, toilet paper, rubber flip-flops, brassieres, bolts of cloth, belts, plastic water bottles: you name it. After that, we lost all sense of direction as we choked up narrow streets by crumbled buildings and finally approached the sea. A raucous fish market sat beside the Castle. Against its walls, several men mended their blue nets.

We entered the Castle through a narrow passageway with stone-laid floors. A courtyard fanned out from it toward the sea, edged by a battery mounted with a dozen rusted cannons. Standing on the battery, I gazed out at three painted canoes straining to get to shore. They seemed to be racing the rain building up in the dark clouds overhead. Far below the battery, the sea rushed against the Castle with a boom, and the flying spray hit me in the face. I tensed at the pounding surf, the bravery of the fragile canoes, and the defiance of the Castle against ocean and Africa through centuries of foreign domination.

When I turned back to the courtyard, Kwafu had secured a guide. He said the town and then the Castle, built in 1643, had been named after Charles the First of England. Then he showed us the Castle's vaults, halls, cannons, and graves. We stopped at a door marked, *The Dungeons*. Our guide opened it with a large key and invited us to enter. Sheer darkness gaped beyond.

"Are we going in *there*?" Kay whispered, grabbing my arm.

"Sure. If he can, we can." I nodded toward the guide who was fast disappearing into the cold gloom with his flashlight. I held David's and Lisa's hands as we groped our way down the mud-packed ramp into the bowels of the Castle.

Although we couldn't delineate them at first, we stood in one of five rooms, each about 30 by 15 feet. The guide led us to the far right one, designated for female slaves. "They were chained here." He held the light over worn, iron stobs in the dirt floor. "The women were in total darkness, except for that small, small light." He indicated the vertical slits in the outer wall, about twenty feet above our heads. "They were given only bread and water. They had no toilet. They lay in their own excrement."

Lisa began to whimper, and David begged to climb up into my arms.

But we didn't leave just yet. We passed another dungeon, splashing through small puddles in the uneven floor. "The male slaves were placed in these three rooms," the guide intoned. "The outer wall formerly was a barred window. Through it the slaves could see the ships that would carry them to Europe and America. They had to wait for as long as two weeks between ships. Many died here. They lay where they died."

"How many were in here at one time?" I asked.

"1500," he answered.

In the last room, the guide also showed us the former passageway that led from the dungeons directly to the sea. It had been walled over since the close of the slave trade in 1807. An eerie chatter startled us.

"Bats!" Kwafu giggled.

The guide held his flashlight up, and we could see them swirling around us. Lisa broke into open sobbing. "Get out, Mommy. Get out of here. I want to get out!" Kay picked her up, and we followed the guide swiftly up the ramp into the light and the warm, salty air.

Outside, the guide motioned us up to the chapel, which stood directly over the dungeons. At the entry to the chapel, he picked up a trapdoor, which led back down into the dungeons." A guard was posted here," he said, "to listen to the slaves below. He would listen for plans of insurrection during worship, when the entire Castle staff would be occupied." He put the trapdoor back into place and announced that the tour was "finished."

We turned away and descended the steps into the courtyard. I could hardly look Kwafu in the face. For in fifteen short minutes the tour had penetrated the fog of my Southernness so that I understood a little about Black rage. Meteoric impressions from my boyhood streaked across my mind and fell in an order now made logical to me. First, the obeisant, "Yassah, Misteh Lat'meh," coming from Black people on my father's chicken farm. The "WHITE ONLY" and "COLORED ONLY" barriers erected across my youth. Then, gradually, the NAACP. Civil Rights. Sit-ins. Freedom marches. "We shall overcome." And from a well-known tombstone: "Free at last, Free at last, Thank God Almighty I'm Free at last!" All these, my fellow Southerners had accused as evidences of *the Negro problem. the Martin Luther King problem.* And more recently, more personally: *the Moses Awulu problem.* Now I saw clearly and irrevocably that the problem was never *Negro*. Rather, it was scathingly *White*.

But Kwafu reacted no more to our tour than to a stroll through an amusement park. "We have more castles and forts. Around forty in Ilaria. Aren't they marvelous?" he chattered on the way to the car. "Would you like to see Fort San Paulo as well?"

"Perhaps," I murmured. "But not today. Perhaps some other time."

It began to drizzle, so we quickened our steps. At the entryway, we startled four hideous vultures. With majestic effort, they flapped their tremendous wings and soared to perch on the Castle roof in the rain. Ever after that, whenever I saw vultures in Ilaria, I would think of Charlestown Castle.

Chapter 2

The tour around Charlestown only whetted our appetites for additional activity. Instead, we faced more homebound days of inertia. A week passed before I finally took the bull by the horns and marched to the Administration Building to announce my presence.

I did not know where to begin once I reached it. Who would know anything about the chaplaincy? I asked an Ilarian woman at the information desk in the foyer. She gave me a name and an office number, which proved wrong. I was shuttled to six more persons before I found a Mr. K.M.B. Akru-Frimsa, the Acting Assistant to the Junior Assistant Registrar, in a small basement office. He smiled broadly and welcomed me to sit down in the chair beside his desk.

He had a pencil-lined mustache and wore a Masonic ring on his left middle finger. I told him who I was and that I wanted to know details about my work: what was expected of me, when I was to begin, where I was to be located.

He soaked in all my questions. Then with considerable stumbling, he told me that I would begin with the opening of term, that I would work out from an office, and that I would perform the regular duties of a "priest," as he put it. I asked him specifically did I have an office assigned to me. He looked blank and said it could be arranged "in due course." He reminded me that I was the first full-time chaplain. "We have no . . . uh . . . precedent to work from, you understand." He flashed a smile at me. "You must bear with us in making the necessary arrangements regarding your work."

"Aside from the Sunday services, what does the University expect me to be responsible for?"

"I should think that will be largely up to you," Mr. Akru-Frimsa responded.

"Do you know what services are held on the campus on Sundays?"

"As for myself, I do not attend divine worship on the campus. So I do not know the Sunday schedule."

"You have no idea when the services are scheduled?"

"Yes."

"You do know?" I was confused.

"I do not know, Rev. Lattimer," he said.

"Is there a faculty or administrative committee that I will be responsible to?"

"Yes, the Chaplaincy Board." Rummaging through some papers, he withdrew a University *Calendar* and showed me the names. "Unfortunately, two are on study leave, one has returned home to Ceylon, and the remaining two have rotated off."

I frowned. "So there is no Board at present?"

"Yes."

"There is?" Again, the confusion.

"There is not," Mr. Akru-Frimsa sighed.

"Will a new one be appointed or elected soon?"

"Yes. During the first term. The Faculty Senate will appoint one in due course."

"When does that meet?"

"Whenever the Vice-Chancellor calls a meeting."

I took a deep breath. Then after a moment, I asked, "Is there no one, then, that I am responsible to in the meantime?"

Mr. Akru-Frinsa shifted wearily in his chair. "Not at the moment, Rev. Lattimer. You, of course, are aware of the fact that your appointment has not yet been made official in the first place."

"Not official?" I exclaimed with surprise.

He shook his head.

"Why not?"

"It must be regularized."

"What does that mean?"

Again he sighed. "Your curriculum vitae must be presented and approved by the Appointments Board."

"But wasn't this done before I was invited to come?" I sat forward on the edge of my seat.

"Of course. It was tentatively approved by the Executive of the Faculty Senate. But it must be presented to the Appointments Board before it is finalized."

"I don't understand," I said, trying to control my rising irritation. "You mean you invited me here to work as Chaplain, and after I arrive, it is still uncertain that the University will appoint me?"

He waved a conciliatory hand. "Rev. Lattimer, I can understand your feelings. Believe me, I do. This is just the way things are, unfortunately," he said kindly. "Very few staff members have been turned down, Rev. Lattimer. It is all a matter of procedure."

I nodded. "Well, when does the Appointments Board meet? How long do I have to wait?"

"Whenever the Registrar calls it to meet."

"And in the meantime, what do I do?"

"Why, carry on with your normal duties," he said. "I shall be glad to help you in any way."

"I see," I responded. I thanked him, got up, and left. I wandered over the campus absentmindedly, my thoughts jangled. I wound up at the auditorium and inspected it more closely. A door led to the back of the building on one side of the platform. It opened into a storage room, dusty and thick with cobwebs. Broken-down chairs from some lecture hall were piled to the ceiling. A second closed door faced me, which was locked. I peered through the keyhole and saw more chairs in it. I wondered if it could be used as my office.

I beat a hasty trail back to Akru-Frimsa. I asked him about the possibility. He suggested that I get a key from the head custodian to check it out and told me where to find him.

I started to get up but then thought to ask, "Tell me. Are you sure I'm entitled to an office since I'm not . . . since my appointment is not official?"

"By all means, Rev. Lattimer," he assured me.

"Would you mind telling me what else I am entitled to as chaplain?"

"Aside from office space, you are entitled to access to the University stores where you can secure paper, office supplies, etcetera. You will have an annual budget for chapel expenses and a table allowance for entertaining visiting ministers. And, of course, as per the original agreement with the United Church, we will pay half the rent on your bungalow, and they, the other half."

I tried not to show my surprise. Instead, I thanked him and left. I tracked down the head custodian, who promised to secure the key for me as soon as possible. Convincing myself that I had done everything possible toward securing an office, I walked home.

Kay stirred around in the kitchen, getting lunch together, more or less the same thing we had eaten every day. Bread, cheese out of a can, something like Spam, and fruit. At the table, I related a sort of "Where did you go?" "Out" "What did you do?" "Nothing" conversation. She told me of her activities in about two phrases: housework and childcare. At first she didn't mind the daily routine. But as one day melted into the next and she could predict all of a day's events the moment she got up in the morning, it began to eat at her. At least I could get out.

I became her link with the outside world, although my connections were hardly viable.

If only our freight would arrive and we could settle in. If only we had transport and could explore our new surroundings. If only we could get to know somebody, Ilarian or expatriate. In those early days, we had to put the lid on a lot of "ifs" and wait it out. We knew such unreal suspension could not last forever. School had to begin; work had to start. This kept us going.

I stuck around the house most of the time to help Kay out. Particularly when it came to washing out sheets and towels by hand. But when I got the fidgets and/or we needed something at the store, I lit out. Or when I thought headway was being made to pry open my new job. Headway came, though, in low gear. For it was after eight days and three trips to the custodian's office and one more to Akru Frimsa's that we unlocked the mystery room behind the auditorium. By then the suspense had mounted rampantly, and I would have grabbed the room even if it had no windows or lights. As it turned out, though, the room made an ideal office. I secured Akru Frimsa's approval. Within his "due course," the office was ready. Only I wasn't. For there again, our freight still had not come, and I had nothing to move into my new quarters. I spent one morning rearranging the furniture, a mere four pieces. When I realized the inanity to which my vigor and brain power had stooped, I went home in disgust. I found the house topsy-turvy, for Kay too, driven by boredom and despair, had moved all the furniture around.

We stumbled through the remaining days until school began on October thirteenth. At that time, the University abruptly woke up from its vacation lethargy. Cars plied the roads more frequently. People emerged from their houses. Students appeared in the dining room, the halls, the lecture rooms. On a personal level, during that opening week we managed to hire a cook, secure our freight, and enroll David in the University nursery school.

With all that accomplished, Kay's walk became lighter; her face beamed with contentment. "What's with you?" I teased.

"My cup runneth over," she laughed.

"Mine, too," I admitted.

"Thank the Lord."

On the first weekend after the opening of school, the Vice Chancellor staged a party honoring new members of staff. The printed invitations read: "Dress: Formal." I wondered if a suit and tie were "formal" enough, since it never entered our minds to bring evening clothes to Africa. A University driver took us to the Vice-Chancellor's home on its own private knoll alongside University Hill. We stopped to pick up another new lecturer on the way, a Black man. I thought he was Ilarian until I heard his voice.

"Hello," I said as the newcomer climbed into the jeep. He wore a Nigerian-styled outfit with tight-fitting pants and a loose piece of matching cloth over them. A skull cap of the same print sat cockily on the side of his Afro hair.

"Good evenin'," he drawled, and I knew he was a Southern American. I introduced Kay and myself.

He swung his head to look at me. Shaking my hand limply, he said, "My name's Jones. Kanu Jones."

"Kanu?" I asked, for it was an Ilarian name.

"Right," he answered.

"Sounds like we all come from the same part of the world."

"Not anymore," he threw over his shoulder.

"Oh? Have you immigrated to Ilaria?"

"Sure have."

"You been here long?" I asked.

"Just four weeks," he said.

"Where did you come from before?"

"Birmingham."

"And you don't think you'll ever go back?"

"Not if I can help it," he laughed. "I consider this place home."

His accent did strange things to me. It conjured up images of gold teeth and flashy clothes, of hog jowls and collards. I realized instantly the stereotype I had put him in: the Negro of my youth. So far I had not pigeon-holed any Ilarian in this manner. I thought I had disentangled myself from that hang-up, but now Kanu Jones proved otherwise. I shuddered to think that the way one pronounced his words would revive a latent prejudice within me.

We rode the rest of the way in silence. A half-moon gleamed in the sky, and from an outlying village, drums throbbed. The jeep carried us up to the Vice-Chancellor's hill and dropped us on a sweeping drive edged by crimson-flowered bushes. The large house sparkled with dozens of lights on dozens of windows. At the side, colored lights and lanterns twinkled on the lawn where the party was held. We stepped in that direction and were met at once by an Ilarian gentleman and his wife. He was dressed in a white dinner jacket and she in the typical two-piece, long Ilarian dress. An obvious wig towered on her head.

"Good evening," murmured the man, whom I assumed to be the Vice Chancellor. "Welcome to Western University and our home. And you are . . . ?"

"Mr. and Mrs. H. W. Lattimer," I responded as we shook his and his wife's hands.

"Excuse me," he said with a smile. "But do tell me which faculty you are with. I must apologize that I find it exceedingly difficult to attach the proper names with the proper persons." His speech was suave and Cambridge-cultivated.

"I am the Protestant Chaplain," I returned.

"Of course, of course!" he exclaimed. "You are the Reverend and Mrs. Lattimer. That is what confused me. Why, welcome to Ilaria. We are delighted to have you in our midst and hope your stay will be most satisfying." His wife confirmed his words with gracious nods of her head. They hovered over us briefly and turned to greet Kanu.

We approached the lawn and saw thirty people clustered on it, chatting and sipping drinks. The Ilarian men wore evening dress or their rich, toga-like _lemna_, the Ilarian national dress. And most of the women, expatriate and Ilarian alike, had on long dresses, which stirred in the warm breezes about us. Many of the expatriate men sported suits or highly embroidered African shirts. One such shirt appeared on Sean standing in a corner by himself with an Ilarian woman. He waved us over.

"And how're ye keeping yourselves?" he boomed while shaking my hand. He looked a bit more subdued with his hair tucked behind his ears.

"Oh fine," I said. "Things are on the upswing. We're finally getting settled." I introduced Kay and Kanu, who had followed us.

The Ilarian woman beside Sean was small with light colored skin and a beautifully delicate face. Her name was Elizabeth Lutterodt.

"Your name sounds European," observed Kay. "Something like German."

"It is Dutch," she said softly.

"Oh, really?" I said. "How is that?"

Kanu had appeared. "Some dirty Dutchman raped her great-great grandmother," he sniffed.

Sean bristled, I gaped, but Elizabeth only laughed. "Yes, to be blunt about it, that is precisely what happened. I come from San Paulo," she explained. "In my town is a fort which the Dutch occupied after the Portuguese. Many of the officers slept with the native girls. As a result, numerous townspeople are descendants of the Dutch."

"And you still choose to retain the Dutch names?" I asked.

"Of course. As a matter of pride," she said, smiling.

"Pride!" cried Kanu. "Pride! Why should you be proud of that?"

She turned, half-amused, to Kanu. "Because the descendants of the Dutch are highly educated, highly respected people. The mulatto children were well cared for by their fathers and educated, even in Europe. Many became wealthy merchants along the coast. It was a mark of distinction to be born of mixed blood."

"But why should it be that mark now?" exclaimed Kanu. "You all are way past the Colonial era. What's the point of hanging on to a

European link with the past? Africans must assert their Africanness! None of this Colonial bit," he glowered.

"But it's nevertheless part of our heritage," insisted Elizabeth. "Something we are proud of."

"But it's foreign," said Kanu.

"Not any more foreign than your suggestion to ride roughshod over our history and our ancestry."

"No, what I'm suggesting isn't foreign. It's African!"

"Not from our point of view," she said. "Perhaps from your point of view as an American."

"I don't consider myself an American any longer," Kanu declared.

Elizabeth smiled sweetly but said no more. Sean took advantage of the pause and offered to take Kanu, Kay, and me to get some drinks. Excusing ourselves from Elizabeth, we strolled over to the long, linen-covered table. On it sat a huge assortment of bottles and glasses. Cognac, bourbon, sherry, beer, soft drinks, and fruit juice. Two Black waiters in white uniforms poised with bottle openers to serve us.

"Now, what'll ye have," asked Sean.

Kanu opted for a gin and tonic. But my background at seminary and in the pastorate never included the cocktail circuit. Kay and I settled on Cokes, to the restrained amusement of Sean. As we were turning away from the table, we all drifted apart. A white-uniformed waiter glided past us, carrying delectables of shrimp, egg, olives, and cheeses on a silver tray. I shook my head as I lifted a pastry to my mouth.

"Unreal. Simply unreal," I said, sweeping my eyes around the yard.

"No pith helmets here, huh?" giggled Kay.

"A'tall, as they say. A'tall!"

Joining a group nearby, we introduced ourselves and shook everyone's hands in the circle. A lecturer from India, the Carters from

Canada, the Van Loofts from Holland, and a strapping Ilarian to my right, who did not say his name. He wore a bright green and gold _lemna_ over a white collarless shirt.

"And what faculty are you in, Mr. Lattimer?" he asked in stilted tones.

"I am the Protestant Chaplain."

"Oh? And where do you come from?" asked the man. "Your accent does not originate from U.K., does it?"

"No, we are from America," I responded.

"And what part do you come from, may I ask?"

"We are from the southern part . . . from Georgia."

"And are you on contract with the University? I cannot remember from my files off hand."

"No. Our church pays our salary," I said, taking a drink. His lips slowly curled. "Well. That must mean you are . . . uh . . . missionaries, I believe."

"Yes, we are," I replied. The others in the circle began listening to our exchange.

"Is your presence among us some new crusade started by your mission?"

"No, I'm here at the invitation of the United Church of Ilaria and the University," I said lightly.

"I see," he said with a smile. "And what do you expect to accomplish here . . . aside from converting us heathen, of course, Rev. Lattimer?"

"Why I expect to do as much as any ordinary minister would do," I said. "Preach, be available for counselling, visit, coordinate Christian programs."

"And do you believe Africans will relate to you, a foreigner and a White man?" His eyes flamed in his massive face.

I squelched my more argumentative self and swallowed. "I guess we shall have to wait and see, won't we, Mr. . . . uh, Mr. . . . I don't believe you told me your name," I said with a smile.

"I am Mr. J. B. R. DeHeer-Johnson, the Registrar of the University," he announced.

"Oh, I see. So you're not a newcomer like many of us?"

"By no means. I have been here seven years," his voice drifted off, and he glanced around the lawn. "Now you will excuse me, please," he said to the group. "There is someone I must see."

"Of course," I said.

Rearranging his _lemna_ in a dazzling sweep of color, Mr. DeHeer-Johnson sauntered away.

The silence in our circle was broken by a rasping, "Good Lord!" coming from Mrs. Carter.

The slight Indian across from me waved his hand, which held a giant handkerchief. "Oh, don't mind him," he said. "He struts and crows at every welcoming party every year. Pay him no mind. Pay him no mind." He blew his nose and stuck the handkerchief into the pocket of his bagging pants.

"You're not a newcomer either?" Mr. Carter asked the Indian, as he flicked his cigarette jerkily onto the lawn.

"No. I've been in Ilaria five years. And before that, it was Nigeria . . . for eight years."

"Good Lord!" again from Mrs. Carter.

"Sounds like you like overseas living," chuckled Carter.

"Not so much that," said the graying man, taking off his glasses to polish them. "I just like living in India less! You make so much more money overseas than in my country," he dropped his voice to a loud whisper.

"But don't you get homesick? Don't you miss your homeland?" Mrs. Carter asked, elevating her penciled eyebrows.

The Indian shrugged. "Not really. One gets used to it."

"You'd have to after thirteen years," laughed Carter.

"Well, one alternative," spoke up Mrs. Van Looft, "is to fly home when you can't stand it any longer." She smiled coquettishly and shook her bright blonde hair out of her face.

Her husband, tall and lean, turned to her. "Dear, darling. Not everyone has your kind of money. And Amsterdam is a hell of a lot closer than say, Canada . . . or India." He spoke loudly as if addressing a child.

"I know, darling," she cooed. "I was just suggesting a way to survive the tropics. For conversation's sake." She fluttered her eyelashes.

"How long have you been in Ilaria?" Mrs. Carter asked Mrs. Van Looft.

"Two years."

"And how long do you stay at a time in Holland?"

"About a half year here and a half year there," Mrs. Van Looft said, fingering her lowcut dress. "When the heat begins in January or February, I leave. I don't come back until September."

"But don't you miss your husband?" Mrs. Carter reacted, missing a painful look shot to her by her husband.

"Of course," responded Mrs. Van Looft with a theatric gesture. "We miss each other dreadfully, don't we darling?" She rubbed her husband's sleeve and smiled at him.

"Yes, dear," he laughed. "We miss each other dreadfully!"

"But we have managed to work out a very satisfactory arrangement," Mrs. Van Looft assured Mrs. Carter and then smiled again at her husband. "Haven't we, dear?"

"Yes. Very," he murmured and emptied his glass.

Mrs. Van Looft held her empty glass toward her husband. "Go and get us another brandy, will you, like a dear husband?" When he left her side, she swayed slightly, and I could tell she had already consumed too many brandies.

Others in the group broke to get more drinks, and the circle gradually dispersed. I found a small African at my elbow. He wore rather thick glasses and rarely looked at me when he spoke.

"Are you the new Chaplain?" he asked, after introducing himself as James Gharta from Ilaria.

"Yes, I am."

"We are so grateful that you have come," he said, smiling. "Those of us in the Christian community, certainly."

"Is the community a very large one?" asked Kay.

"Among students, yes. But faculty, unfortunately, no."

"What do you teach here?" I asked him.

"Mathematics," he responded. Then, "You are an American, I believe."

I nodded.

"Where do you come from?"

I told him.

"I have been to America but not to Georgia," he said.

"Oh, really? Did you study there?" asked Kay.

"No, I attended a church seminar in New York. I was there only a month. So you cannot say I know America very well," he laughed. "There is an Ilarian in my department who studied for some time in America. And more recently too, I might add."

"What is his name?"

"Awulu. A. S. Awulu."

Something flipped inside me, and I said nothing for a while. "Do . . . do you know if he is also called Moses?"

He thought for a moment. "Not that I know of."

"Do you know him very well?"

"Hardly at all. He keeps to himself."

"When was he in America?" asked Kay.

"Two years ago. He has been here only for one year."

I looked down at the twinkling lights on the campus far away. "I may know him," I murmured. "Where can I find him?"

"In the science faculty. On the second floor. But I have no idea where he lives."

"I shall try to find him . . . ," my voice trailed off.

"Will you be preaching tomorrow night?" Mr. Gharta asked.

"Yes. I'm going to give it a try," I said with a smile.

"Shall I come collect you before the service?"

"That will be fine, Mr. Gharta," I enthused. "We have no car yet."

"If I can assist you in any way, I shall be only too happy to do so," he said. "And please call me James, Rev. Lattimer."

"Only if you call me Hank." I said, smiling.

We agreed on a time for the next night. He then excused himself, saying he had to go.

When he left, Kay tugged at my arm. "Moses! Do you think he could be here . . . really?" Her eyes widened.

"He could be. He could be," I said distantly, shaking my head. "When you consider there are only two universities in Ilaria and he was preparing to teach in one of them . . . , it's quite . . . logical. I guess." Kay grabbed my hand, and I hoped she could not detect its clamminess.

We refurbished our drinks and sandwiches. Then we circled around to various groups on the lawn. The Ilarians we met were friendly enough, but the conversation generally foundered after the chitchat of nationality, length of stay at the University, what one taught, and where one lived. We stayed for another hour and then got a lift home with the Van Loofts. Mrs. Van Looft gripped her husband's arm on the way to the car.

As we rolled down the hill from the Vice-Chancellor's, he looked in the rearview mirror at me and said, "It's very interesting that you have been appointed Chaplain."

"Oh? How is that?" I asked.

"We all thought an Ilarian would be."

"Well, you know why they did it, darling," giggled his wife.

"Now, Elsa. That's only hearsay, you know."

"Which is fairly reliable around here . . . ," she said.

Kay and I looked at each other. "Well, tell us more. If I may be so bold," I said.

"It was rumored that two factions in the administration were in disagreement over which Ilarian was to be appointed Chaplain," Van Looft explained. "There was ever so much palaver about it. Then when the Ilarian Church offered your name for Chaplain, both sides eagerly invited you to eliminate their opponent!"

"Mmmm, very interesting," I chuckled. "So I came by default, did I?"

"It seems that way. But don't feel badly," he said. "Expatriates are not really people in the eyes of Ilarians. Only objects . . . to be used and shunted about."

"I see," I said.

We fell silent for a while. Then Mrs. Van Looft offered to take Kay to the market the following week, saying something about "enjoying going" since she found the native women so "colorful."

Chapter 3

The next night, James Gharta took us to the auditorium. Several hundred seats were occupied. Both Kay and I were amazed at the congregation. For if we had been in America, only a scant number of students would have turned out for Sunday worship.

Since it was the opening of term, the service was a joint Protestant-Catholic one. In the processional, it amused me that the priest, a Black Ilarian, wore a white robe, and I, a White man, a black one. As we moved down the aisle, the distance to the front seemed interminable, for I grew more and more self-conscious along the way. Around me floated a sea of black faces. The only White person in the crowd was Kay, looking extremely conspicuous on the third row. Again, the stigma of white skin gripped me. What did those here equate with whiteness? Would it be an obstacle to proclaiming the universality of the Gospel? I realized then that DeHeer-Johnson's questions surpassed mere rhetoric.

Because Ilarians speak a unique English all their own, I wondered whether they could penetrate my Georgian drawl. During my sermon, I grew acutely aware of my own voice and my pronunciation of words. In an effort to make my speech more distinct, I stumbled all the more. It reminded me of the first agonizing sermon I preached to my fellow students and teachers during my second year in seminary.

The service ended and we marched out. I stood at the back door with Kay beside me to greet the students. But most of them left through the side doors. Those who did pass our way limited their greetings to a formal, "Good Evening." I introduced myself only as Rev. Lattimer, resisting the urge to explain myself, for during the service no one announced who I was. I supposed word would eventually get around that they had a new Chaplain.

Kwafu and James, our only acquaintances among the crowd, approached us. With them came three students, whom Kwafu introduced as Memka, Comfort, and Oparu. They shook our hands and greeted us warmly.

"We have a meeting now of the Christian Students Association Executive," said Memka. "We should like for you both to attend."

His wide forehead and cheeks sloped sharply downward to his protruding mouth with its wide, toothy smile. The group of about ten students slowly assembled at the front of the auditorium. James came too, for he acted as an advisor. The Association—commonly called the CSA—welded together the University's Christian community. A counterpart of the United Church of Ilaria, the CSA grew from the various denominational groups on campus a year after the Ilaria churches united in 1964. The Executive represented the different committees of the CSA: service, worship, music, and program. When we were introduced to them, the names matching the proper persons escaped me, for at the time I still found it difficult seeing individuality in African faces.

A student named Samuel acted as chairman of the group. Soft-spoken and dignified, he had parliamentary procedure down pat. Right off, he introduced us formally, including a résumé of our background. I responded by expressing our enthusiasm to work with them. Samuel then adroitly led the group through their plans for the first term. They had scheduled programs on African art and Christianity, a discussion on "witnessing," and a symposium led by two faculty members on the debate over the-government-versus-the-church control of Ilarian schools. They asked me to be the moderator of the symposium.

"I really would rather not," I said. "I know nothing about the church-schools debate. I would rather spend this first term learning about the University and Ilaria . . . and getting to know all of you."

Samuel along with a few others stared at me for a few moments. "Is . . . is that all right?" I asked.

"Yes. Yes, of course," Samuel put in quickly. "It's just that, that . . . ."

"What?"

"We were expecting you to more or less take over, Rev. Lattimer," Samuel said with a smile.

"But I think you all are doing a very effective job yourselves. In fact, I was just marveling to myself how efficient and self-directing you seem to be," I said.

"But Reverend Lattimer. We need your help greatly," said Memka smiling. "We have been praying for the past year that a Chaplain would come to help us. And you are a real answer to our prayers!"

"I'm glad to hear that, Memka," I said. "But actually, I'm here to help you do your own work more efficiently. Not to take it away from you and do it myself. O.K.?"

They nodded, but whether they agreed with my words, I didn't know.

The Service Committee reported. Their activities consisted primarily of a campus Sunday School led by students and weekly visits to the local prison. They discussed future visitation among lecturers to encourage them to send their children to the Sunday School.

"But we must visit the lecturers too, to invite them to Sunday worship," stated Memka earnestly. "We must try to evangelize them as well."

Oparu, the chairman of the Service Committee, shrugged his large shoulders and scowled at Memka. "How do you know they don't go to church in town?"

"Indeed, I don't," Memka said, smiling. "Only the Lord knows their hearts. I thought we could invite everyone to church, believers and non-believers as well."

At this point I asked, "How many lecturers do you have participating in the campus church?"

"Only four or five," James put in.

"Do many expatriates ever come?"

"One Englishman and his wife attended last year. But none came tonight," said Samuel. "Perhaps later, more will come."

"Do you think sending out Sunday bulletins to faculty members ahead of time might help?" I asked.

"I should think we could certainly try that," said James.

"Is there anywhere we can mimeograph a bulletin?" I asked.

"To do what, Rev. Lattimer?" asked Oparu.

"To duplicate . . . to run off a bulletin, " I explained. "You know, you cut a stencil and then ink it up."

"Oh, you must mean cyclostyling," said someone.

"Is there one available to us?"

"Yes, at the Printer's Office."

"Where is that located?"

"Near the library."

There was so much to learn. Locations, terminology, strategy, points of view. Inwardly I thanked God I didn't have to do it all in Akarti, the local common vernacular. If I had a new language to learn on top of everything else, it would take years before anything could get started. Still, wouldn't there be an advantage to knowing a little of it? I asked the group.

"Only for contacts among the University labor force: the stewards, the cleaners, the grasscutters," they observed.

"Have you made any efforts to include them in the Christian community? Or to reach out to them in some way?" I asked.

"Generally the Chaplains have ministered only to the students and the academic staff," said Comfort.

"We should consider the others, though," said Memka. "But how?"

"I'll appoint you and your committee, Memka, to study the idea and let me know what you come up with. How does that sound?"

He nodded, grinning broadly.

We finished our business, and I showed them my office. I explained my plans for developing the outer room into a lounge with chairs, a table for literature, bulletin board, and pigeonholes. They liked the idea. After that, our meeting broke up.

On the way to our house, I asked James if he knew whether the Mr. Awulu in the math department ever came to church. "I've never seen him there," he answered.

When we arrived home, he said in his serious manner, "I shall drop by from time to time to see how you are faring."

The next morning, I tried to find the Mr. Awulu to see if it was indeed Moses. I climbed a flight of stairs to the second floor of the Science Faculty. But after wandering all over it, I could not find the math department. I eventually learned that, according to the Ilarian and English system of things, their second floor is our third. So mounting another flight of stairs, I soon found the math department. I went down the hallway slowly until I saw an office with the name "Awulu" in neat letters tacked to the door. I stood there a long time wondering if it might be Moses, wondering what to say if it were he. My hesitancy extended to absurd lengths. I finally mustered up a knock, which sounded like a drum in the empty corridor. I knocked two or three times, but no one answered.

I went on down the hall and found two clerks typing at their desks. I asked if the Mr. Awulu was called "Moses Awulu." They said they didn't know. Neither did they know where he lived. I next went to the Administration Building to find out. I was directed to a clerk on the top floor.

"Just a moment, Father, I will check for you." My ears flipped at the unfamiliar title.

He had no record that the A. S. Awulu was also called "Moses." But he did direct me to his house in Charlestown.

I arranged with the University driver to take me there the next afternoon. We wound through the tangle of roads in Charlestown and halfway up a steep hill. I got out and climbed the remainder by foot, skirting rocks and firewood and streams of wastewater trickling down. I passed two old men half-asleep on their wooden reclining chairs and women pounding cassava in their mortars and fanning charcoal fires. They regarded me indifferently, and I could not get even a smile from them when I tried to greet them.

As I slowly progressed, children began to swarm around me. Barefooted, some in ragged clothes, some in neat school uniforms. Several had pot bellies, and one, a horrible harelip. "*Fama, fama* (White man, White man)," they chanted and presently began to touch my shirt and trousers. Two begged for "pennies" and pulled at my pockets. They pressed so close to me I could no longer walk. I tried shooing them away. But they only mimicked my words and stayed fastened around me with gaping jaws and eyes. An old woman in a battered doorway tottered over the rough ground to the edge of the group. She yanked one child out by his ear and blasted the rest with a stream of words that sent them flying. Then she strolled back to her doorway without ever glancing at me. I called "thank you" to her in Akarti, one of the few phrases I had managed to pick up. She whirled around; her face lit up with a surprised, toothless smile. She called to a neighbor and apparently explained to her what I had said. The two nodded and laughed and talked as I continued up the hill.

I found the house, a yellow one with porches around it. The young girl there spoke no English. I said "Awulu" over and over, and she nodded her head. But when I tried to approach, she held up her palm and shook her head. I presumed no one was in, so I returned to the University. Without my own transport, I would more likely catch Mr. Awulu at his office.

The driver dropped me at the Maintenance Yard. I wanted to see about getting the lounge fixed up, so I went to the man in charge of furnishings. As someone else was inside his office, I sat on a bench outside to wait. I could hear the conversation within. A very irate Englishman was scolding two men. In a cutting voice, the Englishman told them precisely that the whole bunch in the Yard were "stupid fools." That if they did not fill his requisition "without further delay," he would write a letter to every man over them, clear up to the Vice-Chancellor.

In a few minutes, the man stormed out, carrying a portfolio and an umbrella tucked under his arm. His white shorts, shirt, and knee socks accentuated the whiteness of his hair and his trim little mustache. He marched straight to his car, looking neither to the right nor to the left. When the car pulled away, the silence inside the office was broken with a tumult of loud words in a vernacular. Soon, one man left.

I got up after a while and knocked on the open door. The man at the desk barked, "Come," and I entered. He was a pudgy man with a scowl and beads of sweat on his round face. Approaching him, I held out my hand and told him I was the Chaplain. For a brief moment he just looked at my out-stretched hand questioningly. Then he took it politely, announced that his name was "Kpemlo," and invited me to sit down. When he asked what I wanted, I told him of my needs.

As he wrote my request down, I said, "I guess some people give you a hard time."

He jerked his head up and frowned. Then in a moment his features softened, and he sighed. "You are quite right. Never end." He mopped his forehead with his handkerchief.

"Why do you suppose?" I asked gently.

He sucked his teeth and looked at the floor. "I suppose they think they still are in Europe," he sputtered.

"And they expect a European way of doing things here in Ilaria," I said.

He nodded. "They do not understand us, Reverend. They see a Black man and . . . and think we are all the same. Did you hear how that man abused me? Among Ilarians, it is extreme impoliteness to call a man a fool."

"I have heard that," I said. "And I rather suspect that many Ilarians think White people are all the same: arrogant and thoughtless."

He reflected a moment and then nodded.

"How do you think we can break down these false ideas about each other?" I asked him.

"By talking and getting to know one another?" he ventured.

"Perhaps this year the Chaplaincy can promote some of that," I said.

He shook his head. "It will never work, Reverend," he said.

"Why not?"

"White people will not want to come and talk with Ilarians," he declared.

"But remember. White people are not all alike," I said with a smile. He returned it.

"I must go now. You are a busy man, Mr. Kpemlo. I'd appreciate your filling my order when you can," I said.

He stood to shake my hand.

"How do you say, *I must go now*, in Akarti?" I asked him. He told me that although he was Mpesi—another tribe—he knew the Akarti language. I painstakingly copied his words. He also taught me how to say, *I'll be seeing you*, when I asked him.

I used the words all that week. They opened doors and melted impersonal formalism like magic. I became solidly convinced that I should try to study a little Akarti. I slowly began to get the chapel in order: a toilet repaired, the piano pedal fixed, a key remade for the cabinet holding communion equipment, choir robes cleaned. Endless time was spent in finding stencils, a typewriter, and then the cyclostyle. The chapel's typewriter was "spoiled," as they said, and I took it to the machine repair shop on campus. Upon seeing the backlog of broken equipment in the oily shop, I never expected to see it again until Christmas. I was finding that if I lowered my expectations and deadlines, a lot of frustration could be defused. Therefore, it came as a surprise when on Friday of that week, the requisitioned lounge chairs, table, and bulletin board appeared at my office.

It was the same day that I went around posting the Sunday bulletins all over campus. I was walking toward the library when I bumped into James coming from it. His face lit up when he saw me.

"Hank! Whatever are you doing walking about on this hot day?" he asked.

I pulled him into some shade, wiped my face with my handkerchief, and showed him the bulletins. He was pleased to see them. Then he looked squarely at me and announced, "Let's go get a drink. You look hot." He took me in his car across the campus to the senior staff room. We both ordered Cokes and sat down under a cooling overhead fan.

"How is your family adjusting to Ilaria?" James asked.

"Well, the children seem to be doing better than we are," I chuckled.

James took a swallow of his drink. "That's because they are too young to compare former experiences with present ones."

I nodded. "That sounds logical. It's the former experiences in shopping which rise up and haunt my wife ever so often!" I laughed.

"Is she having a hard time finding things?"

"Yes, she sure is."

"And does she work additionally?"

"No. She spends most of her time tending to us. Still, she feels like she ought to be doing something useful. There appear to be so many needs."

"It's a common feeling among expatriates," observed James. "There are needs, certainly. But it is difficult to find ways to alleviate them. Has she been able to meet other wives yet?"

"Not much. We are rather tied down without a car."

James said nothing for a while. Then, "I shall bring my wife over one day."

The following week, James not only introduced his wife to us, but he also took us to town to shop several times. He never talked much when he was with us. But he had a way of being at ease and giving himself undividedly to us. He also showed thoughtfulness in bringing us vegetables or fish or a student magazine we may have missed seeing.

Sometime later he dropped by my office one morning. "I thought you might like to see this. I borrowed it from Mr. Awulu," he said, handing me a book. I looked at it, decidedly puzzled, for the title said *Advanced Calculus*.

"Look at the name inside the cover," he instructed.

I opened it. In the top corner was written, "Moses Awulu, 204 Tibbs Hall, Georgia Tech."

I dropped the book and stared at James.

"So he is here," I said, after I had regained my breath.

"Yes. A. S. Awulu is the same as Moses Awulu. But why does he not use that name now?"

"For any number of reasons. You will find that Ilarians often change their names. Usually in connection with some event or another," he said.

I arose from my chair and looked out the window, then toward the sea. I stood there for some time. Then James said, "This Mr. Awulu. I take it he meant something to you."

"Yes. Very much." I turned and sat back down at my desk. "I suppose I should tell you about him."

"If you like," James said with a smile. "I have the rest of the morning free."

It took that long to relate to him about Moses and me.

Chapter 4

I suppose my friendship with Moses Awulu crystallized that night we were tossed out of a Georgia restaurant because he was Black. It happened in Pointer County in 1967, thirteen years after the fateful Supreme Court decision had shattered the mystique of Southern hospitality and gentility. Our rejection threw me. I had not realized that some Southerners still clung so desperately to a delusion. Then, too, you know how easily you see the speck in the other fellow's eye while failing to note the log in your own. For on that night, I raged against the bigotry, the hard-heartedness, the arrogance of the White restaurant owners who refused to serve us. And yet I could not anticipate that within two months I would be responsible for doing the same thing to Moses.

I first met Moses earlier on the same day. We were both attending a conference on the global church and its mission. Ample barriers stacked up between us to turn off any real communication. He was African, and I, a homegrown Georgian, having never set foot out of southeastern America. At least we both spoke English, although his version rang with British precision. The difference struck me the moment we introduced ourselves, for never before had I heard anything but a drawl coming from a Black man.

"Hello. I'm Hank Lattimer from Greenwood, Georgia. And you are . . . ?"

"Moses Awulu, from Ilaria . . . and Atlanta," his deep voice enunciated carefully. He shook my outstretched hand firmly and looked at me eye-level. Over his short beard, a broad smile revealed bright, even teeth, making vivid his very black skin. Broad-shouldered and trim, he bore himself in a dignified manner with his head held high. Although he looked regal in a purple and yellow tie-dye shirt embroidered in gold, he demonstrated an openness and a certain humility. Or was it shyness or perhaps uncertainty?

"From Ilaria! How glad I am to meet you," I said, smiling. "Are you a student in Atlanta?"

"Yes," He beamed. "At Georgia Tech. I am a graduate in mathematics."

"Have you been in America long?"

"A'tall. Only two months. I'm still quite a green newcomer," he laughed. "Are you a student, too?"

"No," I said. "I'm a Presbyterian minister, an assistant in a large church at Greenwood . . . in mid-Georgia. And I'm the convener of this upcoming discussion group. Will you be able to help us from an African perspective?"

Moses smiled. "By all means! I should be glad to help you in any way possible."

I showed him where to sit in the fast-filling room. He took his place by three other members of the panel, all missionaries from Africa: two from Congo and Rev. Everett Clarke from Ilaria. I had known Everett through my church, for it supported him and his wife during their fifteen years in Ilaria. He and Moses knew each other by name only. Thirty or so teenagers also crowded into the room, with miniskirts, bellbottoms, long hair, beads, a few bare feet on that October weekend. From high schools and colleges all over the southeast, they were attending the largest mission conference of our church. Over 900 had jammed the auditorium the night before under the platform banner: "To the Ends of the Earth." Additionally, thirty-two missionaries, thirteen nationals, and five staff members from our Board of Missions challenged the youth of our church to consider overseas service. I and a dozen other pastors and laymen acted as counsellors and discussion leaders.

When everyone assembled, we started the forum on Africa. The kids, as at most church conferences, showed more interest in the opposite sex than the opposite side of the world. Some, however, proved the exception with their discerning questions. One asked why hadn't the missionaries turned over their work to African nationals and come on home. And another—a Black youth—accused the White missionaries of exploiting the Africans. The two questions triggered an explosion. Within moments, missionaries were vehemently denounced for their short-sightedness and narrow-mindedness, their arrogance and ignorance. I could feel the defensive sweat popping out all over Everett Clarke, next to me. I wanted to help him out. Yet I knew the kids would see through my pat answers and my lack of firsthand experience. So I could not come to his rescue.

But Moses did. In the middle of the controversy, he asked to speak. In gracious tones, he told of the genuine dedication and trustworthiness of missionaries in Ilaria. He described himself as "a product of missionary labors," one who was greatly indebted and devoted to the missionaries he had known. His bearing, his rich voice, his conciliating manner, and, above all, his Africanness sewed up the case. For who could dispute his authority? Everett Clarke glowed. The two from Congo settled back. The discussion turned to other issues.

"It's too bad we don't hear your kind of testimony about missions more often," I exclaimed to Moses that afternoon. I had invited him along with me to view the famous Indian mound on the other side of the conference ground.

"Oh, is it not a popular one?" He seemed surprised.

"No. Neither from nationals on our mission fields or even from many of our church members . . . as you witnessed this morning."

"But why? I rather thought your church was very mission minded."

"It is, compared to other churches perhaps. But there is the growing feeling that we Americans shouldn't *interfere*, both in international politics and religion. And also the feeling that we have too many problems right here at home."

Moses sighed. "Indeed that is difficult to believe. Of course, I'm speaking only from my own experience. But our church, though it is large and self-supporting, still needs your missionaries!"

"Do the majority in the Ilaria churches agree with you?"

"Certainly," his eyes widened. "Else why should we continue to ask missionaries from your church and others to come? Of course, however, there are some who don't agree. Perhaps due to a bitter experience or personal grudge."

"You don't think the missionary's white skin gets in the way?"

He frowned. "What do you mean?"

"Don't Africans these days associate Whiteness with Colonialism and paternalism?"

He smiled. "You cannot generalize, Rev. Lattimer. It depends entirely on the individual missionary. But really, I cannot speak too highly of the missionaries I have known in Ilaria. Particularly one of your church."

"Who is that?"

"Miss Luella Watson. Do you know her?"

"No, not personally."

"If it were not for her, why, I would not be here today! I can never repay her for her many kindnesses to me."

"How did you know her?"

"She and I worked together in the same Training College. I taught maths, and she, education. She's a deeply spiritual woman. It was she who told me about your church's scholarship program through your Board of Missions. It was her idea that I get an advanced degree in order to teach at one of our universities. She not only helped me to secure the scholarship but also the necessary documents to come to America. I am so thankful to God for her!" He told me of some of the other missionaries he had known, but I did not recognize their names.

The forest clipped by us as I drove. I noticed Moses observing the oaks, pines, and red-berried dogwoods intently. He commented on the beauty of my country. That led to more of his observations of America and into his problems of adjustment. I could tell, too, that he greatly missed his wife and small son back in Ilaria,

"But by far the biggest adjustment, Rev. Lattimer, is just in being a foreigner—an outsider. Always being conscious of the acute difference between myself and Americans."

"Do you mean by being Black?"

"No, it's not so much differences in skin color, as in outlook . . . in understanding. We have a proverb which expresses it: *A stranger's eyes may be big, but he will not understand enough*, meaning, no matter how much you understand, as a foreigner, you'll never understand everything. You will always remain on the fringes."

His frank sharing moved me. He was the first communicative, non-hostile Black person I had met in recent years. By then we reached the Indian mound and got out. We circled the mound in the shape of an eagle, built by pre-Indian peoples about 5,000 years ago. A small observation tower nearby enabled us to visualize it better. Moses was astounded that the stones making up the eagle had been in the same position for so long a period of time. We peered at the eagle and the forest for a while from the tower, before descending the damp stairs. Then halfway down, Moses slipped on a step and fell to the landing. I rushed to help him up. When he put his weight on his foot, it hurt so that he could not walk. So I tried to help him by holding his arm. But the stairway was too narrow. At one point I tripped, almost lunging us down a second flight of stairs.

"That will never do," I said. "Both of us can't afford to be crippled. We'd freeze up here in the winter, and no one would find us 'til spring!"

"And then you would have one rock eagle and two iced chickens," Moses commented, sending us both into gales of laughter. Finally, we decided he'd have to sit his way down. When he lamented that his pants were getting wet, I assured him that I had an extra pair he could wear.

At length we made it to the car and returned to the conference center. The dying sunset glimmered in the conference lake as we rounded it. I went straight to the cabin where I had been staying. Inside, I found the extra shorts and slacks for Moses to try. They fit perfectly. I then examined his ankle by gently moving it in all directions.

"I don't think it's sprained. But I have just the thing for it." I took an elastic bandage from my suitcase. "I always carry one of these with me," I explained. "I have bad ankles myself, left from my soccer days."

"Soccer! Did you play soccer?" Moses exclaimed.

I nodded. "During my university days."

"So did I! What position did you play?"

"Right back. And you?"

"Center. My, what a coincidence!"

"We had a good many internationals on our team at Georgia . . . the University of Georgia. Mostly Europeans and Iranians, though."

"It is a pity we could not have played together, Rev. Lattimer." Moses shook his head.

"Forget the *Reverend* bit." I grinned.

"I keep forgetting. In America you call your mister *minister* instead of *reverend*, as in Ilaria."

"That may be true. But even so, you can call me Hank. I'm probably not much older than you."

"Oh, really?" Moses gaped at me. "I am 28. How old are you?"

"The very same."

"The same! Why, I had no idea. But then I have always had difficulty judging a White man's age."

"And I the same about a Black man's."

We both laughed. I looked at my watch. "It's almost suppertime. Shall we go together?"

"That will be fine," he said. "I will just hobble on your arm, OK?

At the cafeteria, we ate with some of the gang I had brought to the conference from my church. Bud Maxwell, a student from Tech and also a member at Trinity, joined us too. Bud was an all-American-boy type, whose wholesome freshness shone in his eager smile. He readily accepted Moses, along with the rest of the group. No doubt Moses's manner had something to do with his ease at making friends. For he was always delighting in new faces and experiences.

At the table, the kids enjoyed not only listening to Moses tell about Ilaria. But with hilarity, they also related their misconceptions about Africa. Gradually, our images of jungles and witch doctors and round mud huts faded in the easy-going encounter.

After supper we joined the evening meeting in the auditorium. Bud excused himself from us, as he was a guitar player in the special music ensemble. Other items on the program included a lengthy songfest, brief reports from three of our mission fields, and a talk by a mission executive of another denomination.

When it ended, about an hour and a half later, I felt a strong hand grip my shoulder. I turned.

"Davis! When did you get here?" I blurted as I looked into the face of a doctor from my church: Davis Howard. He was casually dressed in a wool plaid jacket, looking like a woodsman just come in from the hunt. He never pronounced words right, and his speech flowed with a western North Carolina hillbilly twang. People always reacted with surprise to learn he was the leading diagnostician in Greenwood. But his interests extended far beyond the medical world to include international and race relations. He was also the youngest man on our Session, the governing body of our church. I secretly suspected that Davis rather liked to shock people with all his inconsistencies.

"Just this afternoon. The trusty Howard Cessna flew me up."

"Where did you land it?"

"Over'n a pasture. Half mile away," he said puffing on his pipe.

"Here. Let me introduce you. This is Moses Awulu from Ilaria. One of our Mission Board's scholarship students."

"Pleased to meet you, Moses," Davis said, shaking his hand. "Are you the only one from Ilaria on scholarship this year?"

"Yes, that is correct," said Moses, his face wreathed in a smile.

Davis grunted and cocked his head in Moses's direction. "Say that again."

"I said, that is correct. I seem to be the only scholarship student from Ilaria," he clipped his words.

Davis whistled and turned to me. "Sounds like King's English there!" And to Moses, "Beautiful!" shaking his hand again.

The Ilarian's eyebrows knit in bewilderment.

"He's remarking about your accent, Moses," I explained. "He enjoys hearing it."

"Oh, I see," he laughed.

Suddenly Davis leaned away from us and yelled across the aisle. "Rufus! Hey, Rufus!" A Black man extracted himself from the crowd. "I want you to meet a soul brother, from Ilaria. Moses Awulu, this is Rufus Hill, a pastor in Atlanta," Davis said, holding Rufus by the arm.

The two Black men greeted each other enthusiastically. Rufus, heavily built with bulging muscles, looked more like an athlete than a minister. He wore a dashiki of colorful African print and a modest Afro hair style. A somber expression hung over him like a cloud, which vanished temporarily as he shook my hand. Davis explained that they knew each other through some church committee on race relations. Suddenly an exchange passed between them which caught me off guard.

"How's dis heah be-yoo-ti-full Negro been doin'?" Davis asked Rufus, punching him on the arm.

"Dis heah Negro's been having' mighty rough time keepin' White folks offin ma back!" answered Rufus.

"White ain't so right no mo'," said Davis, shaking his head. "Naw, son. They ain't. . . . Black is beautiful!"

"Yeah, man. Black is beautiful!" echoed Rufus.

Then they both waved clenched fists into the air simultaneously and burst into laughter. They slapped each other on the back and reverted to their normal speech: Davis, his countrified talk, and Rufus, his urbane manner of speaking. I had no idea what Moses thought or how much he understood of the episode. But I was dumbfounded. Davis and Rufus evidently shared a camaraderie based on common concerns. Still, the thought of joking with and using these words baffled me, for they were words I considered and—I thought—Black people considered insulting. The exchange illustrated my dilemma of talking with Black people in general. I always stood on a swampy ground of uncertainty, even in a trivial conversation about the weather, for no longer did you know what gesture or word or insinuation would offend a Black person. You wanted to be honest, to really care, but so often your efforts backfired. And not so much because of who you were or what you said, but rather who you represented, which I found infuriatingly unjust. Perhaps I needed more exposure to Negroes—or "Black people," as they were preferring to be called—and I was having a hard time remembering. Then maybe I'd learn the ins and outs and not be put off. But in my work at Trinity Presbyterian Church, I rarely related to Black people, except for those on the custodial staff of the church.

As we stood there, Davis suggested we go get a cup of coffee down the road. On our way out, he nabbed Everett Clarke to join us as well as a Mexican he knew, named José. Outside, the night air was brisk. The stars sparkled in the sky, and the quarter moon bobbed in the ripples of the lake across from us. On the way to the car, Rufus asked Moses where he was located and what he was doing. Then he wanted to know how the African's stay in America had been so far.

"Very fine, thank you," said Moses.

"I'm glad to see more from Africa on mission scholarships. I hope more will come from your country."

"Perhaps they will in the future."

"You fellows from Africa are real missionaries to us in the South, you know," I heard him tell Moses.

"Oh, really? How is that?" Moses asked with a surprised tone.

"We need to hear your prophetic word on this race thing."

"Pardon me?"

Rufus repeated his statement a little slower.

"I heard what you said," said Moses. "But I . . . I do not understand you."

"What I mean is," said Rufus, "the Church in the South needs to hear your observations and judgment on racism."

I could tell that Moses was puzzled. "I have no judgment on racism, as you say," he assured Rufus. "In fact, I've encountered nothing but kindness and acceptance in the churches since my arrival. How can I criticize something that I've not encountered?" he asked kindly.

Out of the corner of my eye, I saw Rufus swing his head sharply to peer at Moses in the semidark. He didn't say anything for a long while. "Perhaps not," he murmured finally.

At the car, Rufus, Moses, and I climbed into the back seat, and the others squeezed next to Davis at the wheel. He warmed the motor a bit and then steered through the conference grounds to the main highway.

"Well, José, my friend," Davis said with his pipe between his teeth. "What did you think of the evening speaker . . . as a national from one of our mission fields?"

"Truthfully, I was surprised that he should speak his mind at a foreign missions conference," responded the Mexican. "Of course, mission boards of other denominations are recalling their missionaries along the lines he was suggesting."

"If our Board did that, would it seriously affect the work in Mexico?" asked Davis.

José chuckled. "Yes . . . in the right way. In fact, many of the younger pastors want the missionaries to leave. They want to try their hand at running their own church."

"Well, I think it's scandalous," inserted Everett, trying to see both Davis and us in the back seat. "Theologically, the speaker's premises were in error. The Lord didn't say, 'Clean up Israel first and then make disciples of all nations.' He did not even say, 'Convert Israel first.'"

"No, he didn't, did he?" put in Rufus. "He said, 'You shall be my witnesses: in Jerusalem, in Judea and Samaria, and to the ends of the earth.'"

"Precisely!" exclaimed Everett.

"But that does not mean that when we send missionaries abroad that Jerusalem and Judea should be neglected," said Rufus.

"No, I agree with you," said Everett. "But I see no point in recalling missionaries to do stateside work. Land alive! Just look how many Christians and churches and pastors we have in the States to do the work. And where I am in Ilaria, only 20% of the population are professing Christians!"

"Do you think a greater percentage of the population in America are genuine Christians?" pushed Rufus. "You certainly can't say the Black population is being reached. Nor even the White racists who dominate the churches, I might add."

Everett didn't respond for a while. Then chuckling, he said, "That sounds like a pretty sweeping generalization you just made about the White people in the churches."

"Not at all," retorted Rufus.

Davis looked into the rearview mirror. "And what would be your opinion, Moses? Do you think we should recall our missionaries from Ilaria to tend to the ills of the Church here at home?"

"By no means!" exclaimed Moses moving to the edge of the car seat. "Christians and pagans alike would be far poorer without their presence in our country. Of course, I know very little about the problems in America. But I should think that a balance could be struck between home and foreign missions."

Everett nodded vigorously. By then, we had reached a fork in the road, and in the point sat a truck stop with its gas pump beaming like a lighthouse into the night. We entered the building, half of which was a restaurant, and the other half, a small store. A gaudy jukebox separated the two areas. Of the half-dozen tables in the restaurant, one was occupied by three men looking at the menus. Beside it stood a stocky woman taking orders. They all stared at us as we sat down and perused the menus. Out of the corner of my eye I saw the woman disappear into the kitchen.

"Coffee for everyone?" asked Davis looking up from the menu. "How 'bout a sandwich? I'm starved. Everett? Rufus?"

Everett grinned. "Well, a hamburger might taste good on a night like this."

We were discussing what to order when a man stalked toward us from the kitchen. Pale and almost bald, he wore a spattered apron. He stopped at Davis's elbow.

"Oh, good, here we are," said Davis. "We would like five hamburgers and . . . ."

Before he could finish, the man announced in a monotone, "We don't serve no Negroes in here."

Davis gaped at the man, frozen. We all gaped. Even the men from the other table were watching. No one made a move for a while, and it appeared that the whole evening stood still, unable to progress from that point.

Davis ceremoniously closed the menu and methodically folded the napkin in his lap. I could see his jaw clinching and unclinching. Then he pushed his chair out a little and arose to face the man directly. "And why not?" he asked.

The cook pointed to a sign over the cash register. "That's why," he said through scarcely parted lips. It said: "We have the right to refuse service to anyone."

"Now, please go," said the cook. "We don't want no trouble in here."

Davis sighed audibly. "It's just too bad you don't get our business tonight, isn't it?" he said, smiling broadly at the cook, but his voice was cutting.

"This is against Georgia law, you know that," blurted out Rufus, balling up his fists at his side.

"That makes no never mind. Georgia law ain't Pointer County. You can see the sheriff of this county or whomsoever you please." The man met Rufus's angry gaze head on with his faded blue eyes, his mouth set in a defensive line.

We grabbed up our sweaters and jackets and marched out. In the car, Davis was the first to break the silence. "What's the name of this place anyway?" He rolled down the car window and strained to look at the sign over the doorway. "Dunbar's Roadside Cafe," it read.

"What was all that business about the sheriff of Pointer County?" asked Everett.

"What it meant was it's no use to see the country sheriff," stated Rufus. "He no doubt supports this establishment!" And he hit his knee with his fist and muttered, "Damn!"

"But how can that be if it's against the state law?" asked Everett.

Davis chuckled. "Brother Everett, you've been outta the country too long!"

Everett smiled over at him. "I guess you're right about that! The last racial incident in Georgia that I know anything about was when Lester Maddox forcibly kept Black people out of his restaurant in Atlanta. That was some time ago," he laughed.

"Uh-hmmmm," nodded Rufus.

"When was that? 1950 . . . what?" asked Everett.

"1964," retorted Rufus.

"Moses, how're you doing back there?" Davis searched for him in the rearview mirror.

"Oh, quite well," Moses announced cheerfully. "I presume they did not want us because we were a biracial group. Is that correct?" he asked.

"Yep. Lamentably correct," stated Davis. "I think we ought to report it to the FBI. And perhaps to the company selling gasoline there. After all, they sell in Africa, don't they?" Rufus asked Moses.

"Yes, they do," chimed in Everett before Moses could answer.

"If they sell in Africa, they might want to know about something like this," said Rufus.

"Why, whatever good would that do?" reacted Everett, turning to try to look at Rufus.

There was a long pause before Rufus answered. "Mr. Clarke, when you're on the bottom of the trash heap, you try just about anything," he said in a strained voice.

"The bottom of the trash heap! I . . . I don't understand," Everett sputtered.

Silence hemmed in Rufus's words for a few moments. Then, "I'm afraid I can't explain. Just skip it," he snapped.

Everett remained in the half-turned position waiting for the conversation to resume. But when he saw that Rufus preferred to remain silent, he slowly settled back beside Davis, shaking his head in the semidark. Davis jabbed at his pipe as he drove, and we passed down the highway in silence.

Chapter 5

Early the next morning, I drove over to Moses's cabin to pick him up for breakfast. He answered, "Come," to my knock on his door. He dropped the Bible he had been reading when he saw me.

"Hank! Good morning." He took my hand in both of his and greeted me with genuine warmth. He had on a heavy cloth wrapped around him. It gleamed of rich blues and golds, woven in a fantastic design, almost like a plaid.

"Wow! What have you got on there?" I exclaimed, examining the cloth, woven in long strips and then sewn together.

"Our national dress, a *lemna*," he beamed. "How do you keep it on?" I asked. "It looks ever so long!"

"It is. It's six yards of material," Moses said, undoing it. Let me show you how it's done." He swirled it deftly around his collarless shirt and his shorts and ended by draping it over his left shoulder, leaving the right one free. It fell in folds down to his ankles, much like a Roman toga.

"How's your ankle?" I asked.

"Somewhat stiff," he said and held it out so I could examine it. The bandage had slipped a bit overnight, so I redid it. We then went to the cafeteria for breakfast.

"Moses," I said while driving. "I can't tell you how sorry I am about what happened last night."

He swiveled his head in my direction. "Oh, that's all right, Hank. I understand."

"Do you understand, really?"

He laughed. "If you press me, I guess I don't understand. But I'll try to accept it and go on from there. Besides, it was not directed entirely at me. After all, Rufus was there, too. It is he who should have our sympathy."

"Oh? What do you mean?" I had not even considered Rufus.

"Why, it was his countrymen who rejected him," exclaimed Moses. "Do you suppose that sort of thing happens to him often?"

"I have no idea," I murmured.

"But tell me something, Hank. The sign in the restaurant . . . what did it mean? I didn't understand it. It said nothing about Black people not being permitted to eat there."

I explained to him the sign and its ruse. I also explained how an establishment that catered to the public could not legally designate whom it would or would not serve. Then he asked the same question Everett Clarke had asked: How could the restaurant still operate if it was against the law? So I told him about local Georgia politics and how politicians managed to stay in power by winking at the law.

Moses was quiet for a long while. Then, "Perhaps the owners are not Christians," he declared.

"I doubt that," I blurted. "They are probably hard-shelled, Bible-carrying, go-to-church-every-Sunday Christians!"

"No!"

My eyes jerked towards his. I scanned his serious yet utterly sincere expression. "Moses," I said. "I don't know what you know about our South and our churches. But racial discrimination does exist among Christians, I am sad to report."

He sighed, "Yes, I suppose." He knitted his brows and rubbed his beard. "But I have difficulty accepting it. I mean, how can real Christians—evangelicals—love God and yet hate their brother? For we read in 1 John 2:9: *He who says he is in the light and hates his brother is in the darkness still.*"

I did not know how to answer. For one swift moment I was even tempted to let him live in that false assumption. Instead, I tried to tell him that, although scripturally, prejudice stood condemned, it nevertheless existed. Men are still men, flawed and sinful. "Have you never run across prejudiced Christians before?" I asked him.

"Why, no! Not among evangelicals," he looked stricken. I then asked him what he had been told about the South before he came to America.

"Only what Miss Watson told me," he said. "She said that discrimination towards Black people indeed existed here. But that I probably would not confront it in Atlanta, because it is a progressive, broad-minded city. She could not speak for the more rural areas of Georgia, however. I guess she was right about that!" he chuckled. "She also said that I would not encounter discrimination either in the Presbyterian Churches, that your General Assembly had strongly denounced racism and that the churches, for the most part, abided by its pronouncement."

"Was the progressiveness of Atlanta the reason you chose to study there?" I asked.

"It was Miss Watson's idea, really. She comes from Atlanta, and she wanted me to be associated with her church there: Second Presbyterian. She thought I would be better cared for."

"And have you been?"

"Oh, yes. They have been most kind to me there."

"Has anyone invited you into their home . . . or taken you around town?"

He paused. "Well . . . no. No one has. I have been there every Sunday to worship. When I introduced myself to the minister for the first time, he already knew about me through a letter from Miss Watson. He welcomed me most cordially and introduced me to a number of people. I sit with a certain family every Sunday. But aside from them, I don't know anyone else."

"Have you been to any other churches in Atlanta?"

"Yes. To St. Andrew's Presbyterian with the Jackson family. They were my host family for two weeks before classes began at Tech. They became like a real family to me," he said with a smile.

"And how was their church?"

"About the same. Friendly and hospitable."

"Tell me. Did you see any other Black people in these churches?"

"No, in neither church. I talked with the Jacksons at length about it one Sunday."

"And what did they say?"

"They told me how St. Andrew's has opened its doors freely to Black people, but they just have not come. They mentioned something about socioeconomic factors that make Black people feel out of place and uncomfortable. The church is in a White neighborhood in the suburbs. Mrs. Jackson says that they have tried many ways to attract Black people to their church, but they will not come. However, they took me to a church in downtown Atlanta which does have many Black members."

"Which church is that?"

"Bethel Presbyterian."

"I've heard of it. It's biracial, isn't it?"

"Indeed it was! I never saw anything quite like it. It made me feel ... well, gratified that the church actively tries to alleviate the community problems through classes, clinics, and that sort of thing."

"And did you see the community?"

"Oh, yes! The copastor, a Black man, Mr. Bankins took me there."

"And how did that hit you?"

"Pardon me?"

"How did you react to the community?"

He thought for a while. "It made my heart ache," he said softly. "I never expected a slum like that in America. We have them in Ilaria, particularly in Kwa and the larger cities. But not in America," he shook his head.

We had reached the cafeteria, and I was parking the car when he said, "But something Mr. Bankins said . . . really troubles me."

"What is that?"

"He said that it is White racism that perpetuates the slums. Is that true, Hank?"

I studied the creases of concern on his face. "Partly, I suppose. But I frankly think that is an oversimplification. I think the Black man could really help himself more if he sincerely wanted to."

"But the ghetto doesn't give him much opportunity, does it?"

"No, No, I guess it doesn't," I said.

At the cafeteria, we had to wait awhile in a long line outside before we reached the food. It was another lovely autumn day, which filled you with joy and gratitude, despite Dunbar's. I think Moses felt it too. He seemed to savor every cloud and tree, every person who passed by, noting their mannerisms, their dress. I caught myself seeing my compatriots through his eyes. What would he think of the couple holding hands coming down the walkway? Did Ilarian young people show affection in public? How did he react to the outfits people wore? Pants on girls, shorts on men on Sunday, long hair on boys? Moses became a mirror by which I could see my own society objectively for the first time. Its peculiarities, its hang-ups, its hypocrisies.

We went through the line, collected our food, and found a place to sit. Along the way, heads turned and eyes stared at Moses and his *lemna*. Many people came to ask him about it. He explained it and how it was made and worn, always patiently and proudly. I looked for Bud in the mob, but I failed to find him.

During breakfast I quizzed Moses about his life in Ilaria: where he had been to school and worked. He described the University of Ilaria to me, near the capitol city.

"Is it the only university in the country?"

"No. There is one other at Charlestown in the west. It is called Western University, and it teaches science and technology almost exclusively."

"Do any of our Presbyterian missionaries work in the universities?"

"I'm not sure," he cocked his head.

"What do most ordained missionaries do in Ilaria?"

"Some supervise churches. A few actually have individual congregations. But most of them act as teachers in secondary schools and universities."

"Oh, really? What do they teach?"

"Bible . . . what we call Religious Knowledge. We don't have Christian education in our churches as you do here in America," he said. "Much of it is done in our schools."

"Are they church schools?"

"Most of them are. But not the universities. The schools were begun by missionaries, mainly from Europe, in the 19th century. The local churches control them now. There have been threats from the government to take over the schools. It says it will still allow Religious Knowledge to be taught, but the churches are skeptical. It will be a real battle if the government ever acts on it."

I gulped down the last swallows of my coffee and rocked back in my chair. Then something which had been brewing for a while in me spilled out. "You know what, Moses," I said. "I may end up in Africa someday . . . as a missionary."

He almost dropped his cup. "Hank! That's wonderful! Do you think it will be Ilaria? Or Congo?" his eyes grew big. "Oh, I hope it's Ilaria!"

"I have no idea at this stage," I said, "It's not that far along in my thinking. But I have considered it for a long while . . . since I was a teenager."

"Why didn't you tell me sooner?"

"I guess I had no real reason to," I said, smiling.

I watched him finish up his meal. He piled his grits and egg on the back of his fork held in his left hand, the way English people do. When he finished, he sat looking at me, smiling but saying nothing. Finally,

"Oh, I hope it's Ilaria!" and he shook his head for emphasis. "Will you stay in the church in Greenwood for a certain length of time?"

"No. I can stay as long as I wish."

"Have you been there long?"

"Two and a half years."

"Do you plan to stay there much longer?"

"I suppose so. I have no real reason to leave at the present."

"Do you like it?"

"Hmmm . . . yes. But not for too long."

"What do you mean?"

"I'd like to branch out on my own someday," I said. "Be my own boss you might say."

"In your own church?"

"Maybe. Or on a university campus."

"I see," said Moses. "You can tell I'm just figuring how soon you may be coming to Ilaria!"

"I really don't know, Moses. It may work out. It may not. I'll just have to wait and see."

"Well, I shall pray that it will work out!" he declared, and I knew he meant he would.

After breakfast we went to the auditorium. The morning worship came as the final meeting of the conference. It would be the last chance for the young people to hear the high-geared sales pitch for missions. The preacher for the morning had been carefully chosen to bring the weekend to a climax. He was one of the most articulate missionaries in our church, a minister in Brazil. He read the lesson:

> *The Spirit of the Lord is upon me, because he has anointed me to preach good news to the poor. He has sent me to proclaim release to the captives and recovering of sight to*

"Who are the oppressed?" the preacher asked. "Who are the captives?" He graphically pictured those "bound in the darksome prison house of sin ... the people that walk in darkness." And in each instance, those who were chained and oppressed, those who were blind and poor were somewhere "at the ends of the earth": namely, those living in the Presbyterian mission fields and beyond. Again, with Moses sitting beside me, I tried to imagine the sermon from his viewpoint. What did he think of it?

Afterward, he told me. "It was a wonderful sermon," he said. "I hope it calls many students out as missionaries."

And it did. For nearly 100 fellows and girls went forward at an invitation to prayerfully consider world missions as God's plan for their lives. Bud was among them.

Moses ate lunch with a group from Selma, Alabama, who wanted to talk with him about Ilaria. I nabbed Bud and ate with them.

"Congratulations on your decision," I told him.

"Thanks, Hank." His boyish face brimmed with more than his usual exuberance. "I feel real good about it. Say, where's Moses? He's supposed to ride with me back to Atlanta."

I told him and said I'd get Moses to him at the designated time and place. Then I related to Bud what had happened to us the night before.

Bud gasped in horror. "Man, how low can you get!" he exploded. "I guess those owners didn't know he was from Africa."

"What difference would it make?" I said. "A Black man is still a Black man in their eyes."

Bud's eyes drifted off. "'s funny. I don't think of him as Black. How did he take it?"

"Apparently, OK. He was more concerned with the other Black person in our group."

"Great! He's a keen Christian, isn't he? I guess he influenced me a lot in my decision this morning. And now what you told me confirms it."

"Oh? How's that?"

"Black people have suffered too long, Hank." His brow furrowed. "We owe them an awful lot. That's why I'm considering Africa."

When we finished up our meal, I went around telling the teenagers from my church where to meet me to head for home. Then I picked up Moses and went to the parking lot to wait for them and for Bud. As we sat there in the car, Everett Clarke drove up next to us. He came over and leaned into the window on Moses's side.

"Is Moses here going with you?" he asked me.

"No, he's waiting on a ride for Atlanta. And I'm waiting on the teenagers I brought with me from my church."

"Oh, you're from Trinity, aren't you?" he said with a smile.

I nodded.

"I'll be itinerating there along about March. I'm looking forward to it. Trinity's a mighty fine church. Mighty fine. They really support the cause of world missions, don't they?"

"They sure do," I responded. "I guess, in a way, their mission emphasis attracted me to work at that church."

"I should think it would be a fine place for a young minister to start off," he nodded his head.

"It is. Quite," I agreed.

Then he looked at Moses. "You know," his face grew serious. "I'm real sorry about what happened last night at that café. But I hope you understand."

Moses broke into a large smile. "I'm trying to," he said.

"It will take many years for this race issue to be settled. Many years." Everett pursed his lips. "And the trouble is that so many hot-headed folk want to work wonders overnight. Why, I've learned in Africa you just can't hurry up things before they're ready. Do you know what I mean?" he placed a fatherly hand on Moses's shoulder.

"I guess I do," said Moses.

"I certainly cannot justify the South for its prejudices. Not for a moment. But neither can I justify these social activists in our very churches who push integration at the expense of the Gospel of our Lord Jesus Christ. Why, our whole business as Christians is to proclaim the pure Gospel! It alone will bring healing, won't it, Moses? Nothing else truly matters."

Moses looked as if he were about to respond, when a good-looking blonde fellow called over from the Clarke's car, "Hey, Dad. How are we going to get all this stuff in?" But when he saw that he had interrupted us, he apologized and came our way. Everett introduced him as one of his four sons, all of whom, as Everett explained with pride, were "Ilaria born."

"Well, I guess we'd better be going," said Everett. "So long. Have a safe trip. The Lord bless you." And he left to pack his car.

Soon after that, Bud drove into the parking lot. Moses and I got out and were on the verge of going to Bud's car, when he stopped me. He held out his hand to shake mine.

"I want to thank you for everything," Moses said, gripping my hand hard. "I'm so thankful we met. Will we ever see each other again?"

"I expect so," I said. "I'll be coming to Atlanta, and I'll be sure to look you up."

"Please do," he urged. "I shall be expecting you." His ebony face glowed with his smile.

We shook hands. Then he slid his palm along mine, and when our hands released, he snapped his thumb and index finger together.

"Hey, hey!" I exclaimed. "What kind of handshake is this?"

"It is Ilarian. One used by very close friends. You are supposed to snap your fingers with mine. Shall we try again?"

We did and managed to synchronize the finger snaps perfectly. "Thanks, Moses," I said with a grin. "Thanks a lot." I walked with him to Bud's car and watched them drive away.

Chapter 6

When I went to Atlanta a month later for a church meeting, I found Moses engrossed in his studies and the affairs of the school. He had not been able to meet any other Africans in Atlanta, and it seemed that a tightly knit group of foreign students comprised his friends. They banded together to offer each other mutual solace and the basics of life, like food, money, and facility in speaking English. It disturbed me to see that he was enmeshed in a ghetto of internationals almost exclusively. I asked him, hadn't he met any American students. He confided that, except for Bud and a Bible study he attended, he hadn't. "They are terribly friendly, Hank," he said. "But they don't seem to have time to be your friend."

While I was with Moses, he received a letter from his sister in his home village. Written in limited English, it told of the death of their brother in a truck accident. The news shook Moses visibly. Slowly, he began to tell me about his brother and his life in a Ketumba village, Ketumba's being the tribe he came from. He told me of his uncle, who acted like a father to him, a man made wealthy from timber. He described his uncle's house as the most prestigious in the village because "the mud walls were cemented over and it had a corrugated iron roof instead of thatch." The uncle had bought the truck the brother had driven to his death and financed Moses's education "so that I became the most highly educated man in my village," he said. "Without Uncle, I am nothing."

He went on to relate the awesome pressure over him to succeed, for he did not want to disappoint any of those back home who doted on him. Since Moses's Arab roommate was out that night, I spent the night with him in his room. We went to church next morning—Miss Watson's—and by the time I left for Greenwood after lunch, he appeared a little cheered.

Thanksgiving rolled around soon after that. In spite of extra church duties, I thought frequently of Moses. I wrote him to express my concern for him, as well as to thank him for his hospitality the weekend I was there. The following week, I heard from him. He wrote,

Dear Brother Hank:

I received your kind letter with joy. You will be glad to know that I am keeping well. My sorrow has not been able to overcome me, by the grace of our dear Lord.

Thanksgiving proved to be a very lonely time, with hardly anything to do but to face one's very impersonal books! All of us internationals, who had no place to go, moved into one dorm which remained open during the holiday. I spent most of my time studying: it was a good time for catching up. I also went to church on Thanksgiving morning.

Bud's Bible study group has been a great blessing to me during this time. The students in it have accepted me completely, and in its close fellowship, I no longer feel a foreigner. Isn't that marvelous? I thank you sincerely for introducing me to Bud.

Recently I decided to quit attending Second Presbyterian. I had been attending it primarily for Miss Watson's sake. But I decided there just might be a church that could provide more fellowship. I have gone to Bethel Church, downtown. It is a lively church and has made me feel super-welcomed, if there is such a word.

Then this week we foreign students received invitations to Christmas International House, a program of hospitality open to us during the coming Christmas holidays. Have you heard of it, Hank? It sounds marvelous! None of us has to worry about spending a bleak holiday on an empty campus as we did at Thanksgiving. And to crown it all, I was asked by the Jacksons to be co-director of the House at St. Andrew's Church, which will be a host church. Truly, the Lord has been good to me.

Moses enclosed in his letter a brochure describing the Christmas International House program. About thirteen churches scattered over the country would use their educational facilities to house international students during the holidays. Additionally, the program offered get-togethers with Americans and other nationalities, recreation, tours, and the like. Internationals of all faiths, nationalities, ages, and races were welcome. St. Andrew's was the only participating church in Georgia. The blurb about it said: "We offer good old *Southern hospitality* in the hub of the South, Atlanta, the capitol of Georgia. Tours will be featured to Stone Mountain, the Lockheed aircraft plant, museums, the State Legislature, and other points of historic interest. Ya'll come!"

The program caught my imagination. Suddenly it occurred to me that maybe some of the students staying at St. Andrew's would like to come to Greenwood on a special tour. They could spend two nights in individual church members' homes with a full day devoted to activities around our town, for certainly Greenwood and Trinity Church qualified as "points of historic interest."

Trinity Presbyterian Church, one of the oldest of our denomination, was built in 1798, shortly after Greenwood was settled. As far as I was concerned, I've never seen a mustier, darker, creakier church. But all that just enhanced its appeal to our congregation and to the citizens of Greenwood as well, particularly because in Trinity's walls can be seen fragments of cannon balls fired from the guns of William Tecumseh Sherman when he marched through to Savannah in 1864. For that reason, the church is deemed a Historic Landmark of Georgia. School children and historical societies for counties around periodically view the building. But being a historic landmark carried with it a high price. In an effort to retain the antique chandeliers, costly wiring had been installed. Occasionally it went on the blink, draining yet more from the church budget. Additionally, the sanctuary featured a pulpit perched at the top of a small spiral staircase, pews with doors at the ends of them, wooden floors, and a balcony around three sides of the room originally built for slaves. All of these required occasional mending, refinishing, and a vigilance against termites.

In spite of vast sums spent on its upkeep, most of Trinity's money did not remain on its premises. On the contrary, almost half of the church's budget went to outside benevolences, more than any other church of comparable size in the state of Georgia. These included colleges and seminaries of our denomination, an orphanage in South Carolina, a home for the aged, a college for Negroes, and St. Mark's

Settlement, a mission to Negroes in Greenwood. Above all, Trinity contributed generously to world missions and overseas relief. It supported seven missionaries completely on three different fields, a record which no other Presbyterian church in a four-state area could match. Trinity was widely known as a "mission-minded" church, and it was proud of the fact.

After I received Moses's letter, I went to the office of our senior pastor, Dr. Calvin Rutledge, for our usual 9:30 a.m. tête-á-tête. The occasion always included a ritual of coffee in gold-rimmed china cups served by Hattie, the chief Negro church cook. Then with saucer in one hand and a cup in the other, Dr. Rutledge leaned back on the velvet sofa opposite me and peered in this customary manner through the bottom part of his bifocals. He was a small man with white hair, translucent skin, and misty blue eyes. Every day, he wore a dark blue suit—either a herringbone or pinstripe—and an immaculately starched, French-cuffed shirt.

"Well, what's new with you Henry?" he asked. He loathed nicknames.

I told him about Moses and Christmas International House. As with me, it pricked Dr. Rutledge's imagination. Right then, we put in a call to St. Andrew's Church in Atlanta. They approved our suggestion and earmarked December 27-29 for a tour for 25 students to come to Greenwood. We would be responsible for accommodation and transportation between Atlanta and Greenwood.

I also requested that Moses come down with the group. That, too, was agreed upon. It remained only for the Session of Trinity to approve the idea. When Session convened a few days later, Horace Bull and I met with Dr. Rutledge as per custom prior to the meeting to go over the agenda. Horace was the "Clerk of the Session," the recording secretary, a prestigious position in any Presbyterian church. He was a short, stout man of about fifty with a florid complexion. Whether that came from his collar, which always appeared about to choke him, or his high blood pressure or his staunch activism as a defender of the faith, I used to mull over in dry moments. He inevitably wore a vest, across which hung a gold watch chain. According to our rather outspoken church secretary, Bessie, the vest existed for the watch chain, an heirloom passed down from a Colonial ancestor. Dr. Rutledge leaned heavily on Horace for his opinion, I assumed, because of the pastor's advancing frailty, for he was nearing retirement age, sixty-five, and during that time had been eighteen years at Trinity. It seemed that Horace acted as detective, troubleshooter, and sounding board all in one. Some secretly called him Trinity's "assistant pastor." This again from Bessie.

Horace scrutinized the flyer sent by Moses.

"This appears to be a golden opportunity for evangelism," he intoned and nodded his head with his words.

I visualized additional dimensions to it, like fellowship, service, and dialogue. But I said nothing. Dr. Rutledge suggested that the church's World Missions Committee, of which Horace was chairman, head up the program. Dr. Rutledge appointed me temporarily to the Committee, "since you are the innovator, so to speak," he said, beaming over at me.

Session approved the program. Within a week, the World Missions Committee met. Beside myself, Sarah Dubose, Bea Gilchrist, Malcolm Phipps, and Horace comprised the group. Bea and Sarah, co-opted from the church's Kitchen Committee, represented true Southern hospitality in terms of charming graciousness and cooking proficiency. Malcolm, an elder along with Horace, was lean, lanky, and for fifteen years acting head of the history department of the local Black college. As he unpeeled his wraps on the freezing night and the icy wind clanged the bell in the tower, he expressed concern for his home-nurtured camelias. Horace came last, reddened by and moaning about the cold. But the notes of "Lo How a Rose E'er Blooming" drifting to us from the choir room mellowed him.

"Oh, doesn't that make you feel Christmasy?" gushed Bea, clapping her pudgy hands together.

"It sure does," agreed Sarah. "But it also reminds me of all the shopping and baking I've yet to do!" She laughed, her brown eyes crinkling at the corners.

The two exchanged Christmas recipes until Horace cleared his throat to start the meeting. We began by going over the stack of information St. Andrew's had sent us: information about philosophy and strategy and program.

"I particularly like this," enthused Bea: "*. . . a means to serve the stranger in our midst, the international who finds himself at loose ends during America's busiest time of the year*."

Malcolm, perusing St. Andrew's list of activities, asked, "What kinda thing can we do? I should think Thompson's Landing is a must," he said. He referred to a restored antebellum plantation seven miles out of Greenwood.

Horace agreed. Gradually we built up a repertoire of activities: a visit to the nearby peanut processing plant, the downtown historic area, which included an old slave market and the state's first cotton brokerage firm, and, of course, a tour through our hallowed church buildings.

"I think at this point," said Horace, "we could include a speech about the meaning of Christmas to the group."

I volunteered to act as tour guide around town. Malcolm would secure a bus from the college. That got us around to housing and feeding. We decided to post a list on bulletin boards around the church for members to sign up as hosts. If not enough response came, we would recruit particular families for their services.

"What if some African students show up?" asked Bea.

Everyone looked up, and for a moment Horace had no quick retort. "I mean," continued Bea, "all nationalities come to this thing. And there's even a picture of a Negro in the brochure."

"Yes," I said. "I know one who will definitely come. But I imagine he will stay with Bud Maxwell since they are friends. If not there, with me."

"I'll be glad to take two or even three," said Sarah quietly. "I have plenty of room."

Horace still continued to blink without comment. Finally he said to Sarah, "But . . . but what about Deborah? Will she be OK with this arrangement . . . and safe?" He referred to Sarah's teenage daughter.

"It will be all right," she assured Horace in gentle tones. "I have plenty of room. You know that."

Horace opened his mouth as if to say something more, but nothing came out. He fumbled with the brochure. "That ought to do the trick, then. Surely there won't be that many Negroes among them."

"We might can handle a couple if necessary," said Malcolm. "We have all that family room down in the basement. We can put some cushions or air mattresses on the floor, if need be."

"Very well," said Horace. "Now food. They will arrive . . . let's see. On Thursday afternoon, the twenty-seventh, they will get here. So that means they should go to their hosts' homes right away and have supper there. Then they will be in the homes for breakfast the next day. Now what about lunch? Should they eat with the host families . . . or what?"

After a few moments of thought, Sarah said: "Why don't we have lunch in the church? Maybe it could come after the tour of the church. I'm sure the Kitchen Committee would be happy to participate."

"I knew we co-opted you for a good reason, Sarah," beamed Horace. "Excellent idea! We could have sort of a United Nations banquet for them!"

"We can decorate it all up with flags and international curios. Really do it up!" exclaimed Bea.

"Some of the young people might want to serve or act as hosts here at the church," said Sarah.

"How about making signs in different languages . . . like 'Welcome' . . . or 'Happy New Year' . . . in French and German?" asked Malcolm.

"Maybe Mr. Wong can even do one in Chinese characters," I said, thinking of a family in our church originally from Singapore.

"Perfect!" squealed Bea.

"And music . . . some of us have international records. That in the background would give atmosphere," said Sarah.

"I've got some Latin American stuff somewhere," I said.

"One of my kids has a record with bongo drums on it," drawled Malcolm. "It's pretty gruesome . . . nothing but drum beating. But it might appeal to somebody."

"Those from Africa, maybe," said Bea. Then, "Hey, what will we do with the African students . . . for lunch, I mean?"

For a while no one had anything to say. We put down our papers and pencils and suspended our motions.

"They could eat with their host families," broke in Sarah.

Again, silence.

"That might be best," declared Horace after a while. "Considering present day circumstances. Is that agreeable?"

No pangs of having betrayed the hour, no conscientious objection arose from the five of us. Instead, we all looked at each other; we all smiled and nodded in mutual assent.

The students filed out of the bus the night of December 27th, dog-tired from their four-hour trip. White ones, Orientals, Brown ones, three from Uganda, and Moses. They milled in the Fellowship Hall until their respective families came to get them. Moses looked particularly haggard, for, as he told us that night at the Maxwell's dinner table, more than two hundred students spent Christmas Eve night at St. Andrew's.

"Mercy!" exclaimed Mrs. Maxwell. "Where did you put them all? In the steeple?" she giggled.

"We had secured two hundred cots from a local Boy Scout camp. But as I made the rounds that night, I found some sleeping on chairs, the floor, and even the ping-pong tables!"

"Couldn't you put a limit on how many you'd take?" asked Mr. Maxwell.

"No," said Moses. "Our policy was to turn no one away. As the associate pastor at St. Andrew's said, we won't be telling anyone that there's no room in this inn for Christmas!"

In between our conversations, Mrs. Maxwell anxiously hovered over Moses, hoping to do the right thing. For she had never before entertained a foreigner. I caught Moses gazing and gazing at the silver and crystal and polished antique furniture, the pride of the Maxwell household. After dinner, Mr. and Mrs. Maxwell retired, and Bud, Moses, and I chatted in the den in front of the fireplace. Almost immediately Bud wanted to know how many conversions had they seen at St. Andrew's.

"Conversions?" Moses asked.

"Any Hindus or Muslims becoming Christians? I mean, after all, you have quite a mission field right in your church!" He sat upright with earnestness.

Moses laughed lightly. "As a matter of fact, Bud, I don't know. The program is more service-oriented, as I see it."

Bud frowned. "Yes, but if they don't know the reason behind the service you render . . . well, what's the point?"

"They find out the reason soon enough," Moses said from his languid position. "When their needs are met, when they see the love and concern the church members have toward them, they become extra sensitive to the Gospel."

"Aren't they required to attend church?"

"No, but they come," said Moses. "On Christmas Eve, St. Andrew's had its regular candlelight service. I would say 90% of the internationals attended, and most of them, of course, are non-Christian. They saw

Christians from other lands participating—not just Americans. A Korean choir in their national dress sang 'Silent Night' in their own language. An Indian read the Scripture; I had the prayer. The ushers came from many nations. And as they stood at the front, holding the offering plates with their different skin colors and costumes . . . , why, I tell you, it was one of the most moving experiences of my life!"

"Trinity will present a more direct testimony," declared Bud with a smile. "Mr. Bull will give a talk on the meaning of Christmas."

"Which I don't agree with," I said.

Bud gasped. "Hank! Why do you say that, of all things?"

"I just don't believe in bribing these people to hear the Gospel, you might say."

Bud sniffed. "I don't think it can hurt a thing. These students may never get another concrete opportunity. If they are offended, then that's their responsibility before God. We've done ours!"

Before I went home, Moses pulled out two Christmas gifts for Bud and me. A tie clip each, with an African symbol on it representing the omnipotence of God. I was deeply touched.

The next morning, I sat in the bus in the church parking lot, waiting to get the tour going. The shattering noise of the students talking around me indicated they had all revived. When Moses came on board, he was bundled in his coat, scarf, and hat. He blew into his hands to keep them warm.

"Your hands look purple with cold!" I exclaimed, after we exchanged good mornings.

"I think they're solid ice." He grinned through chattering teeth. "I can't seem to find my gloves."

"Here. Use mine." I fished in my coat pocket.

"Oh, Hank, you'll need them."

"Not as much as you. Take them. I insist."

He took them. "You are too kind to me. You seem to be at the right spot at the right time," he laughed.

I stood up to count heads. Satisfied that everyone was present, I told the driver to move out. We took in a general sweep of Greenwood before zeroing in on particular attractions. The town, about 50,000 in population and nearly two hundred years old, radiates outward on brick streets from central Laurens Square. Edging the streets loom stately houses with decorative grillwork, large columns, and grand stairways mounting to sprawling verandahs. Greenwood prides itself on being "the town with old-fashioned friendliness," as printed on signboards at its city limits. When we finished the town, we drove out to Thompson's Landing on the Oconee River, the ante-bellum plantation of mid-Georgia. It was built in the 1830s by Benjamin James King Thompson, a wealthy cotton farmer and slave trader, whose descendants belonged to Trinity Church.

We returned to the Church about eleven o'clock and bunched in to the Fellowship Hall. The flags, foreign language signs of "Welcome," and colorful streamers elicited smiles and comments from the students. The world map and photo of missionaries supported by Trinity also held their attention. Dr. Rutledge soon glided into the Hall. He welcomed the students in his curious blend of slurred and rolled "Rs." Then he took them on a tour of the church buildings.

When the group returned about forty-five minutes later, Dr. R. mounted the Hall's platform and introduced Horace Bull. He sat down as Horace took over.

"It gives me great pleasure to speak to you today and to welcome you to our fair city and to Trinity Presbyterian Church," declared Horace, rocking back on his heels and twining his fingers around his watch chain. His face flushed, and he pursed his lips in his eagerness to communicate. "I want to share something with you that is very important. Something that means very much to me and that I yearn for you to experience. You who are Hindus and Mohammedans and Buddhists, you who do not know Jesus Christ as personal Lord and Savior, it is to you I am speaking."

He told about the birth of Jesus Christ and why he came to live among men: "to save the people from their sins." He quoted Jesus as saying, "I am the way, the truth, and the life; no man comes to the father but by me," and then John 3:16. He mentioned Jesus's command to "make disciples of all nations," and then Apostle Paul's words, "Woe to me if I preach not the Gospel."

I looked out over the group. They listened politely. When Horace finished, a stack of New Testaments were distributed among the students by the church teenagers, Bud included. That completed, he and I joined Moses and read the inscription inside the Testament. It read, "Jesus said, 'I am come that they might have life and that they might have it more abundantly.' With hopes and prayers that you might have the Abundant Life, from the congregation, Session, and Pastors of Trinity Presbyterian Church, Greenwood, Georgia."

Dr. Rutledge dismissed us. Talking and laughter began swelling under the dome of the Hall to an almost deafening crescendo. The three of us hung together for a few moments, as the others milled about, waiting for lunch to be served. Bud asked Moses what all we saw on the tour, and Moses told him how interesting and memorable Greenwood was.

Turning to me, he said, "And your church, Hank. It has quite an historic past too," he said with a smile.

"Sometimes I think too much for our own good," I laughed.

Our words lagged, and Bud said, "Well, I guess we'd better go. Mom will be waiting."

Moses looked at Bud, surprised when he realized the words were addressed to him. "Waiting? Where?" he asked Bud.

"At our house. For lunch."

"We're not eating here with the others?" Moses asked.

Bud shook his head.

"Why not?"

Bud shrugged. "It's just been arranged that way, that's all," he said. "Come on, Moses, we still have a lot to talk about. We'll never catch up!" and he grabbed Moses by the arm and steered him light-heartedly out of the room.

I turned away. I could not watch them go. For in Moses's "Why not?" my world came slamming down around me.

God! What have we done?

I stayed rooted to the spot, hardly breathing. The room cleared of the jabbering students. When I realized it, I started to follow. But I decided I could not face them. I made my way to the hallway and got my coat. Then I shuffled out to the parking lot. The blast of cold air outside hit me stingingly in the face. I got into my car and turned the key and headed out into the street. Like a horse who knows its way back to the barn, the car practically drove itself to our house. I don't recall doing it.

Kay was surprised to see me. I stood in the family room for a long time, not saying anything, not removing my coat and hat. Soon Kay began to ask me what was wrong? Had I eaten? Was I feeling sick? I went to the bedroom upstairs. After a while, Kay came in and brought a tray of soup and sandwiches. I still had my coat on, and she asked me why I hadn't taken it off. I turned the palms of my hands up and flopped them down again. But I got up to take it off.

"Honey," she gave me a hug. "Please. Please, what's wrong?" She looked up at me with her innocent hazel eyes.

I undid her arms around me and sank back down into the easy chair. She perched on the end of the bed, opposite me.

"I've been through hell," I said.

Her eyebrows flew up. I didn't say anything more for a long time. Finally, "Our church wouldn't let Moses . . . and the other Africans . . . eat there."

"But you knew that before today, Hank. You told me about the lunch arrangements last week."

I ignored her remark. "Our church . . . discriminated against them, Kay."

"Discriminated against them!" she exclaimed. "But, Hank, I don't . . . ."

I held up my hand to stop her. "If it wasn't discrimination, why else couldn't they eat there?" I burst out, "And the damnable thing is that I didn't see it beforehand. I approved it all. And I didn't see it until Moses Awulu was taken out the church door!"

She sat before me, frozen. I couldn't say anything more. She tried but couldn't either. I picked up the tray and ate the cold soup and the sandwich. When I finished she asked me softly, "What are you going to do now?"

"I have the tour again at two. I'll just rest here until then."

I sprawled out on the bed. Kay came and curled up beside me. I was glad that she asked no more questions and made no more comments.

I drove back to the church's parking lot before two. What was I going to say to Moses? This clutched at me all the way. I sat in my car until it was time for the students to come out of the church. I half-dreaded to see Bud driving the Maxwell Chrysler in. When he did, Moses was not with him. I got out and walked over to Bud, my heart in my shoes.

"Where's Moses?" I asked.

"He wouldn't come out of his room," Bud wailed. "The lunch deal threw him."

"What did he say?"

"Nothing. That's just it," said Bud.

"When we left the church, he noticed the other Africans getting into cars, too. And he just said, 'Africans can't eat in your church, can they?'"

And I said, "No," but assured him that they can worship in the church. But the more I talked . . . well, the more he clammed up. He didn't say a word to me all through lunch. And then afterward, he excused himself to his room, saying he wasn't feeling well, and he wouldn't be coming on the tour this afternoon."

I couldn't swallow the lump in my throat. I stood there shaking my head.

"Can you come over this afternoon and try to talk to him?" Bud asked.

"Sure," I replied. I needed to go right then, but I had to lead the tour. No one else was available to take my place.

Just then a car drove up with the three Ugandans. They got out and thanked their host. Then, laughing, they scampered toward the bus.

"They don't seem affected," said Bud. "Is surprises me that Moses should be."

"Surprises you?"

"Mmmm," he nodded. "I thought as a Christian, he would be more . . . more understanding."

"You think he should have lapped up our discrimination toward him?"

My harsh voice jerked Bud's eyes toward mine. Then he dropped them towards the gravel. "I . . . I never thought of it as discrimination, Hank," he said.

"I never did either, Bud. Until today."

He looked up. "Do . . . do you think it was wrong . . . what we did?"

"Is discrimination wrong?"

"But, Hank. I just don't believe our church is discriminatory!" His face twisted in confusion.

"Why not?"

"Because we don't hate Negroes. We don't think of them as inferior or stuff like that."

"Then why didn't we let four Africans eat lunch with us? And one of them a close Christian friend?"

Bud swallowed and looked away. "I . . . I don't know."

I gripped his shoulder briefly and walked toward the bus. It was time to leave. Bud followed.

"Are you coming with us?" I asked.

"Might as well."

"OK. Then afterward, I'll follow you home," I said.

The bus drove us to a peanut processing plant on the edge of town and then to a dairy farm. I was thankful that I did not personally have to conduct the tours, since the owners of the plant and the farm—members of Trinity—provided guides. When the sightseeing ended, the bus took the group to the Howard place for the barbecue. Then Bud and I rattled back in the bus to the church. The sky had been overcast all day. It was growing dark, but the sun appeared briefly as it set. Gold rays of light glinted across the bleak countryside. Occasional tarpapered houses with lightning rods broke the monotony of empty fields. Some had threads of smoke curling from their chimneys and Black children playing on their sagging porches. Others appeared lifeless.

Darkness fell down around us by the time we pulled into the church parking lot. I followed Bud home in my car and nosed into the Maxwell's long driveway behind him. As we entered the house together, Mrs. Maxwell met us at the entryway. "Bud! Hank!" she exclaimed. "Moses has gone!"

"Gone!" echoed Bud.

"Yes. Back to Atlanta. He left with his suitcase. I tried to persuade him to stay. But he said he had to get on back to school."

Bud looked at me briefly. Then, "How did he go, Mom?"

"He asked me to call a taxi . . . for the bus station."

"Was that very long ago?" I asked.

"About four o'clock, I think it was," she replied.

"Was he . . . did he seem upset or anything?" asked Bud.

"Oh, no." She ran her fingers through her bright hair. "No, not at all. He was very polite. He gave me something to give to you, Hank." She scurried away to get it. She returned with a brown paper bag neatly folded up. On it was written, "For Rev. Lattimer." I opened it. Inside lay my gloves. I stared at them and turned them over and over.

"They are yours, aren't they?" asked Mrs. Maxwell.

"Yes. They're mine," I murmured.

Bud grabbed my arm. "Let's go to the bus station, Hank. Maybe he's still there!"

"Sure. We'll take my car."

We sped through the streets to the bus depot. It was empty except for two old women huddled together eating from a bag of peanuts. A neon light cast gloomy shadows across the floor littered with candy bar wrappers and cigarette butts. Seeing no sign of Moses, we went to the ticket window. Behind it, a man sat under a suspended light, wearing a plastic green shade pulled down to his glasses. He was working on a crossword puzzle.

"Do you . . . did you have a bus leaving for Atlanta this afternoon?" Bud asked.

"Yep. One left at 4:40 p.m. The Brunswick 'tlanta Express," drawled the man.

"Did you happen to sell a ticket to an African going to Atlanta?" Bud asked.

The man put his pencil down and leaned over his puzzle. "Sonny boy," he said to Bud. "A lotta Black people ride the busses these days. Now just how could I tell an African from the resta the lot?"

We turned and left.

Chapter 7

The next day, I typed a five-page letter to Moses. In it I tried to explain everything. The church. My attitudes toward Black people. The sudden realization of my blindness when he could not eat at Trinity. I asked him for forgiveness on my part and the church's. I proposed a date when I could come to talk with him.

I never heard from him.

I did hear from Bud. I had written him, asking that he find out about Moses. He wrote in reply that Moses had acted aloof and had not attended the Bible study with the re-opening of school. "I don't know what else to do . . . except to pray for him," said Bud.

In the meantime, I plodded through one day at a time with my usual work, seeing the world around me with a whole new set of eyes. Only Kay and Bud knew what had happened to me. I did not tell anyone else, until our church's Session meeting at the end of January. I did not actually anticipate saying anything there: it just sort of rolled out.

The Session meeting began as soon as Dr. Rutledge strolled into the Ladies' Parlor where we met, followed by Horace Bull. I had not been able to attend the pre-Session briefing due to conflicting engagements. I sat in the back just as Dr. R. and Horace took their seats at the long table facing the rest of us. We had sixteen Elders, all men, on the Session, and true to their title, most of them had white hair or balding heads. Only two were in their forties, one being Davis Howard. I was by far the youngest in the room. For that reason, I contributed very little to the meetings.

The meeting began, and minutes and reports clicked off in rapid succession. Horace reported for the World Missions Committee with a review of the internationals' visit after Christmas. How many students came, how many church members participated, with a fervent hope attached at the end that the unbelievers among the internationals would follow the Lord.

"Thank you, Mr. Bull," intoned Dr. Rutledge at the close of the report. "Your committee indeed performed a splendid job. We shall certainly pray that many will become Christians. Now," he breathed deeply and ran his fingers down his tie. "I regret to say, however, that there is a negative note challenging the positive contribution that our church has made. We received a certain letter, and I shall ask Mr. Bull to read it to you at this time."

He nodded to Horace.

The Clerk arose, and craning his neck over his collar, he began. "It is from the Executive Secretary of the Board of Missions of our denomination. It is dated January 17 of this year, and it is addressed to our Session." Horace read the words of the Executive Secretary, stating his desire to share something with the Session, which directly affected world missions. He then went on to describe the Christmas International House program, saying how the Board of Missions highly endorsed the program. He understood Trinity's part in the program after Christmas but then reacted strongly against the Africans' being excluded from lunch in the church. He stated how Moses Awulu was sponsored on a Board scholarship and how he had been deeply hurt through the unfortunate incident."

It disturbs me greatly (wrote the Secretary) *that such discriminatory incidents still occur in our Southern churches. The incidents alone, if they were isolated to the city in which they occur, are demeaning enough. But usually they extend far beyond the church or city involved. In this case, the Christmas International House program is for the first time placed in jeopardy. Furthermore, the injuries and misunderstanding arising from the incident will spread to Africa itself. The effectiveness of the Board of Missions is greatly hampered. By rejecting a person because of his race, we are in essence cancelling out Christ's command to love our neighbor. Additionally, we make hypocrites out of our missionaries who serve persons of all races.*

I am writing to share these feelings with you, not suggesting that you take any action one way or another. The incident cannot be rectified. But I am appealing to your Christian consciences to try with every means possible to prevent such incidents from occurring in the future. For the sake of the mission of the church, its missionaries on the field, and the cause of Christ Himself.

(Signed) *H. Mackay Bevins,*

Executive Secretary

The dam of silence and decorum among the Elders burst under a torrent of words and outcries. Dr. Rutledge, his voice barely audible above the hubbub, restored order. "Gentlemen, we have heard the letter. Thank you, Mr. Bull," he said. "By your reaction I perceive that you feel with me the seriousness of Dr. Bevins's charges. I would now like for us to discuss the matter and then resolve how we should reply to him."

Several hands waved in the air. "Mr. Thompson, you may have the floor," said Dr. Rutledge.

Matthew Thompson, a descendent of the plantation owner, had a long face and expressive hands. He was senior partner of one of the oldest law firms in town. "I guess what distresses me most in Dr. Bevins's letter is that it is based entirely on false assumptions," he drawled in a high-pitched voice. "I don't think any of us here would consider our church as discriminatory. We accept all races at Trinity to worship. Indeed, it is true we did not plan for the Africans to eat in our Fellowship Hall. But in light of the explosive issue of race today and in light of the fact that our congregational members have mixed opinions on the Negro problem, I definitely feel that what we did was the only realistic course we could have taken."

Several nodded their heads. He sat down, and Dr. Rutledge recognized another elder, a Mr. Hartsell, a well-to-do merchant in a downtown men's store. "I most definitely agree with Mr. Thompson," he said nodding his head as he spoke. "Dr. Bevins sits in his office in faraway Memphis and thinks he knows the situation at Greenwood and Trinity without coming to examine it firsthand. If you ask me, anyone who condemns affairs at a distance without investigating all the evidence is misusing his responsibility!"

Several other hands shot up to be recognized. But before anyone was, Davis Howard arose. "I think it is only fair that the Arrangements Committee for the international visit be allowed to speak for itself."

Dr. R. seemed slightly harassed that Davis had called the play. Still, he followed through and asked Malcolm Phipps to speak for the Committee. Malcolm began by citing the members of the Committee. "We planned the lunch arrangements as we did because it seemed the only natural, realistic thing to do," he explained. "We certainly didn't wish to offend anyone, neither student nor church member. I think we thought that any African who came would understand the race situation in the South. Doesn't the Board of Missions orient them to our problems?"

Davis managed to gain the floor again, as Malcolm sat down. "At the time the international students came, I did not know of the decision to separate the Africans at lunch time," he said. "I would have disapproved it, if I did. I can plainly see how Moses Awulu was hurt. I'm wondering if we didn't consider the feelings of our church members more than the African's. I don't think we can blame the African's ignorance of our race problems, if he was ignorant. After all, we were the hosts, and as every good Southern host knows, you consider your guest first!"

Before I knew it, I raised my hand. "Mr. Moderator, I would like to say something." My voice cracked, and inwardly I swore at it.

"Why, yes, of course, Henry. You may have the floor," responded Dr. Rutledge. Unlike the other members of the Session, he always referred to me by first name. It made me feel younger than ever, and that night, I resented it.

"I, too, think we had a fine program for the students," I started out. "I was glad to see people of all walks of life getting to know each other. I think it was a great opportunity for witness and service. But this incident, which Dr. Bevins has written to us about, troubles me deeply, and I would like to speak about it."

I gripped the chair in front of me to keep my hands from shaking. Horace lowered his pen from his note-taking at the front table, and several Elders turned around to look at me.

"I'd like to tell you something about Moses Awulu, the African Dr. Bevins mentioned in his letter," I said. "Moses was a product, you might say, of our mission in Ilaria."

I told of his education in our mission schools, of his relationship with Miss Watson, and his scholarship at Tech. I described him as a devout Christian, who held many of the ideals of faith as persons in our congregation held. I related to the men how I met Moses at the missions conference and how he and I became close friends. I also stated that Moses could not see how true Christians could be prejudiced. Because of what had happened at Trinity, I said, Moses cut off his relationship with both myself and Bud Maxwell. "I don't see how we can deny a Christian from one of our mission fields to eat in our Fellowship Hall," I ended.

When I sat down, no one moved. Then a rustle began of rearranging papers, of shifting in seats, and brushing lint from suit sleeves. Dr. Rutledge picked up the broken thread of discussion.

"Are there any other comments?" he asked.

Horace squirmed. His face broke his own record for redness. "Mr. Lattimer," he blurted out. "I believe that you were aware of our decision to handle the internationals as we did. You were on the Arrangements Committee. I do not understand why you should criticize the management of the occasion after it is an accomplished fact."

I got up again, feeling more starch in my knees. "You are correct, Mr. Bull. I did approve . . . tacitly. In fact, I guess all my life I have silently approved the way our southland operated. Its schools, its public services, its churches. I knew more or less how Trinity Church stood on racial matters. I never considered my attitudes and Trinity's as incompatible. I saw no problems or inconsistencies. But now I do. When Moses Awulu stood there in our church, asking why he was not going to eat here with the rest of the students, I tell you that I did not have the courage to face him. In a flash, I saw that what we did was . . . was wrong!"

The room stirred. Dr. R. looked out over the group, unruffled. Horace glared. "That is a matter of opinion," the Clerk rejoined icily. He continued, "I would like to remind you, Hank, that you have been with us for only two and a half years, and you cannot possibly know all the angles of the race problem, which this historic church has agonized over down through the years. You have not lived with it as we have. I would therefore suggest that you investigate a few other viewpoints and reasons as to why we at Trinity form policies as we do. Initially I would suggest that you look at our budget. You will find, I am sure, that a large part of our benevolences goes for the betterment of the Negro." The turtle mouth snapped shut, and he settled back in his seat.

Matthew Thompson asked for the floor and was given it. He turned to face me, speaking in a gentle, conciliatory tone. "I'd like to go back a few years, Hank, and tell you about how we adopted the open policy that we have toward our Black brethren," he said, smiling in a fatherly fashion. "About five years ago, our Session agreed to open its doors to Negroes for worship. They were welcome to sit anywhere they chose. But on the very first occasion when they came, they abused our good faith and chose to demonstrate rather than to worship. They were a disturbance to the congregation, looking about, barging in on family pews, singing loudly. They were not even dressed for worship, which showed their intent. So in order to minimize the disturbance, we eventually altered our policy slightly. To those who appear questionable, that is in their manner or in their dress, we seat them in the balcony. They are still permitted to worship with us. Our doors remain open to them, although none have come in the last two or three years. Therefore, as I said earlier, we are not a segregated church!"

Davis stood up. "Gentlemen, the issue is not over our general handling of morning worship," he said through taut lips. "Rather it concerns a specific discriminatory incident in our Fellowship Hall."

I expected an onslaught from the Elders directed toward Davis. Instead, surprisingly, they chose to retaliate with silence. As if he weren't even there. I was additionally surprised that rebuttals would be simmering so soon and so numerous in the back of my own mind. Clearly, I had been catapulted into a different world from them. I used to side with them, or was it more a "drifting" with them, effortlessly, noncommittally? Not that I had arrived, by any means. I knew the taint of racism still clung strongly to me, and it would be years before it wore off. But at least I had recognized it. That was a start.

Dr. Rutledge took the floor. "Dear brethren," he purred, "it is getting late. I think we should conclude our discussion on Dr. Bevins's letter. Does anyone have a proposal as to how we should answer it?"

"I think Mr. Bull should draft a letter," urged Mr. Hartsell. "And after it is circulated among us and approved, then it can be sent."

"I second the motion," rasped a voice.

"Very well," replied Dr. Rutledge. "All who so move, please say aye." The room resounded with the vote.

"Those opposing?"

Only Davis opposed. I could not support him, for as a pastor, I cannot vote.

"Then let us be dismissed with prayer," stated Dr. Rutledge, raising up his arm for the benediction.

In the church parking lot, afterwards, Davis grabbed me by the arm. "Come on, Hank," he said. "Let's go get a cup o' coffee."

"Fine," I replied.

We walked down the street toward the business section. Inside a small restaurant, we ordered our coffee. We sipped it in silence for a while. Then Davis suddenly said, "Well, Hank, welcome to the Underground!"

I put my cup down. "The Underground?"

He grinned. "It's composed of the opponents of the lilywhite establishment at Trinity Church."

"Oh," I said, and drank a bit. "Is it very strong?"

"Fairly. And we're growin'."

"It amazes me, Davis, how I never saw Trinity so racist. Where have I been all this time?"

"You've only been here a short time, Hank. As you were so well reminded tonight."

I smiled.

Davis went on. "It usually takes something . . . well, something earthshaking to knock us out of our miasma."

"I guess so," I said.

"With me, it was my internship. I interned in New York. Black people have the same cotton-pickin' ailments as the rest of us, I soon discovered. And feelings and dreams, too. Segregation made no sense in a New York hospital ward. And it doesn't here in Greenwood, either."

"Do you think Trinity will ever change?"

"Maybe. Slowly. But it largely depends on whether the younger church members will take seriously their responsibility."

"How do you mean?"

Davis put his cup down. "I mean if they will stick with Trinity instead of washing their hands of it. Otherwise, it will die on the vine."

"Have a lot left Trinity because of its racial policies?"

"A lot. And because of its general preoccupation with the past. Oh, the church makes attempts every now and then to swing with the present. Like the current emphasis on inner-city ministry."

I frowned.

"The more I look at our recent decision not to move to the suburbs," he continued, "the more I see it as a cover-up for segregation."

"How?" I asked, surprised. "I mean they didn't have to choose to stay right in a Black neighborhood."

"No, but you know how offense is often the best defense. I think it's just a cover-up. Trinity will stab at being involved in the neighborhood. But you wait and see how it will go about it!"

I took a long drink of my coffee while pondering his words.

"Another thing," he said. "The church desperately needs a younger minister. But I doubt that any will come when they look at it closely. Besides, Trinity is too hard to please. I don't know who they would approve of. I frankly believe that when Dr. Rutledge retires, the church will either fold up completely or have to face a reformation. It can't continue on its present course."

"But all the Elders . . . ," I put in.

"Yep. There're the Elders. But they're reaching retirement age, many of 'em. And it was encouraging when two of us young turks got elected to Session last year. That was no small miracle, Hank!"

"I can see that," I chuckled.

"But even more in that, is your crossing over."

I looked at him and smiled.

"I hope you'll stick with us awhile, Hank. Don't get discouraged. But you should realize one thing. Being under the jurisdiction of the Session exclusively, you're in a real vulnerable position."

"I know," I said. "How do you suggest I play this ballgame?"

Davis sighed and leaned back. "There's no rule book and no referee. Different Southern ministers have tried different tactics. Some preach out openly and immediately get whacked. Others try a more subtle approach. They argue that if they're too open and they are removed, their chances of accomplishing anything positive goes down the drain. So they muffle their voices a bit in the hopes of instigating change. Of the two, I'd say the latter is a more frustrating course. The former's more painful, more traumatic."

I reflected on his words. Then I said, "Well, as far as I know, I plan to stay on at Trinity. For a while, anyway. But I have no idea which way things will go. I'll just have to live it a day at a time."

I found myself telling Dr. Rutledge almost the same thing the next morning during our get-together. He started out by suggesting that I head up the new neighborhood ministry. "I think we need some youthfulness on that committee," he declared. Then he went on to explain how Trinity should encourage new ideas and fresh opinions, "else we will lose our younger folk." I looked at him warily, especially when he ended up expressing gratefulness that I spoke out in Session meeting. I apologized that I didn't come to him first with my opinions. But waving that off, he advised me to "go cautiously" and not to "bulldoze the congregation" with any new ideas,

Then, leaning over and patting my arm, he assured me that Trinity wanted me to stay with them for a long time as its assistant. "But if you ever feel that . . . that things aren't harmonious between you and the church, if you are at odds with us because of your convictions, I hope you will come talk with me about it first thing, all right?"

It was then I responded with my desire to stay "as long as you'll have me. But as for my convictions, I couldn't predict where they would carry me," I said.

His frown clouded his face almost imperceptibly. But I caught it.

Within a week, I was out pounding the pavement on a survey to begin the neighborhood ministry. Coming out of an apartment building one afternoon, I heard a ruckus in a back hallway. In the semidark, I found four Black boys rolling the lids of garbage cans along the hall. Broken bottles, food scraps, and papers littered the floor. They admitted to the mess, saying they were "playing." They came from homes five blocks away and claimed they had no other place to play. After I made them clean up the garbage, I took them outside. There, I saw their patched jeans and sweatshirts too large for them with holes and stains.

I decided to take them to the church to play in our large gymnasium. Of the five more boys we gathered along the way, three were White, filthy and reeking of a sour smell. As we entered the church, we almost collided with two leading women of our congregation. Their eyes widened as they took in the boys' disheveled appearance and mixed skin colors. In the gym, the boys ran and skittered with delight, like birds suddenly released from a cage. Half of them got away from me and entered the showers behind the gym. Within moments, they were soaked. I didn't know how I would get them home with their wet clothes.

In desperation, I called Bessie. She suggested bringing over a box of overseas relief clothing. By rolling up oversized sleeves and legs, she and I were able to outfit them adequately against the weather. As I was preparing to take them out the door and into my car, Bessie stopped me.

"Would you just mind telling me what this is all about?" she asked, her hands on her hips.

After I related the afternoon's experiences to her, she said, "I hope no one saw you come in here with them."

I told her of the two women we had met in the church hallway. Bessie closed her eyes and moaned. Opening them, she looked at me across the top of her glasses and said, "Hank, my boy. You've had it. It's been good to know you," and she held out her hand as if to shake mine.

I winced. "It's that bad, huh?"

She nodded. "I'd bet my last Green Stamp that those two are keeping the phone lines hot right this very minute between their houses and Dr. Rutledge's. What's more, he'll call you into the Holy of Holies first thing in the morning for a cozy little chat. He won't wait even 'til 9:30."

"But, Bessie. What else could I have done?" I asked.

She held back her head and roared. When she calmed down, she said very matter-of-factly, "Why you could have ignored them. Just like this church has been doing for almost two hundred years!"

When I arrived at the office the next morning, a note from Bessie confirmed that Dr. R. wanted to see me immediately. He ushered me into his office, and after the coffee routine on the sofa, he got straight to the point.

"I hear you had a crowd of boys here in the church yesterday afternoon." He tried to sound casual, but I recognized the steely call to arms beneath his smoothness.

I succumbed to the temptation to be difficult. "Yes sir, I did," was all I said.

"And where did they come from?"

"From the surrounding neighborhood," I said, smiling.

His gaze on me indicated that he was waiting for more. When I didn't come across, he said, "And what did you have in mind doing with them?"

"I brought them into the gym to play."

"They had no other place to play?"

"No, sir. I found them dumping garbage over in Casley's Apartments."

"What kind of boys were . . . are they, Henry? What needs do they have?"

I paused. "They were ages six to eleven, or so. Their clothes were ragged; they had no shoes. They come from homes without mothers. Either their mothers work until nightfall, or there are no mothers at all. They stay out of school more than they go. Most of them smoke, half of them have been to juvenile court, none of them go to church."

"I see," said Dr. Rutledge pressing the fingertips of one hand against the other. "And are they of both races?"

"Yes."

Dr. R. picked minute crumbs off his creased trouser leg. "Of course, you know, Henry, we had in mind doing something for the youth of this neighborhood."

"I know. That's what I had in the back of my mind when all this . . . happened."

Dr. Rutledge sighed. "But we did not have in mind, Henry, bringing the children to the church for activities."

"Why not?" I turned to look at him directly.

"We had in mind opening a center more in their neighborhood . . . where it would be more accessible to them," he said. "And our members would voluntarily staff it and make contributions of various sorts to it."

"That sounds somewhat like a duplication of St. Mark's," I observed. "Except that it would be in a slightly different location. In addition, we have all these costly facilities right here. All lying dormant during the week," I said. "It would be a very creative ministry, sir."

"But you must remember, Henry, that our kindergarten and school, scouts, and youth programs take full advantage of our facilities Monday through Friday."

"Every afternoon?" I pushed.

"Almost every afternoon. Besides, there was concern that the neighborhood children would create too great a disturbance and would possibly damage our equipment," he said.

"I would oversee them and teach them to take care of it."

Another sigh came from Dr. Rutledge. "Henry, we are responsible first to our own church members and their needs." He waved a placating hand. "Don't you understand that?"

I looked around the room. My eyes fell on the heavy drapes, the indirect lighting, the gilded bookends on the shelves, and the silver letter opener and pen set on his desk. Every article sat smugly in its assigned place.

"So that means if people disturb our church too much, they cannot come. If we are offended by dirty, smelly, Black and White ragamuffins, then we have to go out to them. Our Christian conscience says we must minister to them. But decorum dictates: *Only at arm's length!*" I blurted out to my own surprise.

Dr. Rutledge sat up straight. For a moment, the inert sword glinted beneath his composure. He compressed his lips together after which he seemed to relax. Then, he leaned toward me and, ever so softly, said, "Henry, what has become of you? What is troubling you?"

I met his gaze without reserve. "I think sir, you know all there is to know. There's nothing to add to what I said at Session."

"Are you quite sure?"

"Quite."

"But what concerns me . . . and many of us, Henry . . . is where this new stance of yours will lead."

I shrugged. "I don't know, sir. How can any of us know from day to day which way the Spirit leads?"

He paused. Then, "Well, I should hope it will be in the best interest of Trinity."

"It seems, though, different ones of us have varying opinions as to what is *best* for the church."

He looked at me sharply for a moment and then at the carpet. "Perhaps, perhaps," he intoned. "Do you think you should talk with the Commission on the Minister and his Work?" he asked suddenly.

"About what?" I returned, startled. He referred to a church committee that aired grievances between ministers and their congregations.

He gestured with his palms upward. "About any, uh, any differences . . . or aggrievances you may now have with Trinity," he smiled.

"I have none, sir," I replied.

"Well, Henry, if you ever feel the need, it can be arranged," he said.

I restrained the impulse to say, *Is that a warning?* Instead, I nodded and said, "All right. I'll take that under advisement."

Our meeting ended. But not the topics discussed. By the end of February, Dr. Rutledge took the initiative to call a meeting of the Commission to talk with me. What precipitated his decision was a presbytery meeting, where ministers and laymen representing churches of several counties meet monthly for business and fellowship. I attended it. During the course of business, a debate arose over the formation of a new church within the presbytery. It appeared that in securing charter members to form the church in Oakview, a neighboring town, a significant number of potential Black members had been ignored. Presbyterian by preference, the Black group sent a letter to the presbytery stating that they were being discriminated against. They pointed out that this contradicted both the Bible and the General Assembly, the highest governing authority in our denomination, for in 1954, the Assembly had condemned discriminatory practices within our church at all levels. The debate over the letter to the presbytery rose to fever pitch. A vote was finally taken, 55 to 6, in favor of continuing the formation of the new church on the present course. I voted among the six.

Although Dr. Rutledge never questioned me about the vote, I am sure that, to him, this represented the final straw. For now I had extended my "new stance" beyond the local congregation at Trinity. And, as he had asked: "Where else would it lead?"

Chapter 8

The Commission met in a new church on the edge of Greenwood. Two laymen and four ministers attended the meeting, coming from other towns in our presbytery. Matthew Thompson, of Trinity and normally on the Commission, remained absent so that the examination would be more objective. Besides hearing grievances between churches and pastors, the Commission sets standards for the ministry in the presbytery. It assesses the needs among the churches and installs and releases ministers as they come and go. But on the day we met, the matter between myself and Trinity occupied the whole agenda. Basically, they met at the request of the Session of Trinity to find out (as the letter to the Commission read) "whether Rev. Lattimer's relationship with Trinity Presbyterian Church will remain compatible." The letter referred to my "recent actions," which, to them, represented "underlying conflicts and deep-seated grievances."

The Commission and I met together for three hours. At the end, they said that they would inform Trinity that conflicts indeed existed between myself and the church. They expressed hopes that the conflicts could be worked out. They advised me to "go slowly" and "try as much as you are able to work for peace and harmony within the framework of your own convictions."

I thought the matter finished. It was, therefore, a great surprise when a month later I received a letter from the Commission recommending that I resign from Trinity. Unknown to me, the Session had held a meeting to read the recommendations of the Commission shortly after it had examined me. Then the Elders voted that I leave the church. Apparently having no guts to inform me themselves of their decision, they bounced it back to the Commission to do so. I could have appealed the decision to the presbytery. But it seemed futile to press it. So by the middle of March, 1968, I complied, and my ties with Trinity were severed.

Davis Howard had been out of town for a month during these series of events. Upon his return, he rushed out to our house where he found us packing up to move. After expressing his outrage, he asked, "Was that Commission really impartial, Hank?" He sat amid the clutter of packing boxes, puffing his pipe.

"I honestly don't know. Only Bradley Wilcox from Wilson sided with me openly. Two of them were obviously pro-Trinity, but the rest you could never really tell. They told me they'd advise the Session that conflicts existed and for me to work for peace. But what else they may have told the Session or what may have leaked back to them, I don't know."

"They didn't send you a copy of the letter?"

"No."

I saw his jaw clinching and unclinching as he shook his head. "Were you surprised when you were asked to meet with the Commission?" he asked.

"No," and I told him of the confab with Dr. Rutledge when he had first brought up the Commission and then how Dr. R. showed me a copy of the letter from the Session to the Commission, asking that I be examined.

"Was it a fair letter . . . or downright slanted?"

"Slanted. You can arrange with Bessie to get a Xeroxed copy of it. I'm sure she knows where to find one."

"So after they read the letter, what did the Commission do?"

I smiled. "Well, interestingly enough, they argued among themselves about how to find whether Trinity and I were compatible! The letter gave no specifics as to what the actual issues or disagreements were. It ended up that I told them what it was all about."

"Sounds like you incriminated yourself."

"That's what Bradley Wilcox said. He protested to the Commission that I was having to testify against myself. They all got miffed that he considered the occasion a "trial," as the chairman put it. But I said I didn't mind talking since I thought more people should know about the matter. I just put it simply that the discrimination against the Africans in our church was a mockery of what Christians believed."

"And then they argued about what discrimination consisted of," muttered Davis.

"Right!"

"Did they ever decide how to define it?"

"The chairman wouldn't let them. He reminded them that the meeting was not held to discuss the 'race issue,' but, of course, 'discrimination' kept popping up repeatedly. Then, Cunningham of Mooresville . . . ."

"Dr. Rutledge's rubber stamp . . . ."

I laughed and nodded. "Cunningham asked if I continued on my present course, wouldn't I alienate many members of Trinity?

"Possibly," I answered

He said that since I took an ordination vow to maintain the peace and harmony of the church, how could I condone actions which would produce the reverse? I countered with how could we condone discrimination? Then Wilcox jumped him with the reminder that I also took a vow to maintain the purity of the church, which course I was apparently pursuing."

"Good for Bradley!" Davis exclaimed. "So what tack did they take up next?"

"To try to determine if I was pro-Black before I ever went to Trinity, you know, if all along I had been a wolf in sheepskins."

"So they asked you if you went to desegregated schools and joined sit-ins and freedom marches prior to Trinity?"

I nodded. "I said I hadn't done any of those things. I don't think they believed I could have changed my tune with the one incident involving the Africans."

"Course they couldn't!"

"So that, too, proved a dead end. The next course to pursue was to find out where I stood theologically."

Davis groaned. "You mean, if they proved you were a liberal, then they could prove you were pro-Black!" Several consecutive puffs of smoke billowed up from his pipe.

"They didn't get very far with that one, either," I chuckled. "When one of them asked, did I believe in the bodily resurrection of Jesus Christ and did I believe in the Virgin Birth—which I answered affirmatively, mind you—Bradley exploded. He reminded them I had been through a theological examination by the presbytery when I was ordained, and it was quite out of order now. He wanted to know why they must inevitably test one's orthodoxy by the Virgin Birth!"

Davis laughed. "Amen, Brother Bradley! Amen."

"The last course was a more forward one. Where would I expect to exert my influence in the future, both in the community and in the presbytery? They had no particular examples in mind, and I refused to predict my actions on something hypothetical. But then Cunningham asked a slippery one: Would I support the Poor People's March, which would soon be coming through town? I said I would."

"And that, dear brother, was the nail in your own coffin!" declared Davis.

"Maybe so. Maybe so. It virtually ended the meeting."

We sat in silence for a while. "Where are you headed now?" Davis asked.

"To the Pilkentons', Kay's parents in Augusta."

"Are they very sympathetic?"

"I think they are more askance than anything . . . that their son-in-law should be classified among the unemployed!"

"Are you hurting for money?" he asked with concern.

"No. The Black-White Fellowship already contacted me. They can support us for several months, if need be. They'll also keep an eye open for job possibilities." The Fellowship was a biracial organization of Presbyterians. Among other activities, they made donations for ministers like myself who were fired because of stands on race.

"And after Augusta, what?" Davis asked.

"I have no idea," I sighed. "It's too soon to even think about it."

"I'll keep up with you, though," he assured me. "And remember this: Though you may be gone at Trinity, the Underground is still at work. Stronger than ever!"

Kay and I plus our one-year-old David moved into the second floor of the Pilkentons' home out in the country. At first we didn't discuss our future. We went through a sort of scabbing over of the recent painful events. And curiously enough, the Pilkentons didn't discuss our future or the cause of our move from Trinity. It would have made life far easier if they had. Instead, their silence only shouted at me: Why did you do it? Where are you going from here?

To keep myself busy, I begged Mr. Pilkenton to let me help with the plowing, for every spring he planted a crop of peanuts, though he was a banker by profession. Only when he was convinced that I asked out of necessity and not out of politeness did he consent.

The days of our back-eddy existence dragged by. In the daytime, between my plowing and her childcare, Kay and I watched the mailbox, hoping something might turn up. At night, we asked each other questions about our future. The idea of going abroad as a missionary kept growing inside me. Every time I alluded to it, however, Kay would emphasize the needs right here at home.

"There are needs everywhere you turn, Kay!" I retorted. "And in each place, you know you can contribute a little, by the Grace of God."

"In that case, why overseas? Why Africa? Can't they minister to their own people more effectively than foreigners?"

"Maybe. But it just seems to me that this is the right time to do it. We're young. The kids are young. And I just don't see going into anything else at the moment."

"Well, I don't see going into missionary service by default!" she said.

"Default? What do you mean?"

"Because something else doesn't pan out."

"But God often leads that way ... by shutting some doors and opening others."

"How do you know all the doors here are so tightly shut?"

"I ... I just feel it, Kay," I replied. "Look. Are you with me on it, or not?"

She sighed, and her features softened. "Sure, honey. I'm with you. But just so long it's not forever."

"How about for three years?"

"Sounds fair enough."

But no sooner did we come to an agreement between us and no sooner did we write our Board of Missions about opportunities than the country fell into a tailspin. Martin Luther King, Jr., was killed by a sniper's bullet in Memphis. His assassination thrust Kay's question of need upon me as never before. Where was it greatest? What should I do? Would going abroad at this crucial time be shirking responsibility at home? And if I should stay, what could I do? I felt hopelessly confused. I needed someone to talk to. But who?

After several days of moping, I wound up in Atlanta. Number one, to try to see Moses. And number two, to discuss the lay of the land with fellow ministers. I spent half the day looking for Moses: his old dorm room, a boarding house, the math building. But I failed to find him. I left a note with a friend of his telling Moses what had happened to me and where I could be reached. I implored him to write me.

I did see Bud. He wanted to know why I had resigned from Trinity. When I told him I was forced to, he could hardly believe it. "Why everyone thinks it was your own doing, Hank!"

"It's supposed to look that way," I said. When I told him I was considering missionary service as our next move, he was ecstatic.

"I'll certainly pray that you find the right opening," he beamed.

I told him I'd keep him posted.

I next went to Bethel Church to see if I could learn anything about Moses. I was disappointed not to find Mr. Bankins, the Black minister. Rather I talked with his White counterpart, a Mr. Todd Wainwright, a tall man in his late thirties. I told him who I was and what I wanted. He said that Moses had not attended church since about January. Then, in late March, he saw an article in *The Presbyterian Voice* that explained everything to him. He showed it to me.

The Voice, a widely-read yet unofficial publication of our church, had found out about Moses and me and Trinity. The article revealed the works: from the day of the internationals' visit in Greenwood until the day I was asked to leave. I strongly suspected Davis Howard leaked the information.

Then Mr. Wainwright showed me responses in letters to the editor. One from Horace Bull, condemning what *The Voice* had said: the same old song about people "not understanding the situation first hand" and "misusing their responsibility." The second letter was written by Rufus Hill. He glibly stated that such repercussions to Moses's rejection were "inevitable" and probably only the beginning of other incidents involving overseas scholarship students.

After I left Bethel, I found myself at Rufus Hill's small church of all-Black members. In his cubicle of an office, I sat opposite him across his desk.

"I frankly don't know why I've come," I laughed nervously.

"I'll be most happy to help you if you can drop me a clue," he said in his sophisticated voice, smiling condescendingly.

I took a deep breath. "For starters, then, I'll say that I just saw *The Voice* article about Trinity Church and Moses Awulu. And your response."

"And what shall I say to that?" he asked, looking at me in a detached way.

I lifted up my palms and then dropped them. "I . . . I don't know."

"You honestly didn't know about the article?" he asked.

"No. It caught me by complete surprise. Todd Wainwright over at Bethel showed it to me just a few minutes ago."

"I had rather suspected you sent *The Voice* the information yourself," he said, as he flipped a pencil back and forth.

"Oh, come on!" I retorted half-angrily.

"So what are you doing with yourself these days, Mr. Lattimer?" he asked.

"Please," I blurted. "Can't you call me Hank?" He closed his eyes briefly and then said, "Very well, Hank." Then I wondered if that gave me liberty to call him Rufus. Or would that insult him?

"You may call me Rufus," he smiled, thawing a little. "Now, what are you doing with yourself?"

"Right now, nothing. And I don't know which direction to go in," I said.

"I see," said Rufus, as he hunched forward. "I guess you are rather in a predicament."

"Exactly." I was silent for a while, and he waited.

"I . . . I want to know," I began, "What you think . . . how you think a White minister can best help in the race problem these days?"

He didn't say anything for a long time. Just fiddled with his pencil. "Hank, most Black people these days don't want help from whitey."

"You mean because of King's assassination?"

"Even before that," he said. "A lot of Black people didn't go along with King."

"How come?" I asked with surprise.

"He taught us to love our enemies. That was all wrong. You know what the Bible says: 'Love your neighbor as yourself.' Well, the Black man loves himself not at all. So how can he love his neighbor?"

I nodded, soaking in his words. "Well, have you any suggestions otherwise . . . about what to do?"

He leaned back in his chair and looked at me through half-narrowed eyes. "Malcolm X would tell you: 'Nothing!'"

I swallowed. "Look. You guys have been hollering for a little repentance from White people. Well, brother, I've got that! But is there no reciprocation from the other side? Is there no shred of forgiveness and . . . and acceptance?"

"What do you want, Hank? Do you want us to receive you with open arms for what you did at Greenwood?" he asked.

I felt hot on the back of my neck. "Well, what do you all want . . . blood?" I stormed.

He chuckled. "Yes. Just about that. That's just about what we want."

I wiped my hands across my eyes. "There must be a Christian, humane answer to all this," I said, gesturing feebly.

"Look," he said and moved forward again. "We are all so damn fed up with words from White people. If you only knew! If you only had an inkling of the sloppy talk, talk, talk we get all the time!" He pounded his desk with his fist. "If you only knew a little of the fury that fires up a Black man every moment of his life!" His face contorted with strain.

I looked at him squarely. "That's what I'm slowly learning about, Rufus," I replied. "I have a little of that fury in me now, too. It's not much. Especially compared to yours. But it's there. And I believe it's a step in the right direction."

He relaxed and then smiled. "I'll back off. I'm sorry."

"I guess that's why I'm here, after all," I said. "To see what action I can get into. To get out of the *words* hang-up."

Rufus swept his hand across the top of his hair. "That's a good question, Hank. Really. That's a good question. It seems to me that the best place for you . . . to make any real impact in the situation . . . is with your own White brethren. With the Trinity Presbyterian types."

"Humph," I retorted. "I've already blown that one."

He nodded thoughtfully. "What about a church in another area?"

"I'm not sure I want a pastorate at this point. I don't think I'd have much freedom to speak out. And I'm not sure a church will be eager to want me! I had thought of the campus ministry."

"Yes, you'd have more freedom to speak out on a campus. But your influence would be zero."

I frowned. "It would be among future Trinity Church types, as well as among Black people who are growing in numbers on the campuses."

"Sure. But it's an easy out. Don't you see? It's among their fathers where the crunch has to come . . . now."

I sighed. "Well, I tried among their fathers. I didn't get very far."

"Why not try again, in another church? It's only after you crack your skull against the wall so many times that it's going to give."

"I . . . I just don't think I can take that route again . . . so soon," I stammered.

Rufus's gaze bored into me. "It would take guts, Hank. Real guts."

I shifted in the chair. "Then, Rufus, . . . I wanted your reaction to this. I've also been considering going to the mission field . . . to Africa."

"You're putting me on!" he laughed.

"Why should I be putting you on?" I fumed.

"That would be even more of a cop-out, Hank. Don't you see that?"

"I see how it could be interpreted that way," I admitted. "But I've been thinking of Africa for years . . . way before Moses Awulu ever came along."

"But what would be the point? To ease a guilty conscience? To help those poor Black people over there simply because neither White nor Black will accept you here?"

I pounded the arm of my chair. "No!" I cried. "I'm not acting from guilt. Why should I be acting from guilt?"

"It's a common reaction among White people," he smirked,

I sighed and hung my head. "Look. It would certainly be a way of staying in this Black-White struggle."

"I'm not so sure of that. It seems to me that more and more Africans are saying, 'Missionary, go home.'"

"But Moses Awulu said that's not true. He said . . . ," I stopped in mid-sentence.

Rufus nodded. "And where did that little naive view get Moses?"

I said nothing for a long while. "Well, I guess I'd better be going. I'm glad I came to see you, Rufus." I stood up, and he followed.

"I'm glad you came too, Hank." He shook my hand with vigor. "I'll be following you with interest," he said with a twinkle. "Keep the faith."

I returned to Augusta late that afternoon. Within a few days, we received a letter from the Board of Missions. It said that Congo had no openings, but Ilaria did. Western University wanted a chaplain for three years. The Board enclosed application papers. After a lot of talk and prayer and pondering, Kay and I filled them out and returned them. We were interviewed by the Board in May and were appointed to Ilaria. Returning to Augusta, we prepared for our overseas move: buying, packing, storing, and shipping. After that, we went through an intensive missionary orientation for three months. When it was completed, we entered an African Studies program at Northwestern University.

So it was a year later, in September, 1970, that rightly or wrongly we arrived in Ilaria.

Chapter 9

I finished my long narrative to James near lunch time. For a while, he did not respond, although he had asked a few questions along the way.

"Indeed, I can see how much Moses Awulu meant to you. I am glad that you told me," he commented.

After he left, I felt badly. Perhaps I jumped indiscreetly into unburdening myself to the first available person. One thing was certain, though: Moses was at Western, and I was determined to find him on Monday.

Nothing held my attention over the weekend, except for the Sunday chapel activities. Rev. Aketu, who had met us at the airport, preached the evening service. Having known him before as a former teacher, Memka helped me plan the evening's activities. I agreed to meet Rev. Aketu and take him to my house for supper. Not knowing what time he would arrive from Kwa, I stayed at the chapel in the late afternoon. Six o'clock passed before a chauffeured black Mercedes pulled up outside. I watched it disinterestedly, thinking some important official had lost his way. To my surprise, it was Rev. Aketu. Carrying a very large briefcase, he climbed out of the back seat, then greeted me heartily.

I invited him into my office to discuss the evening's plans. "By all means!" he exclaimed and instructed his driver to carry his briefcase inside. The minister stood in the middle of my office for a long time, looking at my books. "My, your library is quite large!" he commented.

"It was hard to know which ones to bring with me," I said.

"Oh? You have more in America?" His heavy eyebrows lifted.

"Yes," I answered, embarrassed. "Please sit down. You must be very tired."

"Yes, yes. Quite," he replied, easing into the upholstered chair beside my desk. "I had to travel to Mamsini to preach this morning."

"You've had your share of travels today, sounds like."

"Indeed, yes," he laughed. "It is this way every Sunday, actually. But traveling to Mamsini is no burden, for that is where I come from."

"Oh, really?"

"Yes, yes," he smiled. "My father was one of the first ministers in the Presbyterian church founded by the Geneva Mission."

"And Mamsini was their mission headquarters, am I right?"

"You are indeed," he said, as he fingered his clerical collar. "And our family home is still located in the center of the old Salem, right near to the church."

"The Salem . . . . What is that?" I puzzled.

"Why, it is the area of the town where the Christians used to live."

"You mean, they lived . . . separated from the rest of the townspeople?"

"Oh, yes. Of course," said Rev. Aketu.

"What was the reason for that?"

"So that the new converts could grow in the faith. If they remained with their pagan families and neighbors, well . . . it would weaken their faith, would it not?"

"Did the missionaries demand this sort of thing?"

"Yes, from the very beginning. They quoted from Second Corinthians, the passage about *Come out apart from them, and be separate from them, and touch nothing unclean.*"

I shook my head in astonishment. "Did the missionaries themselves live in the Salems, also?"

"Generally. But many lived in compounds separated from both the Salems and the towns, for health reasons."

"What else did the missionaries consider unclean, apart from living among your neighbors?"

"Why, the traditional ceremonies. Outdooring of infants, puberty rites. And of course many of our funeral rites and pouring libation. Most of our drumming and dancing were considered taboo likewise."

I thought for a few moments. "I guess now that the Ilarian church is autonomous, it can shed some of these European influences in its ministry," I said.

"How do you mean, Rev. Lattimer?" Rev. Aketu frowned.

"Well, aren't there movements to Africanize the church . . . in its vestments and liturgy and music? And experiments to incorporate certain traditional rites—like the outdooring, puberty rites, and marriage—into Christian ceremonies ?" I enthused.

Rev. Aketu looked down and bit his lower lip. "Of course, there are indeed such movements," he sighed. "Mostly from the younger clergy, you understand. But we must be ever so careful. We have had so many difficulties over the years making an impact on the society around us. We must not, under any circumstances, compromise the faith. I'm sure you understand that don't you?"

I nodded.

He relaxed as he changed the subject. "Now, what time do you have? I have 6:25. Is that correct?"

"Yes," I answered.

"Well, perhaps I'd better go to the University guest house and rest a bit."

"My wife and I would like you to eat supper with us, Rev. Aketu," I said.

"That's very, very kind of you," he said, smiling. "But actually I would rather rest than eat. I had a heavy meal at midday, and all I need now, I believe, is a cup of tea. Can I trouble the guest house for that?"

"Oh, certainly, whatever you like," I said half-heartedly, thinking of Kay's all-day effort in preparation for Rev. Aketu.

He slapped the arms of the chair with his hands and then arose. Before leaving, he opened his case and pulled out a black robe to hang up. It smelled of moth balls.

We met again back at the office at 7:15. As we went over the service, Rev. Aketu proposed a lengthy order of worship. It included six hymns, three Scripture lessons (appropriate for the Twenty-first Sunday after Trinity, I noticed), and the various prayers of adoration, confession, and petition. Then we put on our robes, mine a tropicalized Geneva gown I wore over a shirt and tie, and his a heavy wool one with collar and tabs. I remarked to him, didn't he find his rather hot. He shrugged at that, saying that it was the only kind sold by a particular company in Britain.

"No one makes them in Ilaria?" I exclaimed.

"Indeed not," he said. "They must be imported."

"That must make them very expensive."

"Of course. But it's all for the cause, you know." He chuckled as he struggled to adjust his tabs before the mirror I kept in my office. I asked him about the possibility of a get-together with the students afterwards. But he demurred, saying he would be far too tired to socialize.

I, too, was tired by the time the lengthy service ended. Rev. Aketu's sermon staggered under anecdotes and quotations from Shakespeare, Robert Burns, and G. K. Chesterton. Additionally, he delivered it in a finely polished voice, complete with rolled "Rs." When we finished, Rev. Aketu took off his robe in my office and slumped into the chair, wiping his face with his handkerchief. He declined going out among the students milling in the lounge to see him. I excused myself from him to wind things up outside. Memka expressed keen disappointment to me at not being able to see Rev. Aketu. Back in my office, I found the minister thumbing through a book from my shelf.

We walked out together into the night, swept cool by breezes from the sea. Upon seeing us, the driver started up the motor.

Rev. Aketu shook my hand. "It has been a decided pleasure, Rev. Lattimer," he gushed.

I offered to see him off the next morning. But he insisted that he would be leaving before daybreak. As the car pulled away, he called, "Cheerio," to me from the back seat.

I checked by the guest house about 7:30 the next morning to see if Rev. Aketu had gone. Then I walked over to the Faculty of Science and climbed up to the third floor. I crept up to the door marked "Awulu," like a hunter stalking his prey. No sound from within responded to my knock. So I waited around the corner, hidden from view. Mr. Awulu had to come to work some time, and I was prepared to wait for him all day, if necessary.

An hour must have passed before I heard footsteps coming down the corridor. They stopped at the office, and someone went in. I straightened up and swallowed and swept the shock of hair out of my forehead.

I knocked, and a voice said, "Come."

I entered. Working at his desk, he didn't glance up to see who it was. I stood there a moment and then said, "Hello, Moses."

His eyes shot up and met mine. We regarded each other a few moments silently. A sullenness eclipsed the light that used to brighten his face. He seemed years older. No surprise at seeing me registered in his expression.

"Good morning, Rev. Lattimer," he said with a tepid smile. "Won't you sit down?" He indicated a chair. He watched me settle in the chair. Then, "Yes, Rev. Lattimer?" he asked.

"I . . . I thought I'd drop by, Moses, to see how you are," I said.

"I've been more or less expecting you," he said with a coy manner, "ever since I heard you were here."

"I see," I murmured, "and why did you figure I'd come?"

"Because you are a pastor and a missionary," he spit the words out. "It is your *professional responsibility*, I suppose."

"What about out of friendship?"

His eyes glanced away. "I wouldn't know about that," he said stiffly.

I let the silence hang for a few moments and then said, "We cannot consider each other as friends any more, Moses?"

He looked up. "Friendship is a two-way street, don't you think?" he snapped.

"Yes. When one who has offended asks forgiveness and the other gives it. Yes, it can be a two-way street."

He looked out the window, and in spite of his deadpan face, I somehow felt he was churning inside. "Did you receive my letters?" I asked. "While you were still at Tech?"

He shrugged and nodded, still gazing away,

"I tried very hard to contact you in Atlanta. I wanted to see you badly."

Moses swung his head back at me and sighed. "So your letters and notes said. But frankly I had then—and I have now—nothing to say for the incident. Nothing about Greenwood and Trinity Church," he said with increasing vigor. "No reflections. No confessions. No criticisms. Nothing. I have been very happy the year that I have been here. I have managed to bury the past."

"I can't believe that everything is buried."

His eyes flamed and he sat forward. "What is it you want me to say, Han . . . Rev. Lattimer? The past is over. Finished. What do you want me to do? Do you want me to weep on your shoulder about what happened? Do you want me to condemn America, White people, and the church for their racial sickness? Do you want me to be a prophetic voice to your people? Or do you want me to shake the dust off my feet and *accept* and carry on as if nothing happened? What is it you want?"

I sat silently looking at my hands. Then, "No, Moses. I'm not asking any of that from you. I guess I was hoping we could renew our friendship. I do want to repeat this to you . . . in person. I'm profoundly sorry that this thing happened to you. As for me, it changed my life. I saw for the first time my own prejudice and my own people's prejudice. And when I tried to do something about it, I was forced to leave Trinity Church."

"Why, then," he said, "have you come to Africa . . . aside from wanting to atone for your guilt?"

"Guilt!" I cried. "I truly don't believe that guilt feelings have motivated me to come. Right now the chief thing I would like to atone for is our broken relationship."

"I see," said Moses. He sat motionless and then sighed again. "Well, Rev. Lattimer, welcome to Ilaria and Western University. I hope your stay here will be happy and successful. Now I must beg you, please, to excuse me. I have a lecture in the next hour, and I must finish my preparations." He arose from his chair and extended his hand.

We shook hands, limply. "I . . . I hope we may meet again, Moses."

"Perhaps, perhaps," he said with a smile. "As for Moses, I no longer go by that name."

"So I have heard," I said. "What are you called now?"

"My friends call me Kwati."

"I see," I said. "And what shall I call you?"

He looked away and shrugged. "As you wish," he said.

"All right. Goodbye for now."

I slowly closed the door and left. Classes apparently had just changed, and students pressed about me by the time I descended the last flight of steps. Memka, walking among them, waved frantically at me. But I responded with little enthusiasm. I don't know how many others I may have slighted.

Returning to my office, I wanted to sit and think awhile, but three people were waiting to see me. One, my new clerk; another, the messenger; and a third, a student with money problems. So I spent the morning counselling and directing and finding out about files and requisitions.

At lunch time, I related my encounter with Moses to Kay.

"Do you think he still is a Christian?" she asked, when I finished.

"I don't know. I just don't know," I said. "It seems unlikely since he won't open up to me. But just because he's hung up there, doesn't mean he's lost faith in God . . . necessarily."

"Necessarily," echoed Kay.

"I've just got to get through to him, Kay," I insisted.

"But how?" she asked. "He has to meet you part way. You can't force yourself on him."

"Of course," I pondered. After a while, I said, "But if I can't find a way, then . . . then I feel my ministry here is in jeopardy."

"In jeopardy!" she exclaimed in horror.

"Sure." I got up and stalked the floor. "If Moses lost his faith because of racial prejudice and the students here find out about it and if we cannot work out some sort of reconciliation . . . , then, well, I'm living a lie. My message is invalid!" I waved my hands about.

"Oh, Hank. Really!"

"What do you mean, *Oh, really?*" I stopped and scowled.

"I mean aren't you taking this a little bit too heavily?"

"Not a'tall!" I grimaced at her.

"You mean we should pack up and go home . . . because . . . because you can't practice what you preach?"

"That's about the size of it," I declared.

She sighed. "Then how do any of us as missionaries, or . . . or Christians, for that matter, have a leg to stand on? None of us is perfect. Do you think we can't witness until we are perfect?"

I nodded, and then I shook my head. Finally, I held my hands upward in a demoralized gesture of confusion.

Kay got up and gave me a hug. "Honey, please don't brood over this. After all, you don't even know for sure if Moses has lost his faith. Now, do you?"

I shook my head.

In the days that followed I had little time for brooding, fortunately. In empty moments, though, it began to gnaw at me why Moses reacted the way he had. He had been a strong Christian. Why had his faith proved insufficient under fire? At times I wished I knew more about his background. But activities during those first weeks mounted up so that I could only dabble into the question.

I enrolled in the African Studies course, which is required of all first-year students. Then I set about finding an Akarti teacher. James suggested Elizabeth Lutterodt, who, he said, had been looking for part-time employment. So she came to my office on Tuesday and Thursday afternoons for two hours. It was only through her remarkable insight and analysis of linguistic sounds that my reluctant tongue began to produce something resembling the Akarti language.

After two weeks of working with her, she told me that Kanu Jones wanted her to teach him Akarti, also. We arranged that he join our class at my office. During our first lesson together, Elizabeth backtracked to enable Kanu to get the gist of pronunciation. We followed a pat exercise of "Good morning" and "How are you?" with appropriate responses. Kanu quickly remembered the correct answers, but the pronunciation stumped him. Elizabeth and he went over and over the words. Whenever she called on me and I came up with the correct answer, Kanu would turn right around in his chair and stare at me.

For three more lessons, Kanu and I sweated it out, both from heat and intensity. Elizabeth remained unruffled, demure, and terribly patient. Kanu improved bit by bit, but each mistake shook him by the roots. One day, in the middle of a lesson, he jumped up, put his pen in his pocket, and, wadding up his paper, threw it into my waste basket.

"I can't take any more of this . . . this humiliation," he hissed, glaring at me. Before we could respond, he fled from my office.

After a few moments of silence, I said, "I think it would be best if Kanu were in a class by himself."

Elizabeth fluttered her long lashes and then sighed. "Why are Negroes so defensive?"

My ears prickled at her use of the word "Negro."

"White people have given them a reason to be, don't you think?"

"But it's not only White people they are defensive toward," she said. "It's to Ilarians as well."

"Oh? Why is that?"

She laughed a little. "Well, they expect us to still condemn the slave trade! They can't believe we have let bygones be bygones."

"The slave trade with its reminders of it among the castles here is a hard thing for them to forget."

"Then they shouldn't keep coming here and becoming humiliated," she said with a pout.

"But they come to try to find their roots. You understand that, don't you?"

"Of course," she said. "But they hardly ever succeed."

"Why not?"

"They just don't belong here. No matter how much Akarti they learn or Ilarian clothes they wear or native food they eat, they are still foreigners."

"Doesn't their black skin make it any easier for them?"

She laughed. "Not necessarily, Rev. Lattimer. We don't accept ourselves! A black skin doesn't create an automatic brotherliness among Africans. A'tall. We accept the American Negro as another *fama*."

"*Fama*! Does that surprise you?" she asked, amused.

"It sure does!"

"*Fama* really means *foreigner from across the sea*. Of course 99 times out of 100, he's a White man."

"Kanu will flip when he hears that one!" I exclaimed.

"I feel certain that he has already heard it," she declared. "As for now, let us return to the lesson."

The more I studied under Elizabeth, the more she clued me in on life in Ilaria. About marriage customs. Childrearing. Fetish priests. Fishing practices. She was the first to tell me about Wilson, a third-year student who drowned near Charlestown Castle. He was swimming with a friend in the river beside the Castle when he just disappeared in the water. The friend tried to get Wilson but failed. Then he went to shore for help, but the fishermen sitting there mending their nets refused to budge. The police, too, proved immobile."

"Why?" I asked her.

"The river is considered sacred by the people of the town. They believe that the river gods demand a human sacrifice now and again, or else fish will be scarce. If your livelihood depended on fish, what would you have done?"

The customary wake-keeping for Wilson was held that night in the auditorium. I didn't realize it was done in Ilaria among Protestants. The students organizing it asked me to participate with them. It consisted of hymns, Scripture readings, and prayers. At midnight, we dispersed out onto the sleeping campus. James Gharta gave me a lift home.

Wilson's death held top place in conversation around the campus for days. When we entertained the executives of the CSA at our house some days later, they added a few new angles to it.

"How many students from Guinea Hall have now passed away?" Memka asked across the table behind a great mound of rice on his plate.

"Five," came a voice.

"No, it is six," inserted Samuel waving a chicken leg. "You remember Chula was killed in the auto accident last year."

"Aaaah, yes!"

"In a car that slid down the Nkuru Scarp," said Oparu.

"That is the one. Out of the six passengers, he was the only one killed. No one else received a scratch," explained Samuel. "Indeed, it was strange."

A brief silence enveloped the group as they focused on their dinner. The chicken and rice dish, the tomato and okra stew, and the fried plantain were being consumed as if they had not eaten for a week.

"I suppose the hall leaders will certainly sacrifice a cow now," said Kwafu,

"Not if we can help it!" stated Memka, his lips drawn tight.

"What do you mean *if we can help it*?" Oparu put his fork down and sat up straight.

"Why, I should think as the Christian organization at the University we should publicly oppose such a heathen practice."

I asked them what in the world they were talking about.

"Many people, especially the villagers near the campus, believe that Guinea Hall stands on the site where a fetish lives."

Samuel said, "They believe that the god is angry because a building stands there and his followers can no longer sacrifice to him on the spot. Some feel that the god is avenging himself by taking the lives of students who live there."

"Ei! Kwafu!" exclaimed a student at the end of the table. "Isn't that your hall?"

Kwafu giggled, nodding his head. Oparu sucked his teeth in annoyance, and Memka poked deadpan in his rice.

"But I don't understand about the cow," I put in.

Samuel continued, "The students in Guinea Hall want to sacrifice a cow to appease the god so that no more of the students who live there will be killed."

"You mean they will call in fetish priests and go through a ritual ceremony of purification?" I asked, trying to stifle my surprise.

"Yes."

"And all the students are willing to go along with it?" I asked.

"No!" exclaimed Memka.

"We-e-e-ll. That is the contention," stated Oparu. "The leaders of the hall feel that in order to be efficacious, all of the students must attend it."

"But aren't some of the students Christian?" asked Kay.

"Of course." Memka stuck his lip out. "There are many dedicated Christians who will have none of the affair. Then there are others who say they are Christians but who also go along with traditional practices."

"Just in case," giggled Kwafu.

"If the Christians attend the ritual, do they feel they are aligning themselves with black magic?" I asked.

"Of course," replied Memka, nodding vigorously.

Oparu drew himself up again. "I don't agree a'tall." He glowered at Memka. "If we attend as Christians, it does not mean we give sanction to such actions at all. When you go to a funeral of a friend and they pour libation, do you get up and walk out?"

"But that's different," protested Memka.

"It's no different," stated Oparu.

"But I think it is," Memka said, flashing Oparu a smile. "What do you think, Rev. Lattimer?" he turned to me.

"I don't know that much about it," I said. "I haven't looked into libation and ritual sacrifice to know what all they entail. I'm still quite a newcomer, you know."

"But evil is evil, Rev. Lattimer!" Memka pushed. "Whether you are a newcomer or not."

I finished cleaning up the rice on my plate, not at all sure the issue was that cut and dry. "Memka," I said. "What is it you want to do? Do I hear you saying that you want the CSA to publicly oppose the ritual sacrifice?"

"Yes," he nodded, smiling. "How do the rest of you feel?" I asked.

No one else seemed so intense over the subject. "I think we should individually decide whether to boycott the ritual," said Samuel in his most diplomatic voice.

"But that will compromise our Christian witness as an organization," exclaimed Memka.

"By no means," said Kwafu. "If we choose to boycott it as individuals, we don't have to get up and loudly proclaim why we are doing it."

"Then you are hiding your light under a bushel," said Memka with a beatific smile.

Oparu emitted a loud "tsk" but said nothing. The talk turned to a football [soccer] match between halls and then national politics. They mentioned the debate on church versus government-controlled schools coming up on the next Thursday. Samuel assured me that they had secured a moderator for the occasion.

"But you will be there, won't you, Rev. Lattimer?" Memka said, as he beamed over at me.

"Yes, of course, I'll come," I affirmed.

Chapter 10

By the time the symposium rolled around the following week, the controversy over the ritual purification fizzled out. The administration squashed it as being "contradictory to the principles and ideals of the academic community."

Early in the afternoon of the symposium, I waited in my office for my language class. By the end of a half an hour, Elizabeth still hadn't come. I pulled out a new book called *Biblical Revelation and African Beliefs*. I read only a few pages of it when Sean burst into my office, distraught.

"Elizabeth," he said, out of breath. "Her child is sick. Very sick. Can . . . could ye go to see her . . . them?"

"Of course," I responded.

Sean drove us pell-mell down the campus hill to the sea road. Turning east toward San Paulo, we roared along the coast. As we went, I spotted grass-roofed huts under the thick shade of coconut palms. Beyond them, the sun glinted fiercely upon the breakers and canoes drying on the sand. Fort San Paulo loomed bigger and bigger as we approached the town. Along the streets, people, shops, dilapidated houses, and the smell of fish pressed around us. Skirting the old Dutch cemetery, Sean lurched to a stop in front of a shop selling hardware. On its second floor, he knocked at a door. Elizabeth, with circles under her eyes, met us. She invited us into the bed-sitting room, whose sagging double bed took up most of the linoleum-covered floor. A small figure on the bed breathed under a heap of covers. Sean stalked toward it and sat down beside it.

"Thank you very much for coming," Elizabeth said, smiling up at me.

"How is he?" I said, pointing to the bed. "Or . . . she?"

"It's a boy. Come and see him."

I followed her over to the bed. She pulled back the covers so I could see his face. He seemed about two years old, had very light skin and softly curling hair. I realized at once that he was Sean's.

"Have you taken him to a doctor?" I asked.

"Yes, this morning. They gave him an injection, and I will go back tomorrow and the next day for two more. It's probably malaria. He's been so sleepy, so unresponsive. That is what frightens me." She sat down on the bed and began stroking the motionless head. Sean's hairy hand gripped her shoulder. They both sat there looking at the child a few moments before Elizabeth arose and crossed to the lumpy sofa. "Reverend, please sit down," she said softly.

I sat down in a chair while Sean joined Elizabeth on the sofa. I asked more questions about the boy. He was Patrick and had been baptized a Methodist when he was 18 months old, Elizabeth volunteered.

"And he's your child?" I asked Sean.

He gazed at me head on. "Yes, he's my son. He's named after my father."

A heavy silence fell on us, and I saw Sean out of the corner of my eye nudge Elizabeth.

Then she said, "Rev. Lattimer, there is something we would very much like to discuss with you."

"Yes, Elizabeth, what is it?" I responded.

She looked down at her hands, held gracefully in her lap. "Will . . . would you marry us, Rev. Lattimer?"

"It depends, Elizabeth," I said after a moment's hesitation. "We would need to discuss several things, I believe, before I could marry you."

"What sort of things?" she asked with great questioning in her eyes. Sean stared at the floor.

"Like your background. How long you've known each other and your churches, if any. And your analysis of future problems."

"She's Protestant, and I'm Catholic," Sean blurted out, "But she can belong to any church she likes; so can the boy." His eyes blazed at me.

"Well, let's start at another point," I suggested. "How long have you known each other?"

"Three and a half years," said Sean.

"And have you lived together all of that time?" I asked.

"For three years," said Elizabeth, looking back at her hands.

"Have you ever thought of getting married before?"

Neither one answered. Finally, Elizabeth answered, "Yes," as she glanced at Sean.

"Why, then, didn't you do it?" I asked.

Again a silence, broken eventually by Sean. "She spoke of it many times," he clipped.

"But you did not?"

"No."

"Can you tell me why not?" I asked.

He did not say anything.

Then I added, "Sean, I'm not asking these questions to be nosy or to embarrass either of you. I want us to talk these matters out. For they are essential to discuss before you think of getting married. You need to know each other's minds far more than I need to."

He nodded and explained that in the beginning he felt he had no security to offer Elizabeth as a foreigner. But as time passed, he realized that he would always find employment either as a lecturer or as an engineer in Ilaria. "Furthermore, it became increasingly clear that I should never return to Ireland," he said.

"Why not?" I asked.

Sean looked at me with troubled eyes. "Rev. Lattimer, I guess I've not told you what part of Ireland I come from. I am from Belfast, not the Republic of Ireland. As you know, life is becoming unbearable for Catholics in Belfast. What sort of environment would that be for my son?"

I nodded. Then I turned to Elizabeth. She shared her feelings of anxiety about her tenuous relationship with Sean. "I knew if he would leave me to return to his home, then I would manage . . . somehow. It wouldn't be the first time a White man has left an Akarti girl on the coast!"

"But I would have sent you money," interrupted Sean. "I'm not that kind of man!"

"But there's more to life than physical support," she stated, turning to him. "There's more than eating and working and having a room to live in. That is what I could not face, Sean. That is what would be so hard," her voice cracked.

He grabbed her hand. "It won't be that way now, love. It won't be. We shall be man and wife and I shall not leave ye." Clutching his arm with her other hand and leaning her head against it, she began to cry.

I discussed with them where they would live after marriage, as well as their parents' support of their decision. Sean's were dead. Elizabeth's had solidly approved of Sean from the beginning. "They were hoping we would marry," she said. "They consider it a mark of status to be married to a White man."

"And you? Do you consider it a mark of status?" I asked.

She looked at me with searching eyes. "Please believe me, Reverend. I am marrying Sean Finnegan. Not a White man."

"I hope so, Elizabeth. I hope that the question is settled deep inside you. For if you marry a White man for the sake of marrying a White man, many problems would arise."

"Yes, I know," she said. "I have seen that happen to friends of mine. I have seen their hopes built on material possessions and trips to Europe and a fine car and not on their husbands. It only brings tragedy."

"And the church? Will it approve your marriage?"

"It will approve," she affirmed.

"And you, Sean. What is your relationship to the Catholic church?"

He sighed. "I was baptized a Catholic. But I quit attending mass some years ago. I've never attended in Ilaria."

"Do you consider yourself a Christian?"

He shrugged. "I'm not sure. I believe in God. But whatever Elizabeth wants to believe in doesn't matter to me."

"And you are an active Christian, Elizabeth?"

"Yes, Reverend," she said, "I have made many mistakes in the Christian life. But my faith does mean much to me. I want to have a Christian home . . . and maybe even Sean can come to love God too!" She smiled, looking up at him.

"When would you like to be married?" I asked Sean.

They smiled at each other. "The sooner, the better!" said Sean with a grin.

"Oh, no!" Elizabeth exclaimed. "We need time for preparations! We must have a big wedding so that all my friends and family can come."

Sean rubbed his forehead, pseudo-dramatically. "Ah, yes. I quite forgot. When you marry into an Ilarian family, you really marry into a family!"

We all laughed. Then we discussed specific plans as to when and where the marriage would be performed and when they could meet with me for more discussions prior to it. As we finished, Patrick was beginning to stir. Elizabeth asked that I pray for him. Standing, we prayed for Patrick as well as for the forthcoming marriage.

When I was ready to go, I insisted I'd take a taxi back to the University. Sean offered to help me get one, so we said goodbye to Elizabeth. Outside, he spoke in Akarti with a taxi driver, an apparent friend. He introduced me to the man as the *Basela* at the University, the Akarti word for priest or minister. I was glad to see Sean so indigenized, for it made me feel that the marriage would have a better chance of survival. He thanked me for coming and for the prayer before I left.

The driver drove me speedily back to the University. On the way I marveled at the experience I had just come through. For certainly, two years ago, I would have regarded a Black/White marriage as anathema. Why had I changed? Was it not because, in my profound awareness of being White, I was beginning to accept the Blackness of Black people?

The symposium had already started when I returned, so I sat down on the last row of the auditorium. Behind the podium the speaker in favor of church-controlled schools was finishing up a formal speech. I did not know him.

Then, after a brief introduction by the moderator, the opponent to the issue arose. I momentarily stopped breathing when I saw him. For it was Moses Awulu. Contrary to the previous speaker, Moses spoke in an intimate tone to the students, half-leaning on the table before us. He gave a brief history on the schools, telling how they were founded by European missionaries mainly in the late 19th century. He stated that the chief purpose of the schools was "to recruit students into the Christian faith and to make them literate so that they could read the Scriptures. For this reason," he declared, "we cannot tolerate the schools today. For they were founded on the exploitation of the African by the White man."

He went on to focus briefly on missionary history in Ilaria in general. "A history," he stated, "tainted with paternalism and aligned with questionable influences from the outset. From the time the Portuguese defiled us with their presence in the fifteenth century, the missionary had tagged along. First, associated with the merchants and military garrisons in the trading posts on the Guinea coast. Next he accompanied the slave traders and the Colonialists. Always upholding the status quo, ministering to the White predators without questioning the morality of their actions.

"Now, what of the missionary today, the successor to the founders of the schools, the teachers, and the headmasters in our country?" he asked. He quoted figures on how many schools were still run by expatriate missionaries, despite "the tremendous numbers of capable Ilarians who could head the schools if given a chance."

His main antagonism toward missionary-run schools comprised the "inadequate leadership" of the missionaries themselves. This stemmed from two causes, according to Moses: their cultural prejudice toward the African and their racial prejudice toward the Black man.

"Culturally, the missionary has brainwashed Africans to feel uncivilized and inferior. And I contend that most of the brainwashing goes on in our mission schools. Racially, he comes from a society that doesn't give a damn about the Black man. Consciously or unconsciously, the missionary feels superior, or why else would he be here? He is here only to change us, and that, supposedly spiritually. He cares not one shilling for the intellectual or economic betterment of Africans. He only wants to add our souls to the kingdom."

Lastly, he illustrated how missions in Africa were supported by segregated money. "If you or I tried to attend their churches in their homelands, we could not. Because we are Black and inferior. For these reasons this soul has been subtracted from the kingdom!" The last he hissed between compressed lips so that the audience barely breathed to catch his words.

When Moses finished, the first speaker was allowed to rebut what Moses had said. He tore into Moses's idea of brainwashing, stating that if it occurred, it was "all to the good. Integrity and industry and charity are all good biases, which elevate the general morality of the country."

Then a student arose, also challenging Moses. Would Moses please cite more examples of his purported brainwashing?

Moses strolled theatrically to the side of the table and leaned on it with one hand. "Let me describe one situation for you, and you can draw your own conclusions," he intoned. "At a school that I know of, a White missionary had been headmistress for years. But eventually she was replaced by an Ilarian woman, highly educated with many years of experience. But for all practical purposes, the missionary might as well have remained headmistress. She knew everything that went on in the school: from where each student came to how many pieces of cutlery and crockery were in the kitchen.

"Now it appeared that she kept informed about all these things because of her strong devotion to the school and to everyone in it. But the truth of the matter is that she did not trust anyone else. She didn't trust the cleaners, so she counted the kitchen implements. She didn't trust the other faculty members—all Ilarian—so she personally taught and supervised as much as she was able. She didn't trust the students, so she attended all their meetings. She supervised what came and went in the library and the post office. She read everyone's private files. She carried with her a large bunch of keys, which gave her illicit access to all offices and records. Now, as I say, on appearances, her busyness meant interest and devotion. But in actuality, she wanted to control everyone and everything to her own liking and conviction.

"And what were her convictions? Some of them were these: a suspicion of everything African. The refusal to endorse worship services with traditional music because she considered it *pagan*. Uncooperation with any other faith on an ecumenical basis, particularly with the Catholics. A belief that her own fundamentalistic way of Christianity was the norm for everyone else. To me, these dictatorial tactics indicate a repression of academic freedom. The student is never allowed to mature and to think for himself."

As Moses sat down, the room broke into a hubbub of discussion. The moderator had to rap for order to announce that it was time to close the meeting. Comfort, chosen to give a "vote of thanks" as per custom, arose to thank the speakers, the moderator, and the audience for coming. At the same time she urged the audience to weigh the opinions for themselves before coming to any conclusion "on so vital an issue."

The students got up en masse. Several crowded toward the speakers, but most left through the side doors of the building. I slipped out ahead of them toward my office. When I got there, I locked the door and slumped into my chair. My hands felt clammy, and somewhere deep inside, I felt a vise squeezing me.

I sat there for a long time, staring into space, reeling from the impact of Moses's speech. His words had flung fire brands onto my emotions. How had the students really responded to him? Did they swallow his opinions in one lump or only in bits and pieces? They had seemed easily swayed, transfixed by his manner and words. Did they readily accept his indictment of missionaries? And if they found out I was a missionary, what would it mean for my ministry at Western? For curiously enough, it did not occur to most people that I was a missionary. Rather, I was the chaplain, supposedly hired by the University like everyone else.

The unanswered questions tumbled one over the other in no particular order. When everyone had left the building, including my secretary, I went home. Kay trembled with indignation as I told her about the symposium. But sensing my raw reaction to it, she tried to cheer me with a string of maybes and what ifs. Instead of pulling me out of my despondency, though, I dragged her down into it. We went to bed, spent and dejected.

Some days later, I found myself strolling along the beach in front of the University. It was late afternoon, and I was too depressed to study. Walking was difficult, for the beach slanted into the water at almost a 35 degree angle. The waves slammed up on the incline and rushed outward with an overwhelming undertow. I trudged eastward toward San Paulo, looking out over the billows and the roar, trying to find the hazy horizon. A ship interrupted its smooth sweep, and I wondered if it might be heading for America. For a moment, I ached to be on it. To my left, up the steep beach, the thatched huts sat in the sifting rays of sunlight under the coconut palms. Two boys came out to watch me and then to follow at a discreet distance. I bent over, picked up a few shells, and jingled them in my pocket as I went along.

I heard another jangling coming from the beach ahead of me. I discovered that fishermen were pulling in their long seine, which arced out about a hundred yards into the sea. The clanging noise came from two small boys beating pieces of metal together. Their sound synchronized the efforts of a dozen or so men straining at the heavy rope, to which the net was tied. Leaning and walking backward, they moved in unison, each behind the other, taking tiny steps. They would reach a certain point, drop the rope, walk forward toward the ocean, and pick it up again. They sang as they pulled causing me to wonder what their words might be about.

I sat down to watch, caught up in the rhythm and chant and hiss of surf. They served as a pleasant distraction for my lathered-up thoughts. I don't know how long I sat there. But eventually, the net was drawn in and lay stretched out on the sand. Men, women, children, and hungry seagulls hovered over the catch before it was distributed. A mass of fish wriggled and squirmed in the dark blue net, as if part of one great shivering body. The silvery fish trapped in its sides glimmered like stars in a midnight sky. As the sorting began, the women lowered their enamel tubs from their heads for the filling, and children pressed in to have a look and snitch a fish.

As I watched, I began to think of the nets and fish and fishermen of Galilee. The draft of fishes. The torn nets, the sinking boats. Were they any sturdier than these painted canoes of the Guinea coast? Andrew and Peter. The Sons of Thunder. And I thought of the One who called them to be fishers of men. "Follow me," He had said. They dropped everything and obeyed, not fully knowing where or why.

"Follow me." The words reverberated down the hollow corridors of my own mind. Or was it the perpetual swooshing of the waves upon the shore?

I thought of all the agony of decision to come to Ilaria. The kinked-up path that had met us, the uncertainty of my appointment. And now, the symposium. I had followed so far. And what had I met with? What?

"Follow me."

I dug my feet into the sand before me and looked out at the sea. The ship had long gone.

"O.K., Lord," I resolved, without emotion or total understanding.

Chapter 11

When the fishmongers began to disperse, I got up and started along the path through the coconut grove to the highway. A man stepped out from the crowds, calling "Basela!" He wore a neat shirt and pressed trousers. It was Kpemlo from the maintenance yard. We greeted each other cordially. "Have you come to buy fish?" I asked him.

"Oh, no," he smiled. "I was down visiting my brother and his family," he pointed to a clump of huts. "Let me take you to meet them. My brother works as a laborer at the University."

"Fine," I said.

We walked together through the grove, then crossed the highway. We came to a woven, palm-branch wall and entered through an opening into a large, well-swept earthen courtyard. Three sides faced houses of grass and thatch. Each one, I judged, was about the size of our living room alone. Windowless with one gaping doorway, they housed a single family unit, all related to each other in the same compound. In a corner of the courtyard, fish were being smoked in a type of kiln. Elsewhere a fire glowed under a cooking pot.

Kpemlo spoke to the woman stirring the pot, and she trundled into a hut. A tall man emerged with the woman and approached us with a smile. He gave the appearance of a strong, healthy man with the exception of one eye. Ravaged by some parasite, it peered at me as a sclerosed mass of white jelly. He shook my hand and said "Welcome," as Kpemlo spoke to him in their vernacular. His name was Koto, and he and Kpemlo were of the "same father, same mother," as Kpemlo explained. He spoke no English.

Two school-aged boys suddenly scampered out from behind a building. They stopped short when they saw me, and Koto made them shake my hand. They looked at the ground as they did so.

"How old are they?" I asked Kpemlo.

"Eight and nine," he said. "My brother has two other sons, who are older, and two daughters."

"Do they go to school near here?"

Kpemlo's face fell. "Oh, no, Basela. There is no school for them to attend."

"No school at all . . . anywhere?"

"Well, there is a school behind the University. But our children . . . Mpesi children . . . are not accepted there."

"Why not?"

He rested his hands on his hips. "The people in the school are Akarti. They do not speak our language, although we speak theirs. And they . . . they throw stones at our children when they go to school there and trouble them too much."

"There is no school among your own people, then?" I asked.

"Yes, sir," he said in the Ilarian way of answering a negative question.

"How many children live here in the Mpesi villages?"

"In all of them, between here and San Paulo, there must be more than two hundred."

"Can anything be done about it?"

Kpemlo shrugged. "A'tall," he said. "The people here are fishing people. They are all Mpesi people. They have no influence with the local Akarti school officials."

We stood a few moments without saying anything. "I'll see what I can do," I said impulsively.

Then I announced that I had better go. The decreasing light in the sky enlarged the shadows around us, cast by the coconut trees. I shook hands again with Koto, and Kpemlo walked me out of the compound to the highway. The sky flamed orange in the sunset. And from the mangrove swamp beside the road, snowy egrets were rising to wing inland for the night.

The next day dawned with the usual soft coos of doves and coucals. They beveled the sharp edges of sunlight, forcing them into our bedroom. I drew in a deep sigh and plunged into the order of the day, resolving to sweep back self-indictments and depression. A visit from James in my office that morning helped. "Mr. Awulu's speech the other day was a pity," he said. "But we stand solidly behind you, Hank."

As the days progressed, my depression waned bit by bit. I discovered with some horror, though, that it was being replaced with something else. I began to feel stirrings of bitterness and hostility toward Moses. I prayed and hoped and resolved not to let this happen. But in unguarded moments, my mind would suddenly throw a switch, and the harsh feelings would rumble.

I became too busy to ponder much on what had happened. Our car from France arrived, necessitating a week's worth of travel back and forth to the harbor, thirty-five miles away, to get it out of hock. Then the Thanksgiving dinner came for the Charlestown American community—about fifty-five strong—which signaled fresh activities in Advent. I would preach the Christmas service right before vacation. On top of it, I learned that the Appointments Board would meet on December third. This meant collecting required documents for my curriculum vitae. It had all been done prior to our arrival in Ilaria. I couldn't fathom why it had to be done again. "It's all a matter of form," the Registrar's letter requesting the materials had explained. "We expect no difficulties."

On the day of the Appointments Board, I tried to pull together my sermon for the Christmas service. Bibles, commentaries, dictionaries lay strewn across my desk as I worked. They had grown fuzzy with mildew and, of late, smudged and puckered from damp, sweaty fingers. For no matter how high I set my fan, I still dripped with sweat. It would roll off my forehead down onto my papers in front of me. My reading glasses steamed, and my arms exuded with water so that I had to put towels under them when I wrote to keep my papers dry.

A knock came at the door. "Come," I called, omitting the "in" as Ilarians do.

It was Memka. He bounced into the office, smiling and lighting up the room with his buoyance. He, too, glistened with exertion. He greeted me with the customary inquiries about my and my family's health.

Then, "What are you working on, Reverend?" he asked, as his eyes fell on my disarray of books.

"The sermon for this Sunday. Do you have any ideas?" I leaned back in my chair. "What do you think the University needs to hear this Christmas?"

With no hesitation, Memka responded, "Oh, they need the Gospel, Reverend." His face darkened with solemnity. "The pure Gospel so that they might believe in him and be saved."

"But don't you think we should use different terms and phrases to catch their attention? Have some grown immune to the terminology of the Bible and need something else to make them listen?"

"Oh, no."

"Why not?"

Memka seemed startled. He seemed unused to ministers asking questions of him. "Because God promises that if we preach his Word, it will not return to him void," came the satisfied answer.

I sighed and wiped my face and arms with the towel. I looked at Memka's earnest face, his folded hands, one leg swinging over the knee of the other.

"Tell me something about yourself, Memka," I said. "How long have you been a Christian?"

He told me that he came from a pagan family originally, but who now, "by God's grace, have been converted." As for himself, he became a Christian in secondary school under the influence of an English missionary.

"So you think missionaries are pretty helpful . . . in spite of what Mr. Awulu said at the symposium?"

Memka's expression grew heavy. "Indeed, yes!" he exclaimed. "Many of us would be spiritual beggars without them! But as for Mr. Awulu . . . ," he shook his head. "As for him, God have mercy on his soul!"

"What did you think of his remarks?"

"Truly, they came from the devil himself," declared Memka. "Only a devil could say the things which he did!"

"He was once a very strong Christian," I said.

Memka's jaw dropped. Then he sucked his teeth and shook his head. "That cannot be, Reverend!" he said.

"Why not?"

He unfolded his hands and held his light-colored palms upward. "If he was a true, born-again Christian, he would not have lost his faith," Memka explained. "God will not let his own slip and fall into damnation. We have his assurance of that!"

"So what happened?" I persisted. "Why did this man fall?"

"He never was thoroughly grounded in the faith."

I sighed. "But, Memka, I knew the man before . . . in America. His faith was as strong as yours!"

Memka blinked without stirring. After some moments, he said quietly, "It must not have been as strong as you thought, Reverend."

I sat motionless, looking at Memka and inwardly probing his mind. "Perhaps *strong* isn't the correct word after all, Memka," I said, as a growing awareness of the root of Moses's problem took hold of me. "Perhaps *rigid* . . . or . . . or *dogmatic* would be a more appropriate word."

He remained expressionless except for his customary smile. "Perhaps you are right, Reverend," he said. "But I personally believe that none of us can afford to be less than dogmatic about spiritual matters. After all, God himself gives us his promises which are unbreakable!"

Instead of responding to Memka's observation, I changed the subject. "Are you having exams now, Memka?"

That was why he had come to see me: to ask for prayer that he might pass his exams. I discussed with him the importance of study. But he argued that only prayer and total dependence on God would enable him to succeed.

"Reverend, you sound like you are advocating *the Lord helps those who help themselves*," he said. "And you know, Reverend, that is not Scriptural!"

"No, it's not Scriptural." I bargained that I would pray for him if he promised to study. At the same time I told him of my appointment being reviewed, and I asked for his prayers. Surprised, he wanted to know why I wasn't already appointed.

"I'm not at all sure," I said. "Unless it's due to the fact that I'm not on University salary. My church in America pays my salary."

For a few moments, he mulled over my words. Then his face lit up. "Why, you must be a missionary!" he exclaimed.

"Yes, I am."

"Why, that's wonderful, Reverend. Praise the Lord that you were called here by him!"

Shortly after that, our conversation ended, and he asked to be excused. I returned to my work but found it hard to concentrate. I kept thinking of the conversation with Memka, plus the impending action of the Appointments Board. Presuming that I might be called to meet with the Board, I stuck close to my office, even during lunch time. By the time six o'clock came, I still had received no word. So I went home, thinking that the next day I'd hear something.

But the next day brought no news, nor the next. A letter finally came the following week from the Registrar.

Dear Rev. Lattimer: (it read)

The Appointment of Rev. H.W. Lattimer as Protestant Chaplain

The Appointments Board of Western University met on 3rd December to review your appointment as protestant Chaplain. The Board could not reach a general consensus, and it was decided to suspend a decision until their next meeting in the second or third term. At that time, your work and qualifications will come under further review.

Yours sincerely,

J.B.R. De Heer-Johnson, Registrar

I read the letter over and over, trying to make sense of it. What did it mean? I phoned the Registrar's office for an appointment. Luckily, De Heer-Johnson could see me that morning.

I arrived at his office on the top floor of the Administration Building, out of breath and dripping. But the coolness of his air-conditioned office quickly assuaged me. The heavy drapes drawn over the windows provided a retreat from the heat and sweat and the nitty-gritty of campus affairs, far below. The softness of the carpet and the upholstered chair disconcerted me. I felt out of place. Or was it that the office itself seemed out of place in Charlestown?

Behind the polished mahogany desk hunched De Heer-Johnson in a dark suit and stiffly starched shirt and tie. A gold pin pierced his tie in the image of a stool, the kind which Ilarian chiefs sit on when "in state." Beside him sat a male secretary with pencil and pad poised for action.

"What can I do for you, Rev. Lattimer?" he asked, enunciating the "Ts" in my name with precision.

"I am wondering if you can tell me anything about what occurred at the Appointments Board? Namely, why I was not appointed?" I tried to sound calm. I noted that the secretary recorded our conversation, which I thought rather odd.

"No, I regret I am unable to do so," his deep voice resounded in the placid room.

"Was it due to my qualifications or my performance as Chaplain . . . or what?" I pressed.

"I can divulge no information, Rev. Lattimer," DeHeer-Johnson addressed me as a robot. "The matters of the Board are held in strictest confidence by its members."

His gaze bored into me. I forced myself not to fidget or fume.

"Surely you understand, Mr. DeHeer-Johnson," I said. "It puts me in an extremely awkward position. I have no idea of any mistakes I may be committing in order to rectify them."

DeHeer-Johnson leaned forward and forced a smile. "I would not say that a'tall, Rev. Lattimer. You are most welcome here at Western University. You may, of course, continue to carry on as Chaplain. There is nothing to hinder you from that." His voice oozed superficial empathy, though his ebony face remained impassive.

Seeing that I could gain nothing, I forced myself out of the chair. "When will the Appointments Board meet again?" I asked.

"Sometime during the next term. I do not know the date. It is called according to matters of urgency and how many appointments are slated for review," he said.

"I see," I said, watching the secretary take down my empty words.

We shook hands perfunctorily, and I left. The heat suffocated me outside, as I hastened to my office. "You are welcome . . . but not appointed" zig-zagged in my head all the way there. What did it mean? Anything, really? Or everything? I had an office, a budget, supplies, the freedom to do my work. Yet, officially, I was not the Chaplain. What bugged me most, though, was the lack of urgency in the matter. But was anything ever considered *urgent* in West Africa?

I reached my office and slammed the door behind me.

Following the interview, holiday preparations kept me afloat, for they helped me forget my dangling predicament. Right after the University recessed, Kay and I were invited to a couple of parties. One was held at Jim Aiken's, a Canadian lecturer in mechanical engineering. He and his wife, Lydia, staged an eggnog party for about a dozen expatriates at their home overlooking the ocean. I had met Jim in our mutual struggles to get our cars from the harbor. During the many hours of waiting, I had told him something about my appointment coming up for review in early December. So after we joined the party, he asked me about it first thing.

When I announced that nothing came of it, the others in the circle stopped their conversation to listen in.

"For God's sake, why not?" clipped Roger Chesnee, a gray-haired Englishman sitting across from me. I recognized him as the one who had blown his cool at Kpemio that day in the Maintenance Yard.

"I have no idea," I responded. "No reason was given."

"Good Lord!" exclaimed Rick Carter's wife, also in the circle.

"They haven't kicked you out, have they?" probed Rick, beside her.

"Oh, no," I said. "The Registrar said I could carry on as usual!"

Roger shook his head and wiped the eggnog clinging to his tidy little mustache with his napkin.

"Did you actually see the Registrar about it?" asked a young American named Ned. He had long hair and a prying, pointed face. I had not run across him before.

"I sure did," I replied.

"Well, I'm sure you received no satisfaction from him!" Rick exclaimed.

"None whatever," echoed his wife, as she jabbed out a cigarette. "He's impossible, don't you know," she said, turning to Kay.

"And the key to this University," Roger inserted. "He runs it, actually." I figured he must know, having been at the University five years longer than anyone present.

"I hear he's more powerful than the Vice-Chancellor. Is that true?" asked Rick.

"Yes, it is," said Roger. "I don't know why, in fact. The Registrar must have something on the Vice-Chancellor, for the latter is merely a figurehead," he intoned in his most academic voice.

"It's a downright shame," clucked Rick. "He's no more interested in Western . . . than . . . than those Akarti fishermen!"

"Is that right?" inserted Ned in a challenging tone.

"It's common knowledge," blurted out his wife, Helena. She, too, had long hair and wore granny glasses.

"Common knowledge isn't always accurate," he scowled at her.

"De Heer-Johnson is prejudiced as all get out," Rick continued. "I hear he's death on Ketumbas."

"And White people, too, apparently," tittered Rick's wife.

"Hey!" exclaimed Jim, putting down the tray of drinks he was serving. "Maybe that's why you didn't get appointed, Hank!"

"How could that be?" asked Kay. "Would any of us be here if that were the case?"

"There's probably no real reason," laughed Lydia.

"Of course, there has to be a reason," said Ned.

"But you'll never find out what it is," put in Roger, as he flipped his tie. "Assuredly, there's a reason. Some good Ilarian reason, which we *famas* will never find out."

Rick sighed. "Maybe you should consider yourself lucky," he said to me. "No definite appointment means no definite commitment. You can breeze on out whenever you like. Wish mine were like that."

"Hank, what do you propose to do?" Lydia asked.

"Just . . . just *carry on*, as the Registrar suggested," I chuckled.

"What else could he do under the circumstances?" Ned asked the room at large.

"Hell! Go home, that's what!" shot Rick, and his wife giggled and nodded her head.

"No, I don't see going home," I said. "I just need to adjust to the Ilarian way of looking at things, I guess."

"The *Ilarian way of looking at things*! And what the devil is that?" sputtered Rick.

I felt hot on the back of my neck at my sudden gush of exposure. "What I mean is, they're not going to change basically." I fished for words. "They do things their way. We're accustomed to doing things differently. If we don't adapt to their ways, then . . . well, I guess they will break us."

"But if they're not going to change, out of laziness or indifference, then why the hell should we stay here?" demanded Rick, his face contorted. "Hank, you're here to see people change, aren't you?"

"I guess I pretty much leave that up to the Lord," I smiled.

"Oh, come now," Ned objected. "You're the preacher among us. You can't deny that you're not out for conversions!"

"Not really," I replied. "I came here to share my faith and myself in a sort of two-way process with Ilarians. If any words or actions of mine can be of help or of use or if there are any changes or conversions, then it's up to God. Not me."

Rick had no come-back, and surprisingly, neither did Ned.

The conversation faded away. Lydia reignited it. "Come on, folks," she said. "Don't be so serious. Let's forget our troubles. It's Christmas! The season to be jolly!"

Moans of disagreement arose, especially from the Carters. What was there to be jolly about without snow, Santa, Toyland, and evergreens, they asked. Some of the men in the School of Architecture argued over a new policy. Drinks were replenished, and the scratchy Christmas records began all over again.

Kay and I left the party early. Outside, the moon poured out its bright fullness, causing the ocean in the distance to sparkle. The whole sky radiated in the brilliance, as well as housetops, roadways, and lawns. It was a magical night, but I felt morose.

"What a hypocrite," I muttered to Kay. "Do you and I accept *the Ilarian way of looking at things*?"

She sighed. "And I found myself agreeing with an absence of *Christmas spirit*, so called."

"A fine pair of missionaries," I said and squeezed her shoulder in the car. "Shall we drive over to Howard Johnson's on U.S. 1 for a morale booster?"

Kay laughed. "No. I prefer a MacDonald's hamburger, thank you."

As we pulled away from the Aikens', "I'm Dreaming of a White Christmas" drifted out of the house. We sang it together all the way home.

Chapter 12

The heat all but melted our first Christmas in the tropics. The kids clamored for Santa. The lack of toys, culinary goodies, and decorations threw us on our own improvisations. Kay expressed hopes that by next year, we'd be better adjusted.

"You mean if we're still here," I put in.

She chided me for my pessimism, which I termed *realism*. She did succeed, however, in persuading me to focus on brighter things ahead, like new plans for the second term of school. My brightness dimmed somewhat when the CSA held its first planning session in early January, for only five showed up: Comfort, Memka, Oparu, Kwafu, and James. I refused to despair over the absence of the others. You never knew where the kinks occurred, and eventually you learned the futility of asking, "Why?" I did despair to learn that the preaching schedule for the term remained almost empty.

"We've had only three positive responses from guest ministers," said Comfort. "The rest have either not answered at all or have said they had other engagements."

That left me holding the bag for the term. I had wanted to preach more to the community, so, in a way, I welcomed the opportunity. I explained my feelings to the group: how the resident chaplain, knowing the needs of the campus, could preach with more relevance to them. The five responded favorably.

We talked about other programs for the term, including a contemporary worship service using the vernacular and traditional drumming, for in November, Oparu and other students had asked me about arranging such a service. The group expressed enthusiasm, except for Memka. He thought such a service would "compromise our Christian witness." But the others argued him down. Rev. Daniel Quaina was suggested as the guest minister for the occasion.

Near the end of the meeting, I submitted my suggestion for a project in the Mpesi settlements. I described my visit there, along with Kpemlo's describing no school for Mpesi children. Basically, I outlined a program to prepare young children for school. Then, when we secured funds—from what source I hadn't the glimmer of an idea—we could guide the villagers in building a schoolhouse.

"Have you ever done anything like this before?" I asked.

"No," said Kwafu.

"But we have been wanting something to express our social concern for others," exclaimed Oparu. "I know several who would be interested in this sort of thing."

"Yes, but for the Mpesis?" asked Comfort, her lower lip protruding.

I swung my head sharply at her question. "Why not?" I tried to sound non-judgmental.

"Oh, they are such superstitious, idolatrous people. They don't deserve much help," she said and shrugged.

I waited for other reactions.

"Why should we withhold help from another human being for that reason?" Memka argued. "Christ died for us while we were still sinners!"

'Touché!' I applauded inwardly, glad he had said it and not I.

"Well, the fact is, I wonder if they even want to be educated," said Comfort.

"We can certainly try," pushed Oparu. "I am sure some might want to be . . . as Kpemlo indicated to Rev. Lattimer. And who are we—with so much education—to withhold opportunity from them?"

"Just one thing," cut in Memka. "Will there be opportunity for Bible classes and evangelistic services?"

"We'll have to see," I said.

Oparu volunteered to head up a group to see Kpemlo, our logical contact. He promised also to enlist other helpers. "They don't come to church very often, Reverend. Why, in fact, this may be a means to draw them in, eh?" His eyes widened with his own insight.

I nodded. "You are quite right, Oparu. I have seen many drawn to a faith that actively expresses its concern for other people's welfare."

Dates were tentatively set for meetings with interested students and then with Kpemlo. We had no other business, so we adjourned. When the students had all gone, James approached me.

"Hank, I have something to discuss with you," he said.

I invited him inside my office. He continued, "There is a lecturer in the science faculty—an American—who is in desperate need of help."

"Who is he?" I asked. "A Mr. Jones. He calls himself Kanu."

"Ahhh, I know him," I responded. "What's his trouble?"

"Well, his illness seems to be of an emotional nature. I think he has had a nervous breakdown," he said with great concern on his face. "At present he is in the hospital. I have visited him a number of times, but he hardly responds to me or anyone else. I thought perhaps, as Chaplain, you might be able to help him."

"I'm not sure I can," I said, shaking my head. "But I shall certainly try."

"The doctor has also told me that Mr. Jones should return to America. But in his present state of health, well, it seems out of the question."

"Could you take me to see him?"

"Indeed. What about right now?" he asked.

"Fine," I responded, after looking at my watch.

We walked to the campus hospital from the auditorium. "Do you visit the hospital often?" I asked James on the way.

"Oh, two or three times a week," he said, smiling self-effacingly.

"That's great!" I said. "You out-do my efforts, I must say. In fact, I guess I went on holiday during the Christmas break. How long has Kanu been a patient there?"

"Since about Christmas day."

"What do you think is the cause of his problem?"

"General maladjustment, I suppose," he suggested with an embarrassed expression, as if he had passed judgment on Kanu. "But I think the latest problem is with a girlfriend."

"Oh? An Ilarian?"

"Yes. They have been seen together quite often at parties, so I'm told. But suddenly she has taken up with a White man. And of course since he drives a big Mercedes and can offer her many inducements, shall we say, she has dropped Kanu. Apparently, it has crushed him,"

"Is the White man a lecturer here?"

"Yes. A Dutchman. A Mr. Van Looft."

I grunted. James turned to look at me. "Do you know him?"

"Yes, I met him at the Vice-Chancellor's party in October." We walked in silence for a while, as I recalled the Van Loofts's discussion of their "arrangement" at the party.

"It is very sad," said James. I readily agreed.

We reached the hospital, and James led me to Kanu's room. He lay in bed with the sheet pulled up over his head. When James called his name, the sheet inched from Kanu's eyes down to the bridge of his nose. He looked at James and then at me, whereupon he scowled. James told him that he had brought me to visit.

"I don't want to see *fama*," he hissed and turned to the wall. James and I looked at each other, then back at Kanu's form.

"Kanu, I'm sorry you are sick," I said. "I came to find out if there is anything I, or anyone else, can do for you."

A long pause followed before Kanu responded. "Absolutely not!" he croaked toward the wall.

I waited for a few moments. Then I said, "I will come again someday when you are feeling better. So good-bye for now. OK?"

There was no movement of response from him, so we tiptoed out. I met the doctor down the hall and asked him about Kanu. He elaborated on what James had told me.

"Rev. Lattimer, he by all means should return to America. As long as he remains in Ilaria, he will face adjustments he is unable to make."

James and I both pondered the doctor's analysis at length. Then James asked, "Do you think we can give Mr. Jones one more chance of trying to adjust to Ilaria?"

"What do you mean?" the doctor frowned.

"I have in mind . . . well, it may sound like a small thing, doctor," he said and smiled. "But I had in mind what you doctors call TLC: tender, loving care."

The doctor's frown deepened. "And who would administer this TLC?"

"Some of us who are interested in him."

"Well, you should have shown that interest before he got himself in this state!" he scoffed.

"The truth is, doctor, I never knew him until I visited in the hospital."

The doctor deliberated. Finally, "All right. Against my better judgment you can try. But remember this: A man's life and his emotional state are at stake. If Mr. Jones makes a turn for the worse, you shall have to take him to the mental asylum, not here!"

"I'm well aware," insisted James. "That is precisely why I should like to try something."

We left the hospital. I was impressed with James's quiet persistence and his obvious desire to do something for Kanu. He expanded to me his idea of the TLC campaign: chiefly, visits from himself and other Ilarians, whom he would invite. He was convinced that within a few months, Kanu would be better able to cope.

By the next week, Oparu lined up a meeting of students interested in the Mpesi project. True to his estimate, the faces of most of them were unfamiliar to me. They came out of several motivations: Christian compassion, the economic betterment of Ilaria, the chance to bridge the gap between the elite of the University and the ordinary villager in the surrounding countryside.

The group of eight students made contact with Kpemlo, who in turn helped them to gain support from the villagers. The highlight came when all of us paid a formal visit to the chief and elders. Kpemlo instructed me carefully on how to conduct myself in the presence of the chief, how to shake hands from right to left, where to stand, and to speak only through the chief's linguist. Kpemlo and Oparu spoke for our group.

The session lasted over an hour with much apparent haggling in the Mpesi vernacular. Throughout, I wondered if our proposals were being accepted. But when it was finished, Kpemlo and Oparu shared the good news that the chief and elders had readily accepted everything, that what we had just undergone was necessary and only a matter of procedure.

In following days, a crusade began to stir up enthusiasm among the villagers. Needing their wholehearted support, we used every available means to reach them and inform them of the project: through the ringing of the gong-gong, through speeches, house to house visits, pictures, and filmstrips.

But in spite of the enthusiasm generated by both student and villager, in spite of many forays into the villages and the sessions and discussions there and the high hopes on both sides that something could be accomplished, the project came suddenly to an end. It was cut short by a letter written to me from the Registrar.

Dear Rev. Lattimer: (it read)

The Mpési Settlements

It has come to our attention that, in recent days, many students have been making visits into the Mpesi settlements with the expressed hope of building a school for the Mpesi people. It seems that this project has been encouraged and aided by the Chaplaincy. For this reason I am writing to you concerning this matter.

For your information, the Mpesi villages are only temporary settlements. These people migrate back and forth along the coast as they ply their trade of fishing. Furthermore, they are temporary in the sense, also, that Western University officially owns the property upon which the settlements sit. It is the intention someday that the University will remove the settlements and will use the property for University purposes.

With this in mind, I am asking you to call a halt to the project, which you have encouraged. It is not in the best interests of the University. In fact, it conflicts openly with the plans set up by the Administration to remove the settlements in due course. If a school is constructed in the settlements, it would be a waste of money and efforts and would complicate the removal of the villagers.

Furthermore, I find it difficult to believe that you would launch such a project without consulting the authorities of the University. Perhaps you did so in genuine ignorance. I also find it difficult to believe that the Chaplain would engage in activities outside the normal course of his work. Some might interpret such activities as inappropriate to the Chaplaincy. For this reason, also, I am asking you formally to call a halt to the efforts to build a school in the Mpesi settlements.

Sincerely yours

J.B.R. DeHeer-Johnson Registrar

I was shaking by the time I finished the letter. When I saw Oparu later that day, I thrust the letter upon him. He finished it and shook it in his hand.

"Ei! They do not consider the needs of these poor people!" he cried. "And it will take years before they actually remove the settlements. In the meantime, the children will suffer!"

"But we had permission," I said. "What does he mean we did not consult the authorities? We laid our plans before the University Development Committee, and they approved it."

Oparu sighed. "The big man apparently overruled the Committee."

"Then what's the point of a committee, if it has no voice?" I protested.

"I don't know," said Oparu. "But it happens all the time. This University is not run for the majority of the lecturers and staff even. It is run for and by a few in the administration."

His words stunned me. I gaped at Oparu re-reading the letter again, the muscles in his arms tensing in his fury. He threw the paper down, announcing that he would see the Registrar himself.

I tried to deter him or at least to calm him down. But I could not.

Oparu returned to me within twenty minutes time.

"He would not see me," Oparu exploded through taut lips. "He would not give me the time of day!"

"You couldn't even get a glimpse of him?" I asked.

"A'tall! It's the custom," he said, gesturing limply. "The elders rule. The chief has sole authority. And you can never oppose them successfully."

Chapter 13

Rev. Daniel M. Quaina wholeheartedly accepted the invitation to preach at the Contemporary Worship service on February first. About 5:30 that afternoon, he pulled up to our house in his VW, for we had invited him to join us for supper. I met him at the door as he strode toward the house. He had a serious look about him, as if he weighed the situation or your words or you in his mental balances.

"We are so happy to have you, Rev. Quaina," I said.

His lower lip jutted out. "Ei! Don't call me *Rev. Quaina*! *Daniel* will do quite well," he chided. "And your given name is *Henry*, I believe. Is that correct?"

I chuckled. "But no one ever calls me that. I go by *Hank* most of the time."

"Oh, fine," he nodded, as I ushered him to the side of the house where some canvas chairs sat on the lawn. Kay bustled from the kitchen only to greet him and bring us some cold drinks. Gulping at the drinks, we watched two large coucals shyly skirting the bush at a distance. After they disappeared, their liquid cooing fell in a downward cadence so loud that they seemed at our elbow.

"This service tonight," Daniel began. "I cannot tell you how delighted I am to participate in it. How did it come about?"

"The students initiated the idea. So I thought we'd give it a try."

Daniel took a long swallow of his drink, which ended with a tightening of his lips as he set his glass down. "That's good, very good," he declared. "Unfortunately, however, it seems to meet with approval primarily among the youth. Only rarely among the leaders and ministers of the church."

"I must admit it surprised me to find the church not more distinctively Ilarian than it is," I said.

Daniel sighed. "On the contrary. We seem just as much bound to the traditions of the founding forefathers now as we were fifty years ago."

"But why?" I puzzled. "The chief excuse I hear is that the faith will be *compromised*. Do you think that's a valid reason?"

"Not now," Daniel looked at me penetratingly. "It used to be, of course. The early Christians wanted to make a clean break of their lives from the old to the new. To show where their new allegiance lay. At the same time, they were ostracized from their society by their own kinsfolk. So the break came from both directions. It had to come, I suppose, for the church to survive. One was either a Christian, or one was not. And if one was Christian, this meant divorcing oneself from the rest of his culture."

"Is this why the independent, indigenous churches are pulling such large numbers away from the orthodox churches?"

"Yes, one of the reasons. They are more African-oriented. The mainline churches refuse to grapple with this fact. Instead, they wag their fingers and hunt for heresies, smacking of paganism in the independent churches. But you have to define pagan," stated Daniel. "Just because something is traditional does not make it automatically pagan."

I sighed. "Well, I can appreciate the thorny implications of pouring libation by a Christian. Or the debate on whether a Christian can be a chief without contradicting himself. But for the life of me, I can't see why Geneva gowns and King James English and Charles Wesley hymns still have to be retained!"

"It's what we call the *Colonial mentality*," he chuckled.

"Or *missionary mentality*, it seems to me," I said.

Daniel scanned my face, then he laughed. "There is some truth in that statement as well!" he said. "No offense to you, of course!" His eyes twinkled.

"No. No offense, of course," I said with a grin.

When we went to my office before the service, Daniel and I prepared for worship. For lack of anything else, I wore my usual black gown. But Daniel wore neither the cloth he had on at my house nor a black gown. Instead, he brought out a dark green gown with a stole of green and gold *lemna* around his shoulders.

"It's a sort of experiment among some of us pressing for Africanization," he explained. The green, he said, symbolized life and vitality, and the Ilarian symbol at the end of the stole stood for the omnipotence of God. Daniel had an extra stole, not only for me to wear at the service but to keep.

At the service, about 400 students attended, the first large crowd since second term began. Entering into the spirit of the occasion, most of the students attended wearing "cloth," as they say, either the brilliant *lemna* or African printed cotton. The girls had on traditional long dresses with elaborately arranged head scarfs. Their gold earrings and necklaces gleamed against their dark velvet skins. Looking out over the array of African youth, I fully appreciated that Black indeed was beautiful.

Throughout the service, I felt a contagious sense of fervent participation, especially in the hymn singing. For while singing hymns of the traditional vernaculars and tunes, the students smiled and swayed and even clapped to the rhythms. They seemed renewed by the unexpected presence of an old friend. But it was the drums that riveted my attention, for I had not heard them so closely before. I found it all but impossible to keep still as the rhythms welled up from my toes and hammered in my ears. They transfused me with a gladness as nothing else had done. Gladness over living in Africa and working at Western and in knowing Daniel, Oparu, and James.

At the close of the service Daniel glowed when he talked to the many students who greeted him. His sermon, delivered in the fashion of an African storyteller, made a hit with the congregation. Many of the students urged me to repeat such a service. The evening also saw the beginnings of a friendship between Daniel and me. He asked me to come preach in his church in Charlestown on the first date open to me. I booked him, too, for a return visit.

That Sunday represented the peak of my career in Ilaria. For after that, things slid sharply downhill. The first symptoms of decline came with the lackluster expression among the students at worship. Initially, I chalked it up to the drabness of the services in contrast to that exuberant one in February. But then the numbers of students began to drop off. By March attendance decreased to one hundred, then sixty. I knew something must be badly wrong. But didn't this happen in America in the middle of the year? *Sophomore slump* or *winter doldrums*, as we used to call it?

"They must not like my preaching," I commented to Kay one evening after church. "They're tired of the same old preacher Sunday after Sunday." For I had to preach far more often than I had anticipated.

"Maybe they just don't dig your southern accent," came my wife's only answer.

I tried to draw Kwafu—my loyal cheering squad—into the riddle. For among the dwindling numbers, he and Memka remained outstandingly faithful. Oparu, Samuel, and Comfort only occasionally attended services. The CSA never had enough quorum to meet. And the choir, ravaged by non-attending members, straggled in half-embarrassed on Sundays.

"Does this happen every year, Kwafu?"

"No, Reverend. Not in the years I have been at the University."

"Why do you think it is happening this year?"

Kwafu paused. "Truly, I do not know." He shook his head and giggled.

"I don't know either," I reflected. "Yet, I'm beginning to think I do."

He looked at me, puzzled, but had no comment.

James also continued coming to church. I asked him his diagnosis. He readily admitted that something unusual was happening.

"I'm beginning to feel, James, that it's because of me and the indictment Moses made against missionaries and White people last term," I said.

He blinked. "I shouldn't think people would be so gullible."

"But it is a possibility," I said.

His eyes flickered around the chapel lounge, where we were standing. Finally he replied, "Yes, I suppose it is a possibility. But not likely." He smiled, as if trying to cheer me.

But nothing could cheer me. I struggled through the rest of the term, facing only one day at a time. The heat, as if in cahoots with the decline, clamped down on us with smothering intensity in February and March. My midweek prayer services with the workers foundered when the students, who acted as my interpreters, became less available. I continued my classes with Elizabeth (now "Mrs. Finnegan," since January second) and in the African Studies department of the University. A confirmation class kept me mercifully occupied also, for I met weekly with twelve students who joined the church at the end of term during the Easter service. But after Easter, when I faced the emptiness of a two-week vacation with nothing to engage myself in, I hit rock bottom. What was happening to my ministry? What was I accomplishing? Should I continue?

On the first day of vacation, Oparu appeared at our house.

His visit came as a surprise, for I had seen him only a few times during the entire second term. Still, he greeted me warmly. We sat and talked for a while about trivia before he got to his point.

"I was wondering, Rev. Lattimer, if you would like to come home with me for a day or two. To my village in Ketumba."

"Why, yes, Oparu. That would be great!"

"I would invite your whole family," he half-apologized. "But the amenities there are not what you are accustomed to. It may be too hard for your wife and children."

"I understand. When do you wish to go?"

"Would tomorrow be too soon?" he asked.

"No. Not a'tall. I have nothing else to do. Should I bring along anything?"

He thought for a moment. "Yes, perhaps you should bring a container for your own drinking water. Some insect repellant, if you have any. And a pillow or two or something to sleep on. We have none at my mother's house, and we shall be sleeping on the floor."

We then discussed when and where to meet. After he talked with the children for a while, he left.

I picked Oparu up at his hall early the next morning. He threw his canvas bag in the back alongside my paraphernalia. Then we headed east of Charlestown for some miles before turning north into the forest. Gradually we left the palm trees and more open farmlands of the coast. Instead, on all sides towered the mighty forest: verdant, majestic, omnipresent, dappled by bright morning sunlight. Cascading down the tall silk-cotton trees, the light burst into the myriad shades of green amid thick groves of bamboo and tangled vines.

In the midst of the wildness, Oparu pointed out the small cocoa trees with their curious pods growing from their white-bark trunks. Villages broke the density of the forest with almost predictable intervals. They all resembled each other with the rust of their corrugated roofs and their sienna mud walls blending with the hard earth around them. An occasional spurt of color challenged the monotony in the cloth worn by a man or woman, in the piles of tomatoes or palm nuts sold at the roadside, or in a flowering tree or yellow-leafed bush standing alone among the shades of brown.

About three hours up the road, Oparu indicated we were approaching his village. The first sign of it came with the Middle School on the left, almost hidden by a border of blazing cannas. With the school, the beauty and orderliness ended. Instead, houses and chickens and dirt sloped on a long hill toward the forest. After we passed the marketplace, thick with people and confusion, Oparu instructed me to stop. We got out and stretched in the searing sun. I unloaded the car, while Oparu bargained with an old man to watch it overnight.

We climbed a path up the hill through a narrow maze of houses, stirring up curious onlookers in our wake. We passed one mud wall after another, some enclosing open courtyards, the center of family living. Oparu's house consisted of several rooms in the shape of an L, with the mud-packed corner forming the living space. As we approached it, we saw his mother and sister and brothers squatting on the ground, eating out of enamel pans with their fingers.

Spotting us, they licked their fingers clean and ran to greet us. A spiel of laughter and talk in a vernacular ensued before I was introduced. They all shook my hand and said, "Ayisa" (Welcome) right down to the littlest, whose mouth was smeared with orange-colored palm oil left from his lunch. Oparu's mother, whom I was instructed to call "Maamee," found small stools for us to sit on in the shade next to the house. Then they offered us water, though Oparu suggested that I use my own from my jug. After that, they shared their meal with us: some yam mixed with a little fish in palm oil. In spite of the pepper in it, I enjoyed it.

When we finished eating, Maamee took us to an earthen-floored room with a few boxes and flimsy trunks stacked against the wall. Two worn mats lay on the floor. The shuttered window opened out toward the forest. After depositing our things, we lay down to rest. It was quiet, except for the giggling of the small boys outside. I asked Oparu if they went to school.

"Yes, but now they are on holiday like ourselves," he responded.

"Do you think any will go to university like you?" I asked.

"It is doubtful," he said. "My father died two years ago. There is no money to send them even to secondary school. That is, unless, when I finish, I can make the money."

"What work do you plan to go into?" I asked him.

He sighed. "Whatever I can find, Rev. Lattimer. My major is economics, but what I can do with it, indeed, I do not know."

We soon drifted off to sleep and didn't get up until nearly three o'clock. Outside we found only his mother puttering in the yard. She waved us off as we went down the hill. Oparu took me first to the palm wine maker near the market place, where I drank my first taste of the wine from a small calabash bowl. Then we approached the thatched shelter nearby, where the chief and some of the elders sat. I followed Oparu's motions and greetings in the semicircle. Six men sat there, lean, old, and leathery. Three had walking sticks, one appeared almost blind. Rather than working, they sat and deliberated and watched the comings and goings of the villagers.

After our greetings, Oparu talked at length with them in the vernacular, relating what he had been doing. They nodded their heads, blinked their watery eyes, and folded or unfolded the cloth draped around them. I wondered about the encounter: the young university student with a mind stretched far beyond the village, filled with equations, hypotheses and premises. And they, the backbone of Africa who knew how to interpret the talk of drums. How to get the most money from the cocoa bean. How to judge if the rains would be late or early, plenty or sparse in a year. Impassive, authoritarian, timeless.

From there we trekked through the village along its foot paths. We greeted all those we met, and Oparu seemed to know them all. I said the same greeting along with Oparu, and the villager would respond to me as my friend. We encountered shop keepers, selling their tins of milk and packets of matches and bars of soap. Women trading in the market or cooking over fires or nursing their babies. The blacksmith forging farm cutlasses and short-handled hoes. A carpenter fitting a doorframe into a newly dried mud house. And several young men—Oparu's contemporaries—sitting idly by the roadside. And on these rounds we learned the milestones, the woes, and the successes that beset village life.

We heard of marriages and illnesses. Of a boy who had died suddenly in the night, of a barren woman who had gone to a fetish shrine five times but still with no cure. Of a man who would take a third wife. Of a runaway girl found in Kwa, practicing prostitution. Of a young man who had gained entry into a teacher training college. Of twins born the week before. Then of Oparu's friends, the young men. They complained that they had nothing to do but to count passing cars and lorries or play drafts or loaf in the sun. Because they had no jobs, they had no wives. Out of the whole village, they alone regarded me with aloofness, almost with disdain.

We heard more about the young men from Sarka, Oparu's former teacher and now Headmaster of the Middle School. We skirted the lovely school gardens and entered Sarka's disorganized office. Upon seeing Oparu, the Headmaster sprang to his feet and grabbed Oparu's hands with both of his. "Oparu! You have come! How good it is to see you!" he exclaimed in English. Shrieking with excitement, they greeted each other and ended their handshake with snapping fingers. Sarka was the only person in the village with whom Oparu spoke English. He was slight, half-bald, with a touch of yellow in his eyes. He welcomed me enthusiastically when Oparu introduced me. Then he scurried to find chairs for us to sit on.

Apologizing to me, they talked at length of common acquaintances. My ears picked up their frequent mention of people and places and equally frequent "tsks" of concern or disapproval. They discussed one boy in particular who had left the village last year, "as they all do," said Sarka. "We don't know where he went. He wouldn't say when he returned. But he could not find work. He returned here before Christmas, destitute and dejected. His father gave him a piece of farmland, but he refused it. The old man was very provoked with him. He could not understand why any boy would refuse cocoa farming, education or no. He banished the boy from his house, but of course he went to live with his uncle. Now he sits out there with the rest of the bunch, scowling at the world," Sarka said, waving his hand toward the heart of the village.

Oparu had no comment. They both shook their heads and sucked their teeth in silence.

"What troubles me most, Oparu, is that I feel so responsible!" Sarka wailed.

"You! How so?"

The Headmaster strained forward. "Because in the classroom they catch a hope, a vision for a better life . . . from me," his voice quavered. "Then when they go out to claim that vision and there are too many others seeking the same thing and none of them find it . . . well, they become useless misfits. All because of what I've taught them, what I have done!"

"Ei! Sarka," Oparu sat forward. "You cannot take it so personally!"

But Sarka replied only with the pout of his lips and the lifting up of both his palms. "As for you, Oparu," Sarka dropped his voice. "You are very fortunate."

"Indeed!" exclaimed Oparu.

"You are the only one from my classroom who has succeeded, who has broken away from the village in the last eight years," he lamented.

Oparu looked up with a smile. "Take courage, Sarka. Others will come along."

"I doubt it," said Sarka. "I doubt it very seriously."

Shortly after this, we took leave of Sarka. Oparu seemed deep in thought as we walked back through the village along the highway. We trudged up the hill to his house and found his mother and small sister pounding cassava. His brothers energetically rolled an old tire rim around the house with a stick. We sat down on low stools and leaned against the house and looked out over the village. As it grew dark, the tall trees, more stately and somber in the twilight, ringed the village like sentinels. Birds and the cries of animals could be heard in the bush behind the house. Dots of light began to flicker here and there among the houses. Cooking fires, kerosene lanterns, candle flames.

Oparu sat apart from his family. Occasionally his brothers came over to show him something, making him laugh. I wondered if they weren't regarding him with a detached awe.

"Is anyone else in your family Christian, Oparu?" I asked.

"No," he said.

"Does your family give you a hard time because of it?"

"No, in fact they expect it of me," he said with a smile.

"Expect it?"

"Yes. By and large, most Africans regard Christianity as the White man's religion. And when I become educated like the White man, I am expected to take over his ways."

I shook my head and looked at the ground. "What's the answer, Oparu? Will Christianity ever become indigenized?"

"I don't know, Rev. Lattimer. I am trying to help it along," he said, as he smiled again. "I try to keep the lines of contact open between myself and them. I return home whenever I can to show them I am not so different after all."

"A regular missionary, eh?" I grinned at him.

"Yes. Like yourself."

His words blew the smile off my face, causing me to look away.

"It's nothing to feel embarrassed about, Rev. Lattimer," he said with gentleness in his voice.

"Mr. Awulu certainly created some embarrassed feelings with his talk the first term," I said.

"Indeed, it stirred up some ugly rumors about you. After Memka leaked it out that you were a missionary."

"Memka!" I reacted with horror.

"Oh, it wasn't he who said evil of you. He was proud that you were a missionary. But once some of the other students knew of it . . . well, in fact, the rumors began to grow by themselves."

"Which rumors?" I braced myself.

"Some students were saying you knew Mr. Awulu in America, and you personally prevented him from attending your church because he was Black."

I sighed. "It wasn't exactly personal, Oparu. But I did blindly assent to my church's plan to do just that."

He gasped.

"Does that shock you, Oparu?"

"Yes. That there's truth in it."

"And I suppose it shocked the other students."

"Yes. Many turned away from chapel altogether."

"And it circulated among guest ministers so that they, too, refused to come?"

"So it seems," he hung his head. "With the ministers, they reacted to the implications of Colonialism. With the students, to the idea of racism and inferiority."

"And what about yourself? I have not seen very much of you this past term."

"At first, I, too, stayed away because of the rumors," he admitted. "Later on, however, I was busy leading sports activities with the boys in the Mpesi settlements."

"Oh? Did you go there often?"

"Yes, on Saturdays," he said. "In fact, I guess it was seeing your interest in the villages, which changed my mind about you. I saw that what Mr. Awulu said about missionaries did not entirely fit you."

I did not respond; I just gazed at the spots of light which trailed down the hill below us.

"I don't fully understand it all, Rev. Lattimer. I don't even know all the facts. But I'm trying to accept it."

"Thank you, Oparu," I said with a gulp. "Thank you very much."

We ate the pounded cassava for supper with palm nut soup. It took a while for me to get the knack of pulling off a piece of the doughy cassava and forming a little cup in it with my thumb and then scooping some of the soup up in it. I spilled a lot, and the small boys giggled and stared. We ate around the common pot, seated on the ground. Then after supper, in the light of the fire that had cooked the soup, Oparu told the boys stories about mythical forest animals and monsters and tales of brave ancestor-warriors. Eventually the stories spun themselves out; the children grew sleepy. There is only so much one can do by firelight. So we all went to bed.

I lay awake a long time, unaccustomed to the early hour of retirement, for one thing. And for another, my senses kept reacting to the new environment. My thoughts ricocheted back and forth between the world I knew and the world I had seen today. Oparu lay asleep on the floor beside me, wrapped in his sleeping cloth.

After some time, I, too, fell asleep. But within an hour or so, I woke up to some strange cries out in the forest. They echoed hollowly, forlornly, each cry growing louder than the preceding one. Was someone lost in the forest? Was a child crying for help to find his way home? Filled with alarm, I awoke Oparu.

"What in the world is that?" I asked, "Is someone crying?"

"A'tall. Some call it a *bush baby*. Some a *tree bear*," he chuckled. "It's just a small animal in the forest. But, oh, what a loud cry!"

"OK, if you say so," I said, not fully convinced that a *bush baby* could make such a wail. He seemed to be weeping for all the woes and sorrows of Oparu's village. I listened for a while and then turned to go back to sleep.

Chapter 14

For the rest of the Easter vacation in Charlestown, I kept busy with my family, collecting shells on various beaches, going on picnics, taking rides on intriguing roads, and touring every fort and castle for miles around.

One afternoon while we played badminton on the lawn, Rod Allen drove into our driveway. Beside him sat a small, elderly woman. It was Luella Watson, back from furlough. She burst out of the car as soon as it stopped to greet us. "Welcome to Ilaria! It's so good to have ya'll here," she cried in an alternating husky and falsetto voice, hugging each of us after the other.

"We should welcome you instead," Kay exclaimed. "How was your furlough?"

"Just fine," Luella said, trying to corral wisps of her short, greying hair behind the frame of her glasses. "But it just distressed me no end that I wasn't here to help ya'll settle in. There's so much to tend to, and I know you've had a jillion questions to ask and with no missionary around to help answer them. I know it's been hard on you. Oh, you poor dears!" she rattled on breathlessly. "How have you been getting along, really now?"

"We've done very well," I said.

"And I know the work must be getting along well," she said, as she bobbed her head with each statement. "My, we've wanted a chaplain in one of the universities for so long, haven't we, Rod? And to think you dear people have come to fill the post!"

"Please, won't you all come on in?" Kay motioned toward the house. "No sense standing out here."

"Oh, lands, no," said Luella. "No, I'm afraid I'll have to take you up on that some other time. Why, I haven't been out to Buasi yet! I just had to drop by here even for a minute! But I want you to come out real soon. All of you. What about next Friday . . . for supper?"

Kay and I looked at each other. "That will be fine," Kay said. "We have no plans."

Luella moved back toward the car, Kay following her. I glanced over at Rod. "Well," he said, grinning, "I didn't think I'd ever see you all again. How have things been going for you?"

"Not so good," I said. "I'd kinda like to talk to you about it. When do you have to return to Kwa?"

"In the morning, some time. I just brought Luella out. She came in on Pan Am two days ago and has been buzzing around Kwa since then."

"How about coming back here and spending the night with us?"

"Fine! That sounds fine!" Rod said. He got back in the car.

"You sure you won't stay for supper?" Kay asked Luella. "You must not have a thing to eat in your house."

"I have some tins and things, I'm pretty sure. They'll do me until I go marketing tomorrow. Thanks so much anyway. But we'd better push on. I've got jillions of things to do, you know," she tittered.

"I can imagine," I said. "But we'll look forward to Friday."

"By all means," exclaimed Luella. "We'll be seeing you then," and she and Rod pulled away.

When Rod returned at suppertime, we treated him to some fish we had recently bought at San Paulo. Again, I was struck by his vitality, as I had been that first day in Kwa. He had a contagious exuberance. It showed in his quick eyes which mirrored concern and sympathy, despite the lively humor spilling out of them. After the kids went to bed, Kay lit some candles, and the three of us sat at the open end of the courtyard in the semidark. It was cool, and the mosquitoes managed to leave us alone.

Immediately, Rod wanted to know about the trouble I had alluded to that afternoon. So I poured everything out to him, beginning with Greenwood, Georgia. He was the first fellow missionary I had been able to shoot off to. He listened intently and asked thoughtful questions throughout my monologue. When I finished, he looked out into the dark, shaking his head.

"Well, you're still here, friend. That's something!" he declared.

"But I haven't been clearly appointed, either. The Appointments Board still hasn't decided my fate."

"The uncertainty is so . . . so innervating," said Kay. "You find yourself paralyzed to make commitments . . . to get involved."

"I'm not sure that my presence here means anything," I said. "Anything at all."

Rod thought for a few minutes, as he rubbed his beard. "Your presence here means a lot. In spite of what you may feel about it," he said.

"But let's face it, Rod," I argued. "I don't see how I can accomplish anything if the conflicts aren't resolved. I mean, what can I do if I have no congregation, if my words fall on deaf ears?"

"Well, it depends on what you mean by *accomplishing something*," Rod said.

Kay and I both looked at him, puzzled.

"Missionaries can accomplish plenty by being a sort of question or goad. An inert activator. Obscure, behind-the-scenes, unwanted perhaps. But like a catalyst which creates actions and involvements beyond itself."

"Mmmm, I think I see what you mean," I said. "But it's not a very fulfilling role, is it?"

"Nor a very active one," said Kay.

Rod shook his head. "Nor one you can measure the good in or ask, what is the point?"

We sat in silence for some time. "And Moses Awulu, he's never come around . . . you've never gotten through to him again?" Rod asked.

"Not at all," I said.

"It will kill Luella when she hears it," said Rod.

"She doesn't know?" I exclaimed.

"She knows what happened to Moses at Trinity Church. But I don't think she knows he has renounced Christianity over it."

I grunted. "So we'll be the bearer of bad news, eh?"

"Looks like it," said Rod. "She really ought to know."

"Of course."

"Maybe she can get through to Moses, do you suppose?" Kay asked Rod.

"Maybe. We hope she or someone will. Have you talked with Daniel Quaina about it?" Rod asked. "Or have you seen him since last September?"

"Yes, he preached here last February. Seems like a sharp guy," I said. "But I said nothing to him about Moses."

"He might be able to help you," suggested Rod. "He would understand a lot of it, particularly from Moses's viewpoint. For one thing, he was, for a while, a protégé of Everett Clark, very much like Moses was to Luella."

"Oh, really?"

Rod nodded. "Even to receiving a scholarship abroad. But to England rather than America. That was almost ten years ago. He came back a rather torn man. Before he left, he swallowed everything the missionary told him and stood for. He returned a little sadder but wiser. Initially, he had many conflicting loyalties. He wanted to be himself: an African Christian, not a Europeanized one. And yet he knew he owed Everett and our mission everything. It's taken all these years to find himself, and it meant a lot of rejection of the White man's way of things. As a result, many missionaries are all uptight over him, for the truth is, they don't know where they stand with him."

"What has Everett thought about it all?" asked Kay.

Rod sighed. "As far as he's concerned, Daniel is a prodigal son: *one who drifted away and who has never come home*, you might say."

I grunted again. "It sounds like the best thing that could have happened."

"Exactly," agreed Rod. "Daniel is one of the bright hopes for this church, the way I see it."

"You know," I said after a pause, "I just returned a few days ago from visiting in the home of one of my students. He's another sort of Daniel Quaina. Desperately trying to fit his faith into the local framework. It did me real good to go there. I almost wonder if someone arranged it all for me!"

"The Lord, maybe," chuckled Rod.

"Agreed," I said. "For I began to see my troubles were rather pale in comparison."

Rod nodded. "As pale as the White man's skin!"

We followed Rod's directions on how to find Luella when we went out to Buasi the next week. After more than a half hour's bumping on a dirt road, we arrived. I had barely turned off the ignition when the screened door banged, and Luella rushed out.

"You did make it!" She smiled. "You did find the way. So good to see you again." She grabbed our hands and patted the children on the head. "Come on in. I know you're probably dying of thirst. My, but isn't it hot these days! How have you been able to adjust to the scourge of West Africa: our miserable climate?" she laughed a little.

"It's plenty hot, all right," I agreed.

She steered us into her living room through the verandah and directed us where to sit.

"Now just make yourselves at home, and I'll get us something cold to drink. Will Squash be OK for everyone?" She referred to a bottled lemon drink.

"That will be just fine," said Kay, as Luella got up to go to the kitchen.

We sat looking around the room with its brightly cushioned wicker chairs and shelves with worn books and a large desk spilling over with papers, letters, and files. On the wall hung pictures of snow scenes and photos of Luella with various groups of people. She saw us looking toward the photos and invited us to come closer. We stood to view them.

"That was taken before I came to Buasi," she said. "When I worked with women's groups in the north in the early '50s. And this was in 1956, when I first became headmistress here at the Training College." I noted that she looked almost the same now as she did in 1956: with glasses, her hair cropped, and wearing a shapeless, short-sleeved dress and socks and sandals on her feet.

"Then this was four years ago when the new Ilarian headmistress came, Miss Marko—a very capable young woman. See how the student body has grown?"

Suddenly she turned. "Goodness, I'd almost forgotten the Squash. How *inconsiderate* of me!" she exclaimed, her voice cracking on the emphasized word. "You must be dying of thirst."

We sat down again as she fetched the drinks and served them to us. David emptied his glass rapidly and asked for more.

"Now, Hank and Kay. Tell me about your work," she said, settling back into a chair. "Just how are things in Charlestown?"

I glanced at Kay, my mind in a turmoil about what to tell Luella. "I believe I've run into a well-known acquaintance of yours, Luella," I said. "Moses Awulu. He's teaching at the University."

"So that's where he is!" she exclaimed, sitting forward. "I've tried for over a year to get in contact with him. And to think he's right there at Western with you all! My, what a happy coincidence!"

"It's not so happy a'tall, I'm afraid," I said. "You know what happened to him at Trinity Church in Greenwood, Georgia, don't you?"

"Oh, my yes. That dreadful incident. Wasn't that just terrible? And who would have thought it would happen at Trinity of all places. They're so interested in missions you know."

"Well, I was at Trinity as assistant pastor when it happened," I went on. "Moses and I knew each other and were very good friends. But because of the incident, he won't have any more to do with me. Now that we are on the same campus here in Ilaria, he . . . he's trying to get his revenge . . . by ruining my ministry."

"Revenge!" she exclaimed. "What do you mean *revenge*?"

I drained my glass, searching for words. "It will come as a shock to you, Luella. But Moses no longer considers himself a Christian."

She gasped, and her face lost its ruddy color. "Oh, no! I didn't know that at all!" She covered her mouth with a hand and crumpled back against the chair.

"I'm terribly sorry to have to tell you that," I said. "But I knew you would like to know about it."

She didn't say anything for a while; just kept her hand over her mouth and sat shaking her head. David and Lisa began to fidget, so Kay took them outside,

"Forgive me," said Luella hoarsely. "Forgive me, please. This is such a . . . a blow to me personally. I had no idea . . . no idea at all," she choked. "You see, I feel so responsible. It was I who helped him to get the scholarship. But if I thought he might . . . he would lose his faith . . . why it wasn't worth it at all!" She shook her head. "It meant so much to me for him to go. I took such pride in him, like a son . . . in the faith. Oh, I should never have urged him! It's all my fault!"

"I'm sure you only had his interest at heart," I said,

"But where did it go wrong?" she cried. "Did I not prepare him enough? Or the Board of Missions? And to think it happened in one of our own Presbyterian churches! How could I have thought to prepare him for . . . for that!" Then, visibly brightening, she said, "I must try to see him. There must be something I can do."

"I'm not sure, Luella, that he will see you," I said. "You should certainly try, and I hope you'll succeed."

"Indeed, I shall try," she declared. "His soul is at stake! Oh, poor, poor Moses! I must make the effort. I feel certain he will see me. We used to pray together when he worked here with me. He was the only other committed Christian on the faculty, aside from our Chaplain. I feel certain he will see me!"

"I sure hope so," I said. "He regarded you very highly. He told me about you and what you meant to him. So perhaps you, of all people, can get through to him."

She asked me where he lived. Then jumping up from her chair, she extracted a date book from the heap on her desk. After jotting something in her book, she turned to me.

"Now. What can I do for you all?" she looked at her watch. "Supper will be in about 45 minutes. Would you like to look around the campus? I have some supplies to take over to the sick room. Perhaps you'd like to come along."

I accepted her offer. She left the room to get her supplies, as I went outside to check on Kay and the kids. David and Lisa were busy climbing a tree in the yard. Kay thought it best that they all stay put. Luella came out lugging a large box of medicines, which I carried for her.

As we trudged over to the academic side of the campus, she explained about the medicines. "I bought them when I went to Charlestown the other day. When I checked the sick room after I returned here, I found it all but bare. A Miss Narta is supposed to keep it stocked as well as act as infirmarian. I don't know what she's been doing all this time. She probably didn't keep up with it as long as I wasn't here to keep up with her!" Luella sighed.

When we reached the sick room, she pulled from her pocket a large bunch of at least two dozen keys. She flipped through them, and finding the right one, she unlocked the door. Another one unlocked the cupboard inside the small room. She spent a great deal of effort arranging and rearranging the bandages and medicines on the shelves. When she was satisfied, we left.

She took me down the far end of the campus, and in a systematic order, we visited every building, office, and classroom down to the opposite end. She walked as fast as she talked, and although the institution stood at a holiday standstill, from her viewpoint the wheels still ground on. But apparently not fast enough or efficient enough to her liking. On our tour into the dining room and kitchen, our visit extended far beyond a cursory glance. Rather, she guided me through the silent kitchen, poking into drawers and cupboards as we went. The same thing happened in the library, where our tour included her appraisal of the librarian's desk, and in the chapel, where she ran her fingers over the back of the pews to check for dust. She commented to me all along the way about what was missing or forgot to be done or had been overlooked by the appropriate person in charge. And she sighed, saying how she was not responsible, but someone else was, yet she felt it her *duty* to check into everything.

"After all, a lot of good Presbyterian money has been poured into this school, and I, for one, would hate to see it go to waste. Do you know what I mean?"

Our last place to visit was the administration offices. We stopped at the office marked "Headmistress," and she took out a key and opened the door. It surprised me that she had a key, since she no longer acted as headmistress. She let me look in, but we did not enter.

We did enter the admissions office, where she flipped through some files she had unlocked in their cabinet. She complained that the clerk had not arranged them in a more efficient manner. I perched on a desk, waiting for her to finish her inspection and wondering what would happen if someone found us. Eventually, Luella finished, and we left.

"I declare, you just can't trust anybody anymore to do things properly," she declared on the way out. "I just wish someone else would take on some of the responsibility seriously to run the school as it should be. I simply can't do it all. I teach a maximum load as it is without running around all over the place to see what's what!" She laughed, yet I could tell, at bottom, she was dead serious.

Then, suddenly, as we walked back toward the house, something clicked in my mind. The keys. The busyness to the point of prying. The inability to trust anyone else. Luella Watson was the missionary Moses had castigated publicly at the symposium! It was she who had become the object of all his venom and bitterness. I was stunned as I realized the extreme to which Moses had swung.

"Tell me some more about Moses, Luella," I said. "It surprises me that he was teaching in a girls' school. That's a little unusual in Ilaria, isn't it?"

"Oh, yes, yes indeed," she nodded. "Most girls' schools don't want to take a chance with males on their faculty. It's too risky in these days of such overt sexual promiscuity. But, of course, Moses was an unusual young man. He was married first of all. Then, more importantly, he had such an impeccable record of integrity and morality before he came here."

"In what way?"

"Well, he was a most active leader in the Christian Fellowship while a university student. He participated in all sorts of preaching services and volunteer work camp programs. Everywhere he went, not enough could be said about Moses Awulu. Additionally, he was a very bright young man. Very bright. He held honors in math at the University and was the highest in his class during his postgraduate year in education. He could have had any number of prestigious jobs in important secondary schools in the large cities. But he had a missionary spirit. He wanted to serve in an underdeveloped area of Ilaria, and we here were in desperate need of a math teacher. So considering his qualifications—both morally and intellectually—we snatched him up." She paused, then continued, "I'm sure Western considers itself lucky to get him as a lecturer. I always knew that a university was the only place for his abilities. Is he doing well there?"

"As I said earlier, we have no communication between us. I hear from the students that they like him a lot and consider him a good teacher. Other than that, I don't know."

"What a shame," she wailed with a catch in her voice. "What a terrible shame! "

"Yes, it is," I agreed.

"He was the most promising young Ilarian I've ever known. And such a dear, dear boy!"

"Did he get along well with the other faculty members?"

"It's difficult to say, really," she pondered. "In matters of policy, he very often took my point of view, which frequently conflicted with the other Ilarians on the faculty, I might add. But I always encouraged him to stand for the truth. It was difficult for him, I know. But he managed marvelously!"

"You said something about having prayer together. Was this a regular sort of thing?"

"Oh, yes, it was," she beamed. "We met about twice a week for prayer, usually at my house. They always were such rich hours of Christian fellowship when we could both take our problems to the Lord. And we also shared Scriptural promises to encourage each other in the faith. He was such an ardent student of Scripture. So eager to learn. He always borrowed books from me to learn everything he could. I tried as best I could to lead him through a course of Bible study, you know, regular systematic study, as he might have gotten in seminary."

"Why, then, do you think that Moses's faith didn't hold up under the experience at Trinity?"

She cut her eyes sharply over at me, both a question and a rebuke in them. "I just don't know. Indeed, I wish I knew. He seemed to be thoroughly grounded in the faith. He wasn't a doubter; he firmly believed the tenets of his faith. He was nurtured in solid orthodoxy, so I don't know why he should have been shaken."

"I take it he never had much contact with people or writers of a more liberal persuasion, did he?"

"Oh, no! Not when I knew him," she said, frowning.

"What about his contacts with peoples of other nationalities ... were they pretty limited?"

"I would imagine so. I suppose the foreigners he knew best were missionaries, American and British."

"Do you think he was a very astute observer of human nature?"

"What do you mean?"

"Do you think he knew why people behave the way they do, the self-deceptions and rationalizations they resort to?"

"Well," she laughed. "If you mean psychology, I don't think he would have bothered with that. I mean after all, Scripture tells us ample about human nature, now doesn't it?"

"Then he should have known that people were sinful," I said.

She looked at me, her eyes wide behind her glasses. "Why, of course! He believed that."

"But I don't believe he thought that applied to Christians as well," I said.

"Well, it ... it doesn't, does it? she stammered. "Not to genuine, born-again Christians. I mean after all, sanctification is at work within us to control our sinfulness and even to root it out."

"Now, now, Luella," I said lightly. "You sound more like a Pentecostal than a Presbyterian!"

My tone served to relax her, but it also cut off our conversation. She shook her head and smiled. "Well, do I now? I hadn't thought of that. I don't know where I could have picked that up. I don't actually know of any Pentecostals around here," she chuckled.

By then we had reached her house. She held the screened door open for me, and we entered. She excused herself to the kitchen, after which the steward began to bring the southern fried chicken supper out to the dining table. Kay and the children gathered in the room with me.

Sitting down on the sofa, I glanced around the room, deep in thought. I could visualize Moses sitting here, waiting on Luella, looking at the expatriate's home with a certain curiosity. And I could visualize him and Luella sharing their joys and problems with each other. She, the mother hen, clucking and prodding and nurturing the young chick in the faith after her own prescription of Christianity.

At Buasi, he would have few other examples against which to pit his image of the Christian saint. No other laboratory to test his surging questions and observations concerning God and humanity. He would emerge a well-insulated, well-rehearsed Christian, undergirded by a set of pre-concluded formulas. Then, when the mother figure faded and the simplistic Buasi environment exploded into a confusing wilderness of pain and opinions and unfittable pieces of puzzle, which he didn't bargain for on the day he surrendered himself to Christ: then what? Would his faith stand? Could he bend and change course and refocus and still find Christ immutable?

Moses hadn't been able to. His world had collapsed around him. And now he was about to drag mine down along with his. Then—God forgive me—anger began to flame up within me toward the Luella Watsons on far-flung mission stations. For I began to understand why Moses had lashed out at her.

Chapter 15

Luella tried to see Moses the next Friday. At the end of the day, she came around to tell me of her fruitless efforts.

"I found his house, and I'm certain it was the right house," she wailed. "I waited there for hours. And then at his office for nearly two hours. It was just too, too mysterious that no one seemed to know his whereabouts. I think he was trying to avoid me!"

"It could be, Luella," I said. "Did you leave any messages?"

"Why, I left messages all over the place," she said. "I told him how to get in touch with me and how urgently I wanted to see him. But now, I'm wondering if he will respond at all! But I shall return," she threw over her shoulder as she left.

Before she came back to Western, however, Moses was blitzed again. Right before the term began, he was released from his job by the University. James brought the news to me as soon as it was known in the math department.

"It is a very serious, very unusual thing, Hank," he said, shaking his head. "It's not that his contract will not be renewed at the end of the academic year; rather, his contract was broken . . . and in mid-term!"

"But why?"

"For economic reasons, ostensibly. He and about seven others in the University have been sacked because the University is in debt, and by letting some of its employees go, it will save on some funds."

"But why Moses Awulu?"

James raised his palms. "Who knows? No one seems to know."

"Who are the others? Are they all lecturers?"

"No. Some are junior staff members, some clerks. Moses is the only one of lecturer status."

"But there are other lecturers who have been here for less time than he. In English, engineering, psychology . . . ."

"I know." James nodded.

"And the junior staff. Were they all the latest additions?"

"No," he said. "By no means."

"Whatever can be the reason for it all?"

James sighed. "There are many speculations. But one is favored over others. And that is discrimination."

"Discrimination!"

"Yes. Except for one, all of those sacked were Ketumba."

I whistled.

"I have heard that the Registrar doesn't like Ketumbas. Is that true?"

James chuckled. "He doesn't like anyone who's not Akarti, like himself, and/or who will stand in his way."

"Certainly none of these people were in his way, were they?"

"Considering their positions, I don't see how they could be," James conceded. "What he did was sheerly a powerplay, taken out on those most contemptible to him personally."

"How many on the faculty are Ketumba, would you say?"

James sighed. "Not more than ten or fifteen percent, I should think."

We sat quietly for a while. "It's incredible! Two times this has happened to Moses !" I said.

"Indeed, it is lamentable," said James. "I have tried to express my concern to him. But he is a hard one to catch."

I nodded, as my shoulders sagged and my eyes focused on the floor.

"But I also bring another piece of news. This time a cheerful one."

I looked up to find him smiling. "What is it?"

"You remember Kanu Jones?"

I nodded.

"He has been more or less adopted by an Ilarian family. Not officially, of course. But he has been invited to live with them in Charlestown."

"Why, James, that's great news!" I exclaimed. "You are certainly to be commended."

His eyes darted away from mine, as he licked his lips. "No, not me. A'tall! *Nkala me epere.* Do you know what that means?"

It was a traditional Ilarian saying which sounded almost Biblical.

"Yes," I said, "It means, *Through God, I will succeed.*"

He arose to go. "We shall apply the same to Moses."

On the opening day of the term, the news of the dismissed employees engulfed the campus. Students, lecturers, workers, clerks all buzzed with speculation as to why the sacking occurred. Was it really because they were, with one exception, Ketumba? Or was it because, as some said, they were not capable in their respective jobs? Could it be because their superiors were jealous of their work and wanted them out of their way? Of course, everyone desperately wanted to find out why, for their own jobs were pegged to the rationale behind the dismissals.

For about five days, questions and fears ravaged the University community. At its height, some of the students threatened to demonstrate. But being uncertain about what they were demonstrating against, nothing was done.

"They won't march," Comfort said to me, as we sorted through some letters in the chapel. "The Ketumbas among them are not the majority."

"You mean it's no real concern of anyone else?" I rather gaped at her.

She shrugged and stuck out her lower lip. "No. The Akartis, and the Mpesis, and the rest don't particularly care about the issue one way or the other."

"But if it happened to Akartis, you would be concerned!"

"Of course," she replied. "But then, we are in the majority, and something would be done."

I shook my head. "And no one cares about a fellow Ilarian's plight, no matter what his tribe?"

Again she shrugged. "I doubt it, Rev. Lattimer. For tribalism is just a fact of life in Ilaria."

"Even among Christians?" .

She looked at me, startled. "I'm not sure that Christians have even thought about it in terms of their faith."

But Oparu had. When he and I discussed the controversy, he decried the passivity of the campus, particularly among the Christians. He, too, thought faith should make a visible difference. "But tribalism runs too deep, too rampant. Everyone is infected with it, Rev. Lattimer. Many, of course, don't realize it. They would say, 'Who, me? Never!' and then go right ahead making generalizations about another tribe!"

I nodded.

"I would say hardly any action taken publicly is not examined in light of one's tribal background," continued Oparu. "If the person involved is Akarti, they will say, he is treacherous. If Mpesi, he's superstitious and a thief. If Ketumba, he's murderous and vengeful."

"Does this sort of thing come out in the open very often?"

"Not often," Oparu said. "But two years ago a controversy arose over the appointment of a new department head in engineering. Certain factions wanted an Akarti to become head; others wanted a Mpesi."

"And the Akarti no doubt got it . . . if DeHeer-Johnson had anything to do with it."

"Yes, the Akarti got it. But, of course, the issue allegedly revolved around credentials. The Akarti was declared far more competent, which wasn't actually true."

"And the ones recently dismissed were picked because they supposedly were not pulling their load?" I asked.

"Exactly!" exclaimed Oparu.

I considered his words a few moments. Then, off the cuff, I remarked that I might say something in my next sermon about the issue.

Oparu gazed at me. "I wish you well," he murmured.

When I told him that I might say something, the emphasis had been on the *might*, at least in my own mind. I had intended to preach on Jesus and the Samaritan woman the following Sunday. As I spent the remaining days of the week preparing the sermon, it seemed logical that the subject of racial prejudice should be mentioned. Nevertheless, many doubts assailed me about doing so. Who was I, with my own guilt and blindness, to preach about discrimination in the other fellow? And especially since I was a foreigner? For shouldn't a foreigner be reluctant to criticize his host country? Would he not be considered arrogant or nosey to offer his opinions about internal Ilarian affairs? Furthermore, could I say what needed to be said without bringing the wrath of the Administration down around me? And if that occurred, would my appointment be imperiled? Should I risk my ministry for the sake of a sermon?

Kay got the brunt of all my contradictions and questions that week. We stayed up late almost every night discussing the pros and cons. She exhibited more caution toward the matter than I. In the end, I went through with it. But looking back now on my motivations and what finally convinced me to do it, I'm not sure what made me. Of course, it was a *cause*. And sometimes a *cause* dangling before me was similar to a red flag in front of a bull, and I could react only with aggression. Then, too, I think Moses influenced my decision. I still ached to be his friend again. Perhaps the sermon would be a way to mend our ruptured relationship. Or at least set things straight publicly.

On the night of the sermon, it poured rain. The storm was one of those harbingers of rainy season, which rushes in from the sea in a crackling fury. Great sheets of water and blasts of thunder enveloped us about an hour before evening worship. Although the lightning and wind abated by the time we went to the auditorium, the rain still continued. It turned the drains and gutters all over the campus into raging torrents. The auditorium was impossible to enter, for it stood in the way of a great avalanche of water pouring down from the hillside above it. So Kay and I waited in the car, watching the streams and rivulets swirl around us.

"The floors probably will be flooded," I commented. "Are you prepared to mop, my dear wife?"

"Do you have a mop inside?"

"I have a towel, at least. The one I usually mop myself with."

"Fine. But how do you propose to get in? Do you also come equipped with an inflatable raft?" She laughed.

"That's a good question," I said. "Or how is anyone else going to get in. Looks like I may have to call my sermon off. You suppose this is a sign that I should lay low?"

"Of course not," she scowled. "You just go ahead with the sermon. Let the Lord take care of the rain . . . and the congregation."

"That's a euphemism if ever I heard one!" I said. "We'll do good if twenty people show up."

But in spite of my pessimism, the attendance was good. As the rain trickled off, students and some faculty slowly filed toward the auditorium. The first few arrivals helped to mop the floor and sweep water out of the doorways. By the time the service was ready to start, over half of the auditorium was filled, the largest number since the contemporary worship in February. I began to think my blurb in the campus interdepartmental newsletter drew some out. For every week I announced in the paper the weekend activities of the campus church with the sermon topics. But this time, in addition to the title, "Jesus and the Samaritan Woman," I added, "with special reference to prejudices and current events."

I was surprised to find that half a dozen choir members robed and marched in with me. At the front, I separated off from them and sat down facing the congregation. The accompanist at the piano was playing a brief prelude, when in swept DeHeer-Johnson with his secretary in tow. He barreled down the aisle toward me but looked at neither me nor the congregation. Then, standing quite visibly in front of everyone, he gathered his *lemna* ceremoniously over his shoulder and took his seat on the front row.

When I first saw him, my resolution turned to jelly. But after I gulped in a deep breath, I became amazingly calm. During the rest of the prelude, I tried to catch his eye. He refused to look my way. Rather, he concentrated on his bulletin and hymn book and tried to act as if he had worshipped every Sunday among us. Once during a hymn, our eyes did meet, and I smiled. He nodded back ever so slightly, unsmiling. My calmness remained with me, and my voice never quavered once when I led in prayer and read the Scripture and when I plunged into the sermon itself. I felt confident with a strength I had rarely felt in the pulpit. Even when the Registrar's secretary pulled out a pad to take down my words, verbatim.

I began the sermon by expounding at length on the setting and the content of the conversation between Jesus and the woman of Samaria: the *living* water, the proper place to worship, the woman and her many husbands. I then elaborated on how Jesus related with the woman, how he treated her as a person. I pointed out how he had several good excuses not to relate with her since she was a Samaritan, a woman, and a woman of ill reputation at that. I zeroed in on the Samaritan aspect particularly and discussed the prejudice between the Jews and Samaritans. From there I cited the Apostles' examples with those of other races. I read Paul's words: *There is neither Jew nor Greek, there is neither slave nor free, there is neither male nor female, for you are all one in Christ Jesus.*

"I would like to take the liberty to paraphrase this portion from Galatians to speak to our situation today," I went on.

"There is neither Ketumba nor Akarti, Black nor White, expatriate nor African, educated nor illiterate, student nor lecturer, male nor female, for we are all one in Christ Jesus.

"In recent days our University has been torn with questions and fears. Seven employees were sacked, and of those seven, all but one were of the same tribal group. The question arose quite naturally as to why the persons were released. And quite naturally, it has appeared to many that discrimination and prejudice of one group against another were at work in determining who should be released from their work. Furthermore, it has appeared that the Christian people in this University have not stood up to question the dismissals. For as one student told me, 'Nothing will or can be done. Tribalism is a way of life in Ilaria!'

"Now I am not inciting students to go out and protest. By no means. Rather, I am asking that in the privacy of your own consciences you ask yourselves these questions: What are the facts? Were those who were dismissed victims of prejudice or not, or is this pure gossip? In light of the facts, what do I believe as a Christian? What should I do, based on my beliefs?

"It all boils down to our responsibility and obedience as Christians. Do we take seriously our faith and try to live it? Or do we leave Jesus's teachings in the Bible and in the Church on Sundays?"

At this I put my notes aside. I paused and leaned toward the congregation. "Before I close, I have one more thing to say," I confided. "I am not preaching as one without blemish in this matter of prejudice. The words I have preached tonight are as much directed to me and my fellow Christians in America as they are to you. I come from a denomination which is predominantly White. Although our church claims that it loves the Black brother in America, it has in fact showed little evidence of such love. Black men are still excluded from the right to worship in some of our congregations.

"An Ilarian from this campus was excluded from a church where I worked as assistant pastor. He was a fine Christian man, and he and I had been friends before the ugly incident. And because he saw that the church was not acting Christian, he left it and cut off relationships with me. Through this incident, however, the scales of prejudice were removed from my eyes and from the eyes of other Americans. In a real sense, the Ilarian acted as an ambassador, a missionary to America. For the first time in my life, I saw with horror what prejudice does. It humiliates and depersonalizes the victim. It deceives and degrades the perpetrator.

"I left that congregation and have become a missionary to minister to you. I recognize deeply that I am a sinner sent by a sinful church. I confess this to you and ask for forgiveness. And I also ask you as Christians to be aware of the anguish and bitterness which prejudice inflicts on persons."

I offered a prayer and sat down. Only then did my knees seem to shake. Looking out into the congregation, I found Kay. She smiled back at me. In the rear, someone got up to leave. I caught a glimpse of him as he exited through the door. It looked like Moses, but I wasn't sure. My heart hammered at the thought.

The service ended and the congregation dispersed. There was little talking. The Registrar paraded out as he had come. No one offered a reaction to the sermon one way or another, none of the CSA members, not even Oparu. The only comment came from Sean, who surprised me with his presence.

"Can I offer my services to you as a bodyguard?" he said, back in my office with Elizabeth at his side. Our laughter was tinged with apprehension.

As I went home, I despaired that what I had struggled to say meant nothing.

Chapter 16

A note awaited me in my office early the next morning, instructing me to see the Registrar "without delay." I climbed the hill to the Administration Building. The grass, flowers, and sky, washed clean from the rains, glared brilliantly. A warm, rich smell beat up from the earth as the sun brooded over it. On the way, a group of workers took advantage of the softened soil to set in new plants. They saw me, and we exchanged greetings. Many of them I knew from the midweek worship groups. Thinking of them, I continued my trek up the hill and refused to consider what DeHeer-Johnson had on his mind.

The secretary ushered me into the office. From his desk, the Registrar motioned for me to sit down. Declining to shake hands, he greeted me from where he sat with a mechanical, "Good morning, Rev. Lattimer."

The secretary took a seat by the Registrar with his trusty pad and pencil.

"I will get straight to the point, Rev. Lattimer," DeHeer-Johnson clipped. "I have called you here because of your sermon, which you preached last evening and which I heard with my own ears."

Not knowing which signal he was calling, I hung loose. "Yes, I was glad to see you there, Mr. DeHeer-Johnson. I hope you feel free to come again some time," I said with a smile.

"I don't think you realize, Rev. Lattimer," he went on, "how serious an offense you have committed."

"Offense? What offense have I committed?"

He seemed annoyed. "What offense? Do you mean to tell me that you have no idea that you have abused the pulpit by preaching libelous words?" His voice arose; his eyes scowled.

"I preached nothing libelous."

"But I was there, and I swear that you did," he shot back at me.

"There was nothing in my sermon which was libelous," I insisted. "What do you consider libelous?"

The Registrar produced a paper. "Here. I have your sermon written down. My secretary took notes."

"So I noticed. As he is doing now," I said.

He frowned again at me but continued, "Why the part where it says . . . where you say, and I quote: 'Discrimination and prejudice of one group against another were at work in determining who should be released from their work.' Now that, Rev. Lattimer, is a libelous statement, and you have no proof whatsoever to document your flagrant accusation."

"Now just a moment, Mr. DeHeer-Johnson," I said. "That assertion is not true. Your secretary failed to take it down accurately. And I have the manuscript in my office to prove that my words have been misconstrued."

The secretary, raising his head, blinked like a startled barnyard rooster. The Registrar glared at me for a few moments. "What has been misconstrued, Rev. Lattimer?" he asked with irritated reluctance.

I replied, "I know for certain that at the beginning of the statement which you just read, I distinctly said, 'It appears that.' I carefully put that phrase in my statement so that it is speculation and not a conclusive opinion."

With scarcely a pause, the Registrar with his eyes bulging retorted, "Ah, but a question, a possibility, is just as libelous, Rev. Lattimer, as a statement. For the opinion has been formed in the minds of the hearers. You have influenced their minds to consider the issue from only one viewpoint: that of discrimination. Your whole sermon was geared to prejudice, stemming from the historic conflict between Jews and Arabs . . . uh, Samaritans. If you did not consider the issue slanted toward prejudice, then it had no place to be mentioned in your sermon," he said with a smirk.

"I do not agree," I countered. "There is nothing in it which is libelous."

"Perhaps, then we can call in my attorney to judge the situation. At any rate, I am personally appalled that a minister of the Gospel, would . . . would stoop so low to preach as you did, Rev. Lattimer."

I did not answer him. I sat waiting and watching.

"I have cautioned you about intruding into the affairs of the University," he continued. "About participating in activities unsuitable to the Chaplaincy. And I should think that with your appointment still pending, you would be most careful in this regard." He fingered the golden stool pinned to his tie.

"And what do you think the role of the Chaplain is? To stay cloistered in the chapel and never involve himself in the aches and conflicts and triumphs of the University? To preach sterile sermons to an insulated congregation?"

The Registrar leaned forward. "I can assure you, Rev. Lattimer, that we can find an Ilarian chaplain who would follow the mores of Ilarian society far better than you have been able to."

"I don't doubt that," I said. "But Christianity is global. It has nothing to do with the fact that I am a foreigner."

"It certainly does !" he burst out. "It has everything to do with it. I know of no Ilarian minister who would do what you have done."

I refrained from saying that Ilarians knew which side of the bread has the butter. Rather, moving to the edge of my chair, I said, "Look, Mr. DeHeer-Johnson. This University is no isolated African village. It is international, not only in its teaching faculty but in what it teaches. It has to be. As long as you have expatriates here, as long as you maintain the academic freedom necessary to explore truth, you will have international views."

"But the day is coming," he said with a smile, "when we shall have an all-Ilarian faculty."

"Certainly. I am all for that. But I should hope that the University will not become so Africanized that it becomes isolationist."

"We shall decide our own policies in that regard, Rev. Lattimer," he declared. "In the meantime, I would request on behalf of the University authorities that you publicly retract your sermon."

He said it with such an oily voice that it just about slipped through without my catching it. "What did you say?" I asked.

"I am requesting that you withdraw your sermon, publicly, on the basis of misunderstanding and ignorance of the situation."

Drawing a deep breath, I looked down at my hands and then back at him. "And what if I refuse to do so?" I asked.

DeHeer-Johnson glared for a moment in apparent disbelief. Then, taking me by surprise, he jumped up from his chair and leaned on his knuckles until they turned white. "Rev. Lattimer, I should like to remind you for about the sixth time that you are not an official chaplain of this University," he raised his voice. "You are in no bargaining position a'tall. In fact, your temporary appointment can be immediately suspended if you do not comply with the demands of the Administration. Furthermore, I shall personally take you to court for besmirching my reputation and the reputation of this institution!" he cried.

"But there is no evidence of slander! And certainly no mention of your name," I insisted.

"But by inference it is there. Everyone knows it is there!"

"I'm sorry, but I cannot help that," I said. "If what I said happened to fit you, then I cannot help it."

The Registrar looked at me through narrowed eyes. "You are a most insolent White man! And a priest at that!" he waved his hands. "How dare you come to Africa when you need to clean up your own house in America first! How dare you to preach what you did last night and say what you are saying now with all the history of racial discrimination on your hands. Kwati Awulu told me of the hell he endured because of you!"

I flinched. "So . . . so he came to see you?"

Delighted over my discomfort, the Registrar leered. "Maybe yes. Maybe no."

"Well," I sighed. "I admitted to my guilt and to the problem and paradox of being here. And I asked forgiveness of those present."

With that, DeHeer-Johnson burst out in mock laughter and sat down. "And asking forgiveness will set everything aright, will it, Rev. Lattimer? Are you really so naive to believe that? You are not as intelligent as I thought!".

I glanced over at the secretary, who had not taken down the Registrar's last few remarks. Succumbing to a whim, I observed, "And your secretary, why is he not recording all of this conversation?"

Again, the rooster ruffled his feathers a bit, whereas the Registrar froze. He clinched his fists and the veins stood out on his great bull neck. "Rev. Lattimer, you are dismissed! I never want to see your face again," he bellowed. "Now get out of my office!"

The secretary scrambled from his chair to open the door for me. But the Registrar put out a hand to stop him. "He can very well do it for himself!" he cried.

I stormed back down the hill to my office, waving at the workers only mechanically. I slammed the door behind me between my office and the lounge where my secretary sat, bug-eyed, watching me. Upon my entering my office, Oparu and James rose up to greet me.

For a moment we all looked at each other silently. Then shaking my head, I slumped into my chair behind my desk. The other two followed my example.

"Your secretary told us where you were," Oparu began.

"It was a bad meeting," James ventured.

"Yes," I said and wiped my hands over my eyes.

"Did . . . did he threaten you?" asked Oparu, his eyes blazing.

I nodded. "He wants me to retract my sermon publicly. If I do not, he will see that I am dismissed and/or he will haul me into court on a libel charge."

James sucked his teeth.

"Wh-a-a-t!" Oparu cried in a scandalized falsetto. "How does he think he can get away with it?"

"I suppose he considers himself the paramount chief," I grimaced.

"But even chiefs can be de-stooled, you know," Oparu exclaimed.

"Only if there are enough persons with power to do so," said James.

Oparu gaped at him. "I suppose the students and even the lecturers are helpless . . . are at his mercy. Who would have the power?"

"The University Council," James said, referring to a body similar to an American Board of Trustees.

"You don't think student opinion would affect the situation in the least?" Oparu asked James.

"It is doubtful. The students have no real power," stated James.

"I will still tell them," Oparu said.

"What do you expect them to do, Oparu?" I asked. "Do you think they will rally to my support after their months of indifference and negativism toward me?" I was almost angry with his naivete.

"Rev. Lattimer." He jumped to the edge of his chair. "The students have changed their opinion of you . . . because of your sermon. Believe me. It served to blot out much of the ill will they had toward you!"

I squinted at him.

"Really, you must believe me," he went on. "Your confession did it. It took courage for you to do so, and they recognize it. They greatly valued your honesty."

I continued frowning at his words until James intervened. "It's true. I have heard some similar opinions from the students," he said.

"Rev. Lattimer, you cannot retract your sermon," Oparu declared.

"I have no intention to," I replied. "But you realize, of course, you may lose a chaplain because of it."

Oparu's eyebrows flew up.

"I don't think De Heer-Johnson will follow through," said James. "I think it is no more than a bluff."

"But he has done it before," cried Oparu. "He has cut down others who have opposed him."

"Yes, but they were all persons on University salary," James pointed out. "He could very easily stop their pay."

Oparu's face lit up. "And Rev. Lattimer is not on University salary. Isn't that true?" He looked at me.

I nodded.

"Furthermore," James continued, "Rev. Lattimer is called here by the United Church of Ilaria. He cannot be released without their consent."

Oparu eased back in his chair, as if victory lay imminently at hand.

"Another point to bear in mind," James said. "The University Council meets shortly. I think perhaps they can be informed of this. You see, from what I understand, a power struggle exists between the Registrar and three key members of the Council. Since his position is up for tenure at the end of this term, perhaps he will not step too far out of line to oppose his antagonists."

"Do you know any of them?" Oparu asked James.

"One I know quite well. We were University mates. I will pay him a visit," James said with a smile.

"I think, too, I should write the United Church Executive," I said. "They should know about this. Particularly, as you say, they are my chief means of support."

"Yes, that would be a wise move," James said.

After a while, Oparu and James begged to be excused to their classes. I thanked them wholeheartedly for their concern.

"Let me know immediately of any new developments," said James, as he left. He gave me his house and office phone numbers. He also warned me not to give my sermon to anyone, for it would "only be used against you."

I wrote Rev. Aketu that night, explaining the situation to him. It took me three typewritten pages to do so, for I had to repeat the pre-Ilaria history of Moses and me to an extent. In the meantime, I plunged into my work without reservations. The number attending chapel activities picked up. Perhaps Oparu's words had been true, that the students had reversed their feelings toward me. At least a dozen or so had from an all-night prayer meeting organized by Memka. They sent me a card after their meeting saying, "We unreservedly support you," followed by their names and a verse of Scripture.

As for the sermon itself, I continued to hear repercussions from it daily, chiefly from lecturers who had heard about it second hand. Most of them read motives and statements into it, which I had not intended. One Iranian woman in statistics lauded me for my "great courage" in stepping in "where Ilarians refuse to tread" and for calling DeHeer-Johnson's hand. To my dismay, many others quoted the Registrar's name, and I began to see what he meant that "the inference was there, and everyone knew it was there."

That scared me plenty. I began to fear that, without meaning to, my sermon might indeed prove libelous. So I sought a lawyer in Charlestown. It seemed hours as he read my sermon from beginning to end, while I sat in his office. Finally, he raised his white head and announced that the statements were "rhetorical" and the questions "speculative." Therefore, it was not libelous, but he warned that it was "close."

The next day, Rev. Aketu's letter came. He expressed both concern for my difficulties and support for my work. "It occurs to me that perhaps a visit between myself and the Registrar might be helpful at this juncture," he wrote. "I shall make an appointment with him in about a fortnight." He also said he'd ask Daniel Quaina to accompany him for the interview.

The date for the meeting between the Registrar and the two ministers was set for May twentieth. About forty-five minutes prior to the appointed time, Rev. Aketu's Mercedes drew up, and the small plump minister alighted. Along with him towered Daniel, looking cool and self-possessed. He wore a neat sports shirt with his slacks, whereas Rev. Aketu oozed moisture through his dark suit and clerical collar. I invited them to sit in my office.

"Well, indeed, we are happy to see you once more," said Rev. Aketu with a smile, as he fingered his briefcase in his lap. "But, of course, not under the present difficult circumstances." He laughed lightly and gazed around my office, very much as he had done on the night he preached at the chapel.

"And you say the Registrar personally came to hear your sermon?" asked Daniel, his elbows on his knees, his angular face tense.

"Yes, he heard it."

"But what does he think ministers are supposed to preach about? I mean anyone who goes to church should expect to hear some judgment of God . . . if we are faithful to preach his word. And no one makes the congregation come. They come voluntarily."

I nodded.

"And he actually thinks you directed the comments to him?" asked Rev. Aketu.

"Oh, definitely," I answered.

"I'm wondering, in all fairness, if you could let us read your sermon?" asked Daniel.

"Of course," I said and unlocked my drawer to get it out.

The two men sat close together to read it. I suggested that they start near the end, but they insisted on reading the whole thing for the content.

"It is a fine sermon. Very fine. Certainly one we need to hear today in Ilaria, I might add." Rev. Aketu smiled and shifted in the chair.

Daniel raised his eyebrows. "Still, I suppose, considering the circumstances, it's a rather explosive one. I can see how the Registrar might be upset with its . . . its insinuations toward the institution. But there are none toward himself. I don't see how he can call it *libelous*."

"Unless, of course, the Registrar feels somewhat guilty over the accusations," put in Rev. Aketu.

Daniel stuck out his lower lip. "I don't know that we can say that the Registrar is guilty or not. Because he has reacted negatively does not indict him, Rev. Aketu."

The older man flipped his hand down at the wrist. "Indeed, I am sure Rev. Lattimer did not preach it with the intention of indicting anyone. To be sure, he had only the best interests of the University at heart." He chuckled as if to lighten the gravity of the atmosphere.

Then he turned the subject to other matters by asking about the chapel activities during the term. I showed him a calendar of events. He registered surprise upon seeing the variety of things I was involved in. He commented on how I had broadened the scope of chaplaincy far more than he had ever visualized it. Daniel asked questions regarding my relationships with students and staff.

He wanted to know how the students had reacted to the sermon and to my confrontation with the Registrar.

"Why, how should they know of Rev. Lattimer's meeting with the Registrar?" interjected Rev. Aketu.

"I told them about the meeting, Rev. Aketu," I exclaimed.

He gaped, and then, as if to cover up his reaction, he coughed into his handkerchief. "You don't think that might make for agitation and student unrest, Rev. Lattimer? Students, these days, are so . . . so volatile, you know."

"I felt that I should tell them—at least members of our Christian Students Association—so that they should know where I stood," I explained. "If their Chaplain stands in danger of being sacked, they should know of it."

"Oh, you won't be sacked," Rev. Aketu reassured me. "Not as long as we support you. And we do, you know. By all means, we do!"

I felt that if he were close enough, Rev. Aketu would have leaned over, fatherlike, and patted my hand.

Daniel stared at Rev. Aketu remotely. He looked at his watch and announced that they should be leaving. We all stood up. "We shall pop in on you before we go," said Rev. Aketu.

"Fine," I said, and I invited them for something to drink in the staff room afterwards. Daniel declined, saying he had another engagement, but he would return to say goodbye.

I made a stab at my work after they left. But not being able to concentrate, I did nothing more than clean up my desk and drawers. An hour passed, almost two before the ministers returned to my office. Rev. Aketu stood wiping his face with his handkerchief.

"Well, it was a good meeting. Good," he said. "I'm certain things shall be worked out satisfactorily for everyone concerned."

I invited him to sit down while I walked Daniel out to the car. The driver had agreed to take him to Charlestown and then return for Rev. Aketu.

Daniel said nothing on the way out. We stood for a moment at the curb as we shook hands. "I'm sure you did what you thought was right," he said, looking at me with his piercing eyes. "Still, it's rather a difficult position you find yourself in, isn't it? Especially as an expatriate."

I nodded. Isn't he going to tell me more, I thought. Doesn't he sense the unspoken questions pressing against my lips? But because he was in a hurry, I said nothing. I waved him goodbye and returned to Rev. Aketu.

I took the Ilarian to the staff room in my car. He declined a cold drink and ordered tea instead. When it arrived at our table, he spent a great deal of time fussing with the milk and cubed sugar set out before him. He expressed dismay that the milk was the evaporated variety rather than the reconstituted whole milk he was accustomed to. We sat back under the fan, drinking silently. I waited for him to tell me about the meeting. To learn where I stood. To see if any tensions between myself and DeHeer-Johnson had been eased. Instead, he talked idly about the weather and about some of the schools in Charlestown. He asked details about Kay and the children.

As we got up to go, he said, "We have a Personnel Committee meeting the first of June. We shall bring this matter to the attention of the group. I think, therefore, in your best interest, we should have a copy of the sermon."

I agreed, and when we returned to my office, I got it out once more. "Do you have an extra copy of it?" he asked.

"Yes. I made one . . . after it became a matter of dispute. But I keep them both locked up."

"Very good," he said, bobbing his head in approval. He slid the sermon into his briefcase, and then we walked out to his car. The driver roared off after we said goodbye.

I went home, dejected. What had the meeting solved? I asked myself over and over. What?

I was to the point of tears. Kay and I clung to each other in bed that night. Finally, after we made love and lay calmly side by side, I blurted out a prayer. A loud complaint, really: "God, what are you doing to us? What do you have in mind for our life here? We need your help, your peace, your direction. As Jesus calmed the stormy sea, calm us. Give us strength for whatever comes. Amen." Kay echoed my Amen, and we allowed the distant sound of the surf to lull us to sleep.

Chapter 17

When the June first Personnel Committee met, I was called to appear before it. They had just received a letter from the University Appointments Board, asking that I be withdrawn "without delay."

Rod wrote me the news. When I went to Kwa the day before the meeting, I stayed with the Allens, and Rod shared the letter with me. The Appointments Board cited three basic reasons for my removal. One, I did "not qualify," with no further explanations. Next, they stated their "decided preference" for an Ilarian chaplain.

We do not feel (said the letter) *that an expatriate chaplain is in any position to understand the cultural and historical background of our students and faculty. Neither will they relate as freely to an expatriate chaplain as to an Ilarian one. Rev. Lattimer has shown little regard for our customary ways of handling matters at the University. Furthermore, he has not been able to build up a following among the students, demonstrated in the fact that attendance has markedly fallen off in recent weeks at chapel functions. He has also engaged in activities we consider inappropriate for the chaplaincy*."

The third point only alluded to "the recent circumstances wherein Rev. Lattimer abused the pulpit by slandering the Administration."

I whistled as I put the letter down. "It's actually not very specific, is it?"

"That was my immediate reaction to it," agreed Rod.

"How do you think the Committee will react to it . . . , Luella not withstanding?" I asked. Luella, a member of the Personnel Committee, was also staying with the Allens. Upon my arrival in Kwa, I was shocked to learn that she was out soliciting support from Committee members on my behalf.

"She does it every time," Edith Allen told me when I protested. "There's usually something on the agenda she takes issue with, and she leaves no stone unturned to tell the members how they should vote!"

Rod laughed at my question. "You take Luella with a grain of salt! Those men will vote like they please, although they will try to pacify her on appearances."

"That figures," I said. "But seriously, do you think they will buy these opinions without more facts?"

"It's a possibility," said Rod. "A good possibility. Tell me, though, what all did Aketu and Quaina learn when they went down to see you?"

I laughed. "You tell me, and we'll both know! I haven't a clue as to what went on in their meeting with the Registrar."

"Did they see anything of your work . . . something which they could formulate their own opinions about?"

"Oh, a little, I suppose," I said. "I showed them a calendar, and we discussed some of the programs. But as far as my personal relationships with people there . . . I doubt that they got anything along those lines."

"Perhaps they did. Daniel is a pretty astute observer."

"Maybe so," I said. "But he had to rush off when the meeting with the Registrar was finished. And Aketu, well . . . to be frank, he acted completely indifferent. Rod, he wouldn't tell me one thing about that meeting! There I was in gosh-awful suspense about what went on, and he didn't say a thing. Except that he thought things would work out fine. If that didn't ever burn my gizzard!"

"That's the way they do, though, with everybody," Rod explained. "They wait until the official meeting or the official letter to explain what's what. Meanwhile, you dangle and try not to let it get you down."

"But it leads to so much suspicion and distrust. How do I know those two didn't sell me out to the Registrar? I mean if that happened at home, what else would we suspect?"

"But it's not home," Rod said, smiling. "It's just their way. And you just have to trust them. It doesn't mean they sold you out at all."

"Well, I sure hope they don't let me dangle tomorrow."

"Oh, officially, they probably will. But they'll know that I'll tell you everything that happens during the meeting."

"They don't resent that?"

"No," he chuckled. "They rather expect it."

We were interrupted with the arrival of Luella. She explained freely what she had been doing. "I think things will turn out fine, Hank, fine," she patted me on the arm. "I have seen them all, and they have assured me that they thought you did the right thing. They have your interest really at heart, and they don't wish to see you leave the University at all."

I thanked her only out of politeness. We then discussed Moses. She still had not made contact with him. When I told her of his recent dismissal, she reacted with profound horror and retired to her room. Shortly afterward, we all went to bed.

The next morning, Rod drove me down to the offices of the United Christian Church of Kwa. They lie adjacent to Victoria Square, the hub of Kwa. We edged alongside the city's largest market, a big openair sort of Woolworth's, and pressed through mobs of people on tangled streets. At the office building, we met the other members of the Committee. Besides Daniel Quaina and Rev. Aketu, Rev. Pediadu from the Ketumba region, a gaunt, graying man with glasses, hobbled in, leaning on a walking stick. He shook my hand formally. The last to arrive was a Rev. Larson, middle-aged, mild-mannered with a slight lisp. He represented the Kwa region.

All of the minsters wore dog collars and suits, except for Daniel, who had on an embroidered shirt. Two members of the Committee—an Ilarian from the Eastern Region and a Swiss missionary from the north—were unable to come. Rev. Aketu hovered around me a bit to ask about my family and thank me for coming to the meeting. Luella gave me a motherly pat on the shoulder before she disappeared with the men to the conference room upstairs.

I sat on a hard bench in the empty reception room. Fortunately, I had brought some newspapers along with me to read. Before I finished them, though, James Gharta appeared.

"Good morning," he said with a smile. "I told you I'd make it."

"Indeed you did!" I cried, jumping up to shake his hand. "I can't thank you enough." I had shared the summons from the Committee with James on the day I'd received it. He promised to join me at the Church offices "to support you," he said.

"You got the bus this morning all right?" I asked.

He nodded as he sat down beside me. "It made good time. Still, I shall be glad to ride with you on the return journey," he said.

His usual reticence melted as we began to talk a little. I asked details about his background, and he, about mine. He particularly wanted to know about the seminary I had attended, its curriculum and practical experience in local churches.

"You know, I attended seminary myself," he murmured.

"But you were never ordained?" I was surprised.

"No. I attended only two years. Then I quit," he said.

"Why was that?"

He looked at the floor for a few moments and compressed his lips. "There were many reasons, actually. Many agonizing reasons. I guess the chief of which might be termed the *European complex*, even in an African seminary. Do you know what I mean?"

"I sure do."

"The ministers who control the seminary and who are on its Board have no interest in making either the ministry or the church pertinent to Africa." He compressed his lips again.

"And, of course, they don't really have many Africans on the seminary faculty, do they? Since most of them are expatriate missionaries, I imagine that would further weaken efforts to Africanize the ministry," I said.

"On the contrary, that is not the case, curiously," said James.

"Oh?"

"It is an interesting fact that most of today's missionaries are the very ones who encourage the African church toward an integration between faith and life. Like yourself." He looked up at me and smiled.

"Me?" I puzzled.

"Yes. You've evidenced that, in my opinion. In sponsoring the Contemporary Worship. In your interest in incorporating Akarti into services and using it with people across the campus. I don't think many Ilarian ministers would have done that. Certainly not to initiate such a thing as the Contemporary Worship. They might have approved it if the students had asked for it, like an indulgent father pleasing a child's fancy."

"I see."

"Missionaries, after all the pros and cons, are still needed here, Hank. Very badly," he went on. "You are in a unique position to ask questions, to challenge us. You provide us with a needed point of view, chiefly because you are not paid by our church. And because you are not striving after some position. If a young Ilarian minister asked those questions, he would be severely censored by the older clergy. Mainly because he would pose a threat to them. He is tied to an outdated form of ministry. Nothing creative or new or daring is ever ventured. I could not stand that, Hank. So I left the ministry."

"But not really," I said, smiling at him.

He returned a quizzical look.

"You do as much ministering on Western campus as I do," I said. "With your visiting and your personal interest in people. Like Kanu Jones. And like with me, now."

He said nothing for a while. "I try to do what I can. I feel it's no more than what is expected of any other Christian."

"Many other Christians believe that, James. But only a few do something concrete, as you do."

"Well, we must thank God for that," he said quietly.

A short while later, a clerk entered the room and beckoned me to come. I followed him up the stairs to the conference room. Small tables were set in a circle around the large room, and behind each one sat the ministers, Luella, and Rod, with papers spread out in front of them. Luella beamed at me as I entered. Rev. Aketu, the Chairman, arose and indicated where I should sit. When I had settled down, Rev. Aketu began.

"Rev. Lattimer, we have been discussing the letter which we received from the Appointments Board of Western University," he intoned. He passed a copy of it down to me. "And we have had some difficulty in determining the validity of the reasons given for your . . . uh . . . withdrawal. Some of us feel the reasons are valid. Others feel that they have no solid evidence behind them." He glanced around the room. "Be that as it may, there seem to be certain things that only you can tell us about. In the first instance, there is the allusion to the activities 'inappropriate to the chaplaincy.' And secondly, there is the allusion to the 'abuse of the pulpit' in the sermon you recently preached.

"Now in regards to the sermon, I have duplicated copies of it for the Committee members to peruse," and he pointed at the paper each person had. Inwardly I gasped. I had no idea he would distribute the sermon so freely, so unguardedly. "We have, amongst ourselves, aired varied opinions about the sermon," he went on, flashing a beneficent smile. "Some of us feel that it is indeed, uh . . . *abusive*, and others of us disagree: But we should like to hear from you directly about the circumstances that led to the sermon and why you preached it and varying reactions to it which you have observed." He folded his hands and tilted his head back to receive what I had to say. The others also fastened their attention on me.

Briefly and as clearly as possible, I complied with his request. I related the sacking of the employees. The speculations as to why only Ketumbas had been picked out. The indifference of most people to tribalism in the community. I spoke of the sermon, its theme, its intent, and pointed to the sheets in front of them with the actual words of it. I set it clearly in the framework of the relationship of Jesus with the Samaritan women.

I paused, and members began to question me. Were my motives indeed in the best interest of maintaining harmonious relationships on the campus? Was there no other more peaceful alternative than "a sermon," like a "friendly discussion" with the Registrar, demonstrating a "pastoral concern?" All this came from Rev. Larson. Then questions arose concerning sermons in general and the role of the minister. When does he preach peace, and when does he speak out against social injustices? When does he bring the Good News of the evangelist, and when does he bear denunciations of the prophet?

From there, they asked me how I saw my role as Chaplain in general. "I see it as one of involvement," I said. "It is understanding the hurts and fears and hopes of a community and of relating the Gospel to these."

"And what sort of activities are expressed in your involvement . . . aside from preaching sermons?" The question came almost sharply from Daniel.

"Mixing with students, listening and learning from them," I said. "Being aware of needs, seeking outlets for social concern in concrete projects. Incorporating African values into worship services. Participating in campus meetings, whether religious or not: games, parties, get-togethers."

"And would any of these activities be considered *inappropriate* to the chaplaincy?" asked Rev. Larson.

"I suppose you can always get varying opinions on any action of a minister," I said. "Some will like it; some will not. I have tried to take seriously the claims of Christ in everyday life. That is all."

"But is it not true, Rev. Lattimer," continued Rev. Larson, running his little finger around his clerical collar, "that at one point you engaged in a village project at the expressed disapproval of the University authorities? A project which they considered *inappropriate*?"

I felt the hair bristle on the back of my neck. He could have received the information only from Aketu or Quaina, who would have gotten it from DeHeer-Johnson. And the way he twisted it around—had it been his own wording or the minister's or the Registrar's? And why he chose to throw that morsel out to the eager ears of the Committee only irritated me. Calming myself, I emphasized to Rev. Larson how I did not know the village project was forbidden by the University until after we tried it. How I was given permission by the proper University Committee but was overruled by the Registrar, to whom I immediately submitted.

"Rev. Lattimer, . . . Hank, do you not feel that being a foreigner alters your stance a bit on what is considered *appropriate* or *inappropriate*?" Daniel asked with his penetrating eyes and voice.

"How do you mean?" I asked.

"Do you feel you know Africans well enough to be this much involved? Might you be imposing your own interpretations of social needs upon others of a different culture? Are you speaking out on issues when in fact you have been part of the community for so short a time and do not know it intimately and do not know all the implications and the innuendos?"

I caught my breath. "I . . . I don't know. I did what I did in good conscience, as I felt directed by the Lord." I met his gaze with my own. "Rev. Quaina, let me ask you something, if I may," I said and swallowed hard. Heads craned and ears seemed to perk up. "I was invited here on a three-year term by your church. Now, that length of time is very short to accomplish anything. Am I to take it to mean that during those three years, I should do essentially nothing? That I must wait until I become more acculturated, which may take umpteen number of years? That as an expatriate missionary, I can make no judgments, take no actions?"

Silence hung heavy around us for a moment. Then Daniel smiled slightly. "Hank," he said with a softened tone, "indeed that is a most delicate question. A question that has been argued and maligned as long as missionaries have been in our country. None of us Africans can tell you what you in your conscience feel. One major observation occurs to me in relation to this point. That is, you Westerners are more action-oriented, and we Africans, more person-oriented. Do you understand me?"

I nodded mutely.

"But . . . but," Luella sputtered, waving her hand vigorously. Rev. Aketu recognized another hand instead, that of Rev. Larson.

"Rev. Lattimer," he said, "do you not feel that by preaching this sermon your ministry at Western now stands in serious jeopardy?"

"I had considered that ramification before I preached it," I said. "But frankly, I don't know when my ministry at Western has *not* been tenuous."

"What do you mean?" Larson frowned.

Once again, feeling very much like a broken phonograph record, I told about the relationship between Moses Awulu and myself, of the rejection in Georgia, and the symposium at the University.

"And you feel that this has a direct bearing on the conflict at the University?" Rev. Aketu leaned forward.

"Yes, I do. It is not just the sermon. It is who I am and where I come from and who I represent."

A long pause followed, broken by Rev. Pediadu in his rasping voice. "Would you like to remain on at the University, Rev. Lattimer?"

I thought for a moment. "Yes, I certainly would. The potential for a fruitful ministry is great. The students are far more open to hear the Gospel than in my country. I feel that it is a unique, almost paradoxical opportunity that I can baptize a dozen converts into the Christian church as I did at Easter within a stone's throw of Charlestown Castle and all it stood for."

"Rev. Lattimer," continued Pediadu, "do you think any good will be accomplished in the presence of the conflict with the Administration, especially if it continues and if it becomes aggravated?"

"I don't know," I said. "Who can know but God?"

He said nothing, and neither did anyone else.

"Are there any more questions you should like to pose to Rev. Lattimer?" Rev. Aketu asked the group.

Silence.

"Then if not, Rev. Lattimer, you may retire."

Returning to the reception room, I shared what had transpired with James. Neither of us had much comment to make. We sat almost an hour before Rod came downstairs. I could tell by his face the outlook was bad.

"Hank, they voted to honor the University's request to withdraw you. It was three in favor of the withdrawal, two opposed, and one abstention. I'm . . . I'm terribly sorry." He gripped my shoulder, and I looked quickly away. James moaned a protracted, "No," while shaking his head.

Before Rod could say anything more, Luella burst into the room, distraught. "Hank, it's . . . it's just not fair at all! I cannot imagine what happened. They . . . they deceived me! Even Daniel Quaina, of all the ungrateful people! Why, yesterday they all had you in their interest. And now look what has happened!" Her voice cracked, and her eyes took on a fierce expression.

"Easy does it, Luella," said Rod. "I don't think they deceived you. They just voted the way they felt about the matter after they heard all the facts."

"They are heartless people, just heartless!" she exclaimed. "After all the sacrifice Hank has made to come to the field. The Church has no right to be so . . . so flippant with a person's life. Why, he shall certainly appeal it to the home Board!"

"But the Board won't interfere with the Church's decision, Luella," said Rod. "You know that."

She gasped at Rod's words. "You mean we missionaries have absolutely no recourse to a higher authority if they decide to sack us?"

"We have recourse within the structure of the Church, but no more."

She looked out the door, wide-eyed, "Oh, that's perfectly terrible! It's not fair at all! Why, we don't have a chance!"

I cringed even in the throes of my own garbled feelings. I wished James did not have to hear what she said.

Rod changed the subject. He offered to take James and me back to his house where my car was parked. Then he would have to return to the rest of the Committee meeting. Luella retreated back upstairs but not without assuring me that she personally would take my cause before the Board of Missions through a private letter between herself and the Executive Secretary. "Structure or no Church structure!" were her parting words.

James and I silently followed Rod out to the parking lot. Without my asking, he told me what happened in the meeting on the way to his house. "I suppose, basically, they all wanted peace," he began. "They knew you were transient, that they would have to 'live with the University,' as Pediadu put it, long after you left. He hardly said a word throughout. I can't help but think that his being Ketumba sided him with you and your sermon for the most part. But in the end, he put in his plug for peace and how their decision will reflect upon the image of the Church as a whole. He also worried that if they supported you, they would forfeit future openings, which may come to the Church from other secular institutions. I think they latched onto his words and voted accordingly. Being the oldest among them had its influence too. . . .

"It must have been Aketu who abstained. Although he acted as Chairman, he had a right to vote. All throughout, he supported you as a missionary. He asked how could the Committee undo God's call for you to come to Ilaria. He agreed with me that the University's letter gave no examples to back up their assertions and that what the letter said was an opinion of a small group. He and I both pointed this out to the Committee repeatedly, but it had little effect."

"I gather, too, that being a foreigner came into play a good bit," I sighed.

"Yes, Daniel said a lot on that score," said Rod. "When they discussed the section of the letter about the preference for an Ilarian chaplain, he jumped on the bandwagon for that one. He said that it was natural that Ilarians, in time of need, would turn to an Ilarian for help, and Europeans, to Europeans. Then Aketu orated for a while on how Christianity is no respecter of persons. Luella immediately agreed with that and went on and on about how much preparation you had on Africa prior to coming out. And also how we are all one in Christ and that in Him barriers are broken down. In other words, that Daniel was dead wrong!"

I humphed a little and asked, "And how did he rally from that onslaught?"

"Oh, he was his usual unflappable self," chuckled Rod. "He insisted that he was not anti-foreign or anti-missionary or anti-American . . . that they would not invite us here if they felt that way. But he pointed out that after all is said and done and attempted, missionaries are still foreigners with different perspectives from our Ilarian congregations and constituents."

"But did he not see that the difference of perspective could be healthy?" asked James.

"Apparently not," returned Rod.

"You know, I have to admit that I feel Daniel is partially right," I said. "In a way, I'm glad to see him standing up against the establishment and being aggressively pro-Ilarian, though . . . though at my . . . expense." I dropped my voice.

"But it can be carried too far, of course," cried James. "Ultra-nationalism can only lead to a stagnated church!"

We rode on silently for a while. "Then, too," Rod went on, "your statement about the sermon not being the only issue, about its being, rather, who you were and where you came from and such. I think that more than anything clinched their arguments, I'm afraid. They saw no hope for ever having peaceful relationships with the authorities so long as you are at Western."

"I said it sincerely, as the truth," I said. "I could not have left it out."

"I . . . I guess not," said Rod. "And I hope you don't chastise yourself for what you said or left unsaid. I . . . I know it's a nasty pill to swallow, Hank. But I hope you can tie up your ends there at Western and get out as soon as you can and concentrate on better things ahead. And there will be good things ahead for you. I'm confident of that." He said it with deep concern, which I appreciated tremendously. But all I could do at the time was to nod my head.

"Let me add this, though, Hank," Rod said. "The Personnel Committee is quite willing to consider reassigning you to another place in Ilaria. You think it over, and let me know, OK?"

Again, I nodded mutely.

He dropped us at his house and returned to the meeting. Edith had lunch for James and me. Like Rod, she said the right things, which helped me get through the meal. After a short rest, James and I left the Allens. We ran a few errands around Kwa before returning to Charlestown in the afternoon.

We talked very little on our drive west from the city to the country, the rolling, lush country turned green by the rains. We passed a plain swept by winds followed by trees and bush and grass pressing around us in verdant vitality. Village after village flicked by us. At a roundabout we angled off toward the sea and presently glimpsed it through the palms. At one point we crested a hill, below which lay a broad vista of whitecapped waves under a golden sky. Its timeless beauty caught at my throat. But then we plunged down the hill on toward Charlestown into the shadows. And there at the bottom, amid slowed traffic and staring people, lay a lorry in the middle of the road, on fire. The sides of it were scorched, but the slogan over the cab was yet visible. "Still Living" could be read through the flames and smoke. I changed gears and plummeted around it. Somehow, it made me want to cry.

Chapter 18

Upon returning to Charlestown, Kay and I mulled over staying in Ilaria versus returning home. We decided on the latter. The preliminaries of packing began at the office. My secretary trailed me around in stunned silence, as he and I closed up shop. During the course of the day, several workers and students filtered in. They stopped short when they saw what was going on. By the afternoon, the numbers increased as news began to drift across the campus. Most of them I knew, but many were complete strangers. They came to console me, to express regrets, but primarily to ask questions. About the Church's Personnel Committee meeting, about my encounter with the Registrar, my sermon, the symposium, Moses Awulu, Trinity Presbyterian Church, and southern America in general.

It reminded me of an Ilarian proverb, which says, *The knot is untied from the end,* that is, to understand a problem, you have to go to the root of the matter. I became exhausted with the untying of the knot. So I hastened my efforts to clear out and then retreated to our house.

After that, I went out only when necessary. Not only did I wish to avoid explanations even among sympathizers, but I reached the point where I didn't want to stir up any impertinent remarks from those on the periphery of the church. Remarks beginning with "Ah, yes, you know the Church . . ." or "As for the clergy . . ." made with a shake of the head and a gleam in the eye. For from their viewpoint, I imagined, I had failed as a chaplain and as a Christian or as a do-good American at best.

"But . . . but why this . . . this seclusion?" Kay demanded in wide-eyed astonishment when she saw my tactics.

"Well, why not, Kay? There's nothing more to do. We're . . . finished."

"I . . . I just thought we could exit a little more graciously. That's all," she said, smiling brightly.

The look I shot her punctured her smile.

"All right, all right, I'm sorry I said it," she said, turning to something else.

With touches of both dogged determination and good sportsmanship, she began with me the process of uprooting with scarcely a complaint. When I had told her of the decision of the Committee on the night of June first, she cried. But she indicted no one: neither the Church nor the University. I wondered, then, whether she attributed the blame wholly to me. She never let on, though, if she did. The next morning, she had calmly surveyed her now shattered domestic enclave.

"Well. Where do we start?" she had said, smiling wanly. I had muttered something about getting barrels out of the storeroom while I finished up at the office.

The day after I left the office, Memka came, the first of a series.

"Reverend!" he exclaimed, his eyes bulging. "I just heard the terrible news! Why did they do it? Was it your sermon?"

"They did it for many reasons, Memka," I answered tiredly. "My sermon was only one of them."

"But surely the Administration cannot sack you without the Church's approval!"

"But the Church did approve it."

Memka's jaw went slack around his salient teeth. "Eh! That's difficult to believe!"

"No, not really."

He stared at me. Then, sitting back in the chair, he smiled. "Well, at least, Reverend, the Lord is sufficient in our troubles!"

I nodded.

"We don't always know his ways. He is probably leading you to greener pastures."

"Perhaps."

"You must completely trust Him. You must surrender yourself to Him, saying, *Thy will be done*. Then your heart will be at peace."

"I am trusting Him as best I can, Memka," I said. "But my heart is not at peace."

"But Jesus promises to give us His peace. It is a promise we can claim for our own!"

"I know. But He also said, He came not to bring peace but a sword."

"But that is related to unbelievers, Reverend," he argued. "Believers are meant to have His peace."

"I don't agree, Memka," I blurted out. "How can I have peace when I am part of a Church which is blind to its own shams and festering sores? When hostility has driven a wedge between me and another person, and try as I might, I cannot find a way to remove it? And when irrational hatred has destroyed a potentially profitable ministry for the Lord at Western?"

He looked at me with the same smile but said nothing for a while. Then he added, "In spite of these, if you pray to the Lord, believing, you shall have his peace. You must say with Job, *Though he slay me, yet will I trust in him*."

"And by trust alone, my questions will be resolved?"

"By trusting him, the questions will resume their proper proportions. The mountains they seem to be will become as anthills."

"And I should do nothing actively to resolve these questions?"

"Only allow God to work them out," he declared. "Pray that his kingdom come, his will be done. We must pray, Reverend. That is the secret!"

I stared at Memka's confident, glowing face .... "Memka?" I looked down at my hands.

"Yes, Reverend?"

"I can see how you have peace, Memka," I said. "You never expose yourself to the raw edges of human experience."

Astonishment erased the smile from his face. "Why, what do you mean?"

"Memka, my friend, you have insulated yourself with so much Scripture, so many dogmatic formulas, you have lost touch with people and their problems."

"But Reverend, I do not consider myself a monk, a . . . a recluse, if that is what you mean!" he pressed his hand against his chest in a gesture of vindication.

"No, you are not a recluse in the physical sense. But spiritually, you are. You go about your affairs as if you don't want to get your hands soiled. As if you don't want to involve yourself in sin and suffering, except to pray. Do you think the Lord himself was like that?" I demanded.

He thought for a few moments. "His activities with the sufferings of men were only secondary, Reverend," he said, smiling. "His prime mission, of course, was to preach the Good News of God, to call sinners to repentance. And to live the perfect life of the Son of God. By all means, He relied on prayer to accomplish these things!"

I sighed, knowing that we both spoke the truth. Memka seemed on one side of the coin, and I, on the opposite. Both bound together by a basic allegiance yet back-to-back and unable to communicate. The antagonism troubled me, for I knew no matter how strong our differences, we needed each other. I pointed this out to him, begging him to consider my viewpoint. At the same time, I expressed gratefulness for his, by saying I would take his words to heart.

After Memka, others came. Oparu, hot and fuming, wanting to do something on my behalf by igniting a student demonstration. I restrained him and told him and the others to concentrate on their exams and studies. Demonstrating would only bring them trouble and might even end their University careers.

Sean and Elizabeth dropped by. After the usual consolations and explanations, they wanted to invite Kay and me to a farewell dinner at their bungalow. I tried to dissuade them, not feeling up to it. But I didn't want to offend their generosity and their effort to do something for us. So I accepted. They asked me to give them a list of others I would like to invite. Right off, they suggested the officers of the CSA, and we set the eleventh of June for the dinner. We planned to fly out by the fifteenth.

Then, of course, there was James. He came more than once, offering his generous help. It was he who arranged with the University to take our things on June ninth to the harbor. He also helped to pack, to get lumber for crates, and even to entertain the children when they added to the confusion.

On the night of the seventh, Kay and I stayed up late stuffing our barrels, the seven we had brought out to Ilaria with us. James had not come that evening, as he had exam papers to mark. I finished the clothes and toys lying on the dining table and asked Kay what was next.

"There's that pile of sheets and towels on the buffet," she said. "You can start on that."

"You want to hand them to me while I stick them in?"

"No, I'm still sorting through the medicine cabinet," she said.

"Oh, come on, Kay. It'll go faster if we work together."

"Well, who's going to go through the medicines and the toilet articles? Not you, I know!"

"Of course, I can. You can bend over for a while, and I'll take it sitting down," I grumbled.

Kay dropped her work and came over to me. "Let's take a break. What would you like to drink?"

"Nothing. I'm all right. We'd better keep at it."

"But you're getting all grouchy."

"I have a right to be," I said, flinging a pile of towels into an empty barrel.

She watched me silently. Then in a moment, she handed me more. "Here, throw some more in," she said. "The harder the better."

I jerked my head toward her. "I can do without the sarcasm," I snapped.

"I wasn't being sarcastic. I thought it would do you good."

"What would do me good?"

"Letting off some of that bottled-up resentment."

"Well!" I exclaimed, drawing myself up straight. "And what else do you suggest, Madam Psychologist?"

"I don't know. I've thumbed through all suggestions on file, and none of them seem to fit," she said. She looked as grim as I had ever seen her. "What do you suggest?"

"Nothing."

"Are you going to flippantly forge another link in this chain of hate and bitterness?" her lips trembled.

"I hadn't particularly philosophized about it one way or another!" I retorted.

She seemed at a loss as to what to say next. I turned back to the towels. After a while, I asked her what time it was. When she said 10:30, I announced that I was going to bed. I went to the kitchen for a drink of water. I drank out of a cream pitcher since I couldn't find any glasses. I took some water out to Kay, which she received gratefully. Then we both fell into bed, after moving stacks of clothing off onto the floor. A bird clattered out in the dark, and drums from a neighboring village announced a death. I quickly fell asleep.

Along about midnight, something woke me up. I lay in bed, listening. Then I realized, when I heard the noise again, that someone was knocking on the door. I wondered why the night watchman should be waking us up, for I presumed it was only he. I groped my way across the courtyard, knocking something over in transit. Reaching the door, I flicked on the light. As I opened it, I struggled to focus my eyes on the form standing there.

It was Moses.

His presence was like a dash of icy water in the face, for I instantly came to. But the shock of seeing him rendered me motionless.

"May I please come in? I would very much like to talk with you," he pleaded. I strained to catch a note of gloating in his voice, but it seemed to be absent.

"Sure, sure. Come right in." I ushered him into the living room. I moved pots and pans and measuring cups from chairs, making room for us to sit. "We're in sort of a mess around here," I said.

We sat down opposite each other. Moses leaned forward, his elbows on his knees, his fingers intertwined. He looked at the floor for a few moments and did not say anything. His green and yellow printed cloth was wrapped completely around him, for the night air was chilly. He had sandals on his feet, and the flashlight he had carried rested in his lap.

He sat back, smiling nervously. "I . . . I scarcely know where to begin . . . or what to say," he said. The sides of his mouth twitched ever so slightly.

I sat still, expectantly waiting.

"I suppose basically," he began, "I have come to apologize to you for what I have done." The last several words quivered, and I could see that he was struggling to control himself.

I did not know how to respond, so I nodded at him mutely.

Moses looked at the floor, breathing deeply. Then he drew himself up tall in the chair. Looking at me straight in the eyes, he said, "I shall have to explain myself," he struggled. "For you do not know even the extent of what I have done to you. Let me begin at the beginning. Perhaps that is the best way. Let me begin back in Greenwood, Georgia." His voice quavered. "After you last saw me, there at your church, I went home with Bud Maxwell. I confronted him with my suspicions . . . about Black people not being allowed to eat in your church. He confirmed them, saying that he thought I would understand. 'That we still could be brothers in the Lord.'

"But I . . . well, I . . . could not see it. The action did not fit the words. I was furious. I was humiliated. I broke off with him, right there in his home. Back at Tech, I did not attend the prayer group anymore, and soon I did not go to church. I was a completely disillusioned man. All that I had been taught, all that I had believed turned sour in the light of what had happened to me.

"Irrationally, I blamed all Americans and all Christians for the scandal of my rejection. The Church, its missionaries, and Christian friends were part of this horrible hypocrisy. I know, now, that I acted rashly, immaturely. You cannot blame everyone and throw out the whole Church or the entire White race for one humiliation. After all, we are all sinners!" His eyes were large, his face intense with fervor.

"Well, I dropped from the scene as it were. I managed to stay afloat with my studies. But I withdrew into the ghetto of foreigners and aliens. I nursed my wounds and my bitterness in the company of international friends who had had similar encounters. Some of them as great as mine but most of them trivial in comparison. I returned here a year ago and have been very happy.

"And then you came . . . ." He swallowed hard, and his eyes fell to the floor once more. "When you came, I saw that I could take my vengeance out on you," he said. "I had no qualms about it. I began to rationalize that my chief source of troubles stemmed from the missionary. Namely, Miss Watson of your mission. I blamed her for everything. For my naivete toward human nature and human weaknesses. For my narrow faith. For poorly preparing me for going to the States, and for—what I thought—understating to me the extent of racial discrimination there. For you knew how I innocently believed that no evangelical, no saved Christian could possibly be prejudiced. Especially no Christian who supported your missions in Africa. But Bud Maxwell and your church shot that myth to pieces," he said, trembling.

"Then when you came, as I say, I was out to get you. To see you humiliated as I had been. The symposium was bad enough. I knew what I said would catch fire in some of the students' minds. And it did. But then I found out there was one man in high position who basically was anti-White and anti-Church. I decided to use him as my instrument of revenge." He paused.

"And that was DeHeer-Johnson," I said.

He gasped. "Did you know?"

"I more or less figured it out."

Moses swept a hand over his face. "I went to him in confidence and explained everything to him before the Appointments Board was to meet. I told him how I thought a man with a background like yours was unsuitable to be Chaplain on an African campus."

"And my appointment was suspended."

"Yes. DeHeer-Johnson never was keen on having a Chaplain at a state university. But he had been overruled by others on the campus who thought having a Chaplain was *proper*. It was one of the few times he has ever been overruled, I might say. At any rate, I told him about you, and he managed to suspend your appointment for most of the year anyway. He assured me that that was only the first step. That gradually he would find a way to get rid of you. He would find something to use against you. One of them, of course, was accusing you of meddling when it came to the projects in the Mpesi settlements."

"You knew about that?"

"Oh, yes," Moses chuckled. "I knew about everything you did. But there were two things I did not take into consideration in my cleverly devised scheme."

"What were they?"

"One was that I did not figure that you would be the missionary you are. You contradicted all that I said at the symposium. You were so different in fact that you involved yourself in my dismissal. I . . . I was there. I heard the sermon. That more than anything shocked me to my senses."

Words failed us both for several minutes. Then I asked him what was the second thing he had not reckoned on.

"The Registrar himself," Moses replied. "I knew he was prejudiced against White people. But never in my wildest imagination did I consider that he was also prejudiced against Ketumbas. I . . . guess I had not been here long enough to know that. Why, he must have been laughing at me all along while I was informing him about you!"

"What you intended for me happened also to you," I said.

"Yes, it did indeed," Moses murmured. "We are both out of our jobs. Only . . . only you would not be if it were not for me." His voice shook as he lowered his head into his hands.

I looked at the floor. After a while, Moses raised his head again. "I . . . I found my faith again in this crisis," he said. "When I was sacked, I discovered it had not really disappeared. At rock bottom, it was still there. I fell back on it when everything else collapsed. Only . . . only . . . ."

"Only what?"

"Only I cannot be forgiven by God or be at peace with myself until I know that you forgive me." He looked squarely at me with brimming eyes. "Will you forgive me? I know you must hate me instead. But can you possibly forgive me?"

I rubbed my eyes. Hate. Forgiveness. Peace. Of course, hate had been there. But the shell of defensiveness built up against him, where was it now? The hostility toward him, what cause had it to linger? Was this not the bridge I had been trying to span between myself and Moses? Should I not rejoice and be glad?

I slid my hand down to my chin. Looking at Moses, I said, "You have given me far more reasons to hate you than I did before tonight."

His eyes met mine briefly, then dropped. "I can only imagine," he whispered.

"Many of the things you've said I have pieced together on my own. Still, hearing the words come directly from your mouth has cut deeply."

He nodded without looking at me.

I swallowed. "But Moses, I'll forgive you. For how can I do otherwise when I need also to ask forgiveness of you? For what happened at Trinity?"

We gazed at each other, and we smiled, feeling uncertain and self-conscious. Moses eased himself back into the chair. His clenched fists relaxed. In the distance a dog howled against the backdrop of continued drumming. For a long time, we felt no compulsion to say anything. The silence, rather, served to refocus our perceptions of each other.

Presently Moses asked, "What will you do? Where will you go?"

"I don't know yet. But I'll go back to America. The Personnel Committee of the Church is willing to post me to another place in Ilaria. But I feel I should return home. To the Trinity Presbyterian Church type of people, I suppose. And yourself? What about you?"

"I'm not sure. But I must see Miss Watson and set things straight with her. I may look for a teaching position somewhere."

Then, re-arranging his cloth, Moses got up. "I should be going now. It is very late. But may I come again before you leave? I should like to get to know your family."

"Yes, please do. And I want to invite you to a farewell dinner at the Finnegans on the eleventh. Can you come?"

"Yes, I think so. I would very much like to. And I want you to come to my house, too."

"I will," I said with a smile.

At the door, Moses turned to shake my hand. "Thank you. Thank you very much," his voice quavered.

"No, I need to thank you instead," I said . . . .

Our handshake was strong and prolonged. It ended with a snap of the fingers.

END

9 798988 176121